Picking Up the Ghost

TONE MILAZZO

ChiZine Publications

FIRST EDITION

Picking Up the Ghost © 2011 by Tone Milazzo
Cover artwork © 2011 by Erik Mohr and Mara Sternberg
Interior design © 2011 by Corey Beep
All Rights Reserved.

LIBRARY AND ARCHIVES CANADA CATALOGUING IN PUBLICATION

Milazzo, Tone, 1971-
   Picking up the ghost / Tone Milazzo.

ISBN 978-1-926851-35-8

   I. Title.

PS3613.I435P53 2011   813'.6   C2011-902597-3

CHIZINE PUBLICATIONS
Toronto, Canada
www.chizinepub.com
info@chizinepub.com

Edited and copyedited by Helen Marshall
Proofread by Samantha Beiko

Canada Council   **Conseil des Arts**
for the Arts   **du Canada**

We acknowledge the support of the Canada Council for the Arts which last year invested $20.1 million in writing and publishing throughout Canada.

ONTARIO ARTS COUNCIL
CONSEIL DES ARTS DE L'ONTARIO

Published with the generous assistance of the Ontario Arts Council.

Any violation of copyright will release the Three Curses of Izzalom upon the perpetrator: their minds will become as like sieves unable to hold any but the most trivial knowledge, their good fortunes will come at the expense of those they love and the ghosts of their ancestors will rise every night and suck marrow from their bones.

To Melissa Turner Milazzo, who believed in this book long before it deserved such faith.

Picking
Up the
Ghost

1

IT'S A BIG WORLD

Cinque tore through fourteen years worth of junk, trying to find just one more sneaker. At the bottom of the pile he uncovered a comic book his Ma bought for him at a thrift store back before he could read. On the cover the Fantastic Four surrounded the Molecule Man who was counterattacking with a wand in each hand.

He brushed his dreads away and opened to the middle, a picture fell into his lap. It had come with the comic book. Back then in ignorance and wishful thinking he was convinced that it was the father he'd never known and the comic was a secret gift but later on his Ma told him it was an androgynous singer and actress from the eighties named Grace Jones. He smiled at the naiveté of his younger self, and dropped the comic and the picture back on the pile.

Cinque gave up on finding a matched pair. He accused the shoes of abandoning him, though he knew that didn't make any sense. A father might walk out on him but a shoe wouldn't. He still had a black one and a white one; at least they were for different feet. The high tops were from different brands and the mismatched soles made him walk lopsided as he picked up his bag and went downstairs toward the smell of pancakes.

He came downstairs as his Ma rushed past in her waitress uniform. He was about to ask if she knew what happened to his missing shoes but she cut him off, "Are you just coming down now, boy?" Without waiting for an answer she kissed him a quick goodbye and rushed off to work.

With a muffled, "Morning," he joined Darren at the table, and tried to get as much food in him while he could. His older cousin acknowledged him with a nod and a mouthful of pancakes.

"Good morning, Cinque," said Grandma as she wiped the stove. For Grandma, meal time was a lesson in punctuality, not entitlement. Meals were served in windows of time, not amounts. Miss the breakfast window and you went hungry until lunch. Grandma's stern look reminded him of this rule. Her strict timekeeping didn't make the boys especially punctual but it did make them accomplished speed-eaters and that was good enough for her. Two teenage boys shovelling food into their mouths made poor conversation and Grandma didn't try to talk to them; instead she talked at them, reciting pieces of wisdom that she thought the boys needed to know, hoping some of it would sink in.

"You boys should know that Mark Twain said, 'If you tell the truth you don't have to remember anything.' Tangled webs and all that."

The boys reacted their usual way, hearing more than listening as they cleaned their plates and issued hurried goodbyes. Maybe Grandma hoped that starting off the boys with an anecdote like this would help keep them on the right track through the rest of the day. Maybe it did, because for a couple of boys living in St. Jude, Cinque and Darren were pretty good kids. Cinque did well in school and Darren had high hopes for the future.

Darren's long legs carried him over the steps and through

the yard before he turned to give Cinque his daily well-are-you-coming-or-not look. Almost instantly it changed into a what-fool-thing-you-onto-now look.

"Whatcha got on yo' feet, boy?" Darren asked while Cinque closed the door.

"What's it look like?"

"Looks like you gone blind last night. Get back up in there and find some shoes that match."

"I can't. These are all I got."

"What happened to the other ones?"

"They're gone. I looked everywhere. They must of walked off on their own," Cinque said.

Darren looked at Cinque. Cinque looked at Darren. The older boy gave up and turned away. "Do me a favour. Do *us* a favour. Get a new pair of shoes, quick like. I don't want your weirdness to be rubbin' off on me at school. Understand?"

The two boys walked away from their house and out into St. Jude. For all its faults, no one could say it wasn't a green city. Plants filled the empty lots, abandoned properties overgrown with weeds, grass shot up from the cracks in the pavement and most residents let their lawns go wild. But the grass was always greenest over the collapsed sewage lines.

Darren grabbed hold of Cinque at the corner, just as they were about to cross the street into downtown.

"Yo! Hold up here. Gimme yo' bag."

"What for?" His bag stayed on his shoulder.

Darren grabbed it roughly and pushed the younger boy away. "I need you to carry somethin' into school for me. Stay here." With that, he disappeared down an alley between two of the abandoned buildings.

The city was laid out like a big X, around the two main streets where Cinque waited for Darren on the corner of Belmont and Potts. Of the four corners, two of them were abandoned department stores. One was a windowless box, a discreet sign confessing that it was an adult bookstore. Kitty-corner to that, was the -arber Man, with its decaying, pseudo-Egyptian façade. The barber pole shone, bright and clear, day and night like a lighthouse for pedestrians.

Cinque jumped at the horns from the riverboats on the Mississippi. The sounds travelled far and clear in the cold, wet air.

Darren re-emerged from the alley and handed the bag back to Cinque. The increased size and weight of the bag would have told him that there was something else in there if the sloshing sound hadn't.

"What'd you put in here?"

"It's cool." His cousin dismissed his concerns. "I'm bringing it in for science class."

"Since when did you bring in anything for class? And why I gotta carry it?" Cinque reached for the zipper.

Darren grabbed his hand in a hard fist. "'Cause I'll kick your ass if you don't." The younger bit his lower lip, hesitating. Then Darren suddenly softened, "Chill, little man, you ain't got nothin' to worry about. You know I won't let nothin' happen to you."

The boys stepped over the collapsed fence on the west side of Livermore Combined School's overgrown football field, around the spot on the track that was always muddy, even on the hot days, and past the Three Hundred Building, so rank with mould that even the St. Jude School District couldn't use it. A horrible place for learning, the one-two punch of budget cuts and standardized testing had left the school without the resources to teach the students any more than how to fill out bubbles on a Scantron sheet.

When they entered, Darren grabbed the smaller boy by the shoulder and ushered him into the boys' room with the least functional plumbing. The school had written off the toilets, the janitor having bound them in trash bags and duct tape. When the sinks stopped working they'd lock the door for good.

"Give it here," Darren said, opening his bag.

Cinque pulled the mysterious cargo out of his own bag—a bottle of liquor. "You had me carry this for you?" Cinque shouted, angry with Darren for using him. "Why you gotta bring this stuff to school for anyway?"

"School's where the customers are, little man!" Darren smiled as he reached for the illicit prize. "What am I gonna do? Sell outta the house? You really is the smart one, ain't ya?"

"Boy, I oughta smash this bottle across yo face!"

Darren's smile dropped into a scowl, his outstretched hand balled into a fist. His voice went deep and low, and Cinque realized there was going to be trouble. "Maybe you ain't so smart after all."

He counted on Darren keeping his eye on the bottle so he could kick the larger boy in the nuts, but his cousin simply leaned a little to one side. Cinque's foot hit him harmlessly in the leg. Darren grabbed the bottle with one hand and pushed him down with the other.

He landed hard on his butt and Darren stood over him, bottle in hand. Darren's smile returned like it had never left as he put the contraband into his own backpack. "You always kick with the right leg an' you always telegraph by leanin' way back to do it, but that you all over, ain't it? An open book."

Cinque hated the wide smirk of triumph on his cousin's face, but after a moment, Darren gave him a hand up. He stood, shaking his head. "I don't get it."

"I know you don't. You too honest, that's what's wrong with you. Well . . . one of the things wrong with you. Later, little man!" And with that Darren took off.

Still feeling stung and humiliated, Cinque left the bathroom to drop off his homework—one of the few students who did. He did well in all of his classes, but he hid it from the other kids like Darren told him to. He left his homework in the faculty mailroom so no one would see him hand it in.

Unfortunately for him, Imani knew and she was waiting for him, her long, lean form blocking the way to the mailroom. There was a bemused smile on her face. "Sin-Kay!"

Her deliberate mispronunciation of his name was more command than greeting. Cinque suspected the sharp, precise syllables really meant, "Here, boy!"

They'd been in school together for years. While Cinque kept to himself, Imani devoured attention. She was pretty enough to be popular, but instead she seemed to dance above and around the social pecking order. Somewhere in the sixth grade Imani discovered the light-skinned boy with nothing to say, and he hadn't had a day of rest since. She knew he was smart, but more book-smart than street-smart and she used that to make him squirm.

"Did you do your homework, Sin-Kay?" Imani pouted with big doe-eyes as she made the question sound like, "Who's a good boy?" Lightly touching her chin to her chest she looked down at him. As of last year she was taller than Cinque.

Cinque tried to enter the mailroom but Imani blocked the door, head tilted to one side. He tried to duck under her arm and she pinned him to the door jamb with a casual swing of her hip.

"Quit playing, Imani! We have to get to class!" He tried to dodge past her again but she was too quick. Her game came to an end when a teacher rushed in to grab her mail, opening the doorway. Cinque followed the woman and put his homework in the mailbox. When he returned, Imani stood at the door, and her gaze dropped to Cinque's feet. He sighed inside.

"Yes, I know. My shoes don't match," he said in his serious voice and headed for homeroom.

"Nuh-uh, Sin-Kay," Imani followed him, pretending to be appalled. "Pants and shirts don't match. Socks don't match. But one black shoe and one white shoe? That's just wrong! No, it's scary and wrong, it scarong."

Cinque walked away, eyes front, but Imani wouldn't relent.

"That's so wrong you couldn't a thought it was right. I'm guessin' that be a cry for help. Am I right or am I right?"

"I ain't hearing this."

Imani darted around to blocking his way again. "Is this the new tin foil hat? Was the CIA sendin' you messages through yo' feet? And by mixin' up the pairs, you break the signal? Come on! Tell me what's up wit' that? Were they stolen? Maybe they ran off to be with your pops, shoes'll do that."

Cinque winced. Imani had never teased him about his missing father before. Why now? But asking her why would be asking for trouble. He couldn't show her another weakness.

2

TO BE WITH YOUR POPS

Cinque always got the mail when he came home from school, a habit started when he was younger. He thought that if he checked the mail often enough then maybe mail would arrive for him. It never had—not until today. But wedged in the mailbox was a manila envelope from the City of Chicago to *Mr. Cinque Williams*. Excited and confused by the important looking letter, he hesitated. Finally, curiosity got the better of him and he read it on the porch.

Dear Mr. Cinque Williams:

It is our solemn duty to inform you of the passing of your father, Kelly Lee, due to natural causes in his apartment during August of this year.

According to the Cook County records you are the sole next of kin. As such you are encouraged to fill out the accompanying reclamation form and present it and your birth certificate to the Cook County Office of the Medical Examiner to claim his remains and his estate.

Failure to file a reclamation form within 90 days will result in both the remains and possessions becoming the property of the City of Chicago to dispose of at its discretion.

Our condolences,

Cook County Coroner and the City of Chicago

His head spun. He didn't know what to think or how to feel. He didn't know the man. And now he never would.

Letter in hand Cinque stepped back out on the porch and stared north, where the Mississippi came from. His Grandpa had passed away three years ago, now his Pa. If his life was a river, he thought, and his family, all his family including his Pa, was its source then he knew he'd better find that source soon because it was drying up.

That evening Cinque fell asleep on the porch waiting for his mother to come home from school, waking when the headlights lit up the front yard as she turned into the driveway. Ma cut the engine of her little, two-tone brown and primer car and lifted herself out. He liked seeing his Ma come home from school. She looked so pretty and smart in her skirts and button-down shirts, much better than she did in the morning's waitress uniform. The engine ran on for a few turns before finally shutting down. It sounded as tired as Olamide Williams looked. But that didn't stop her from smiling at her little boy.

"Well look who's up. My little soldier is making sure I get out of the car okay."

"Hi Ma." Cinque smiled back, wondering suddenly if he should keep the letter a secret. She looked happy today.

"You hungry, Cinque?"

"Always," he said, thankful for the delay.

Once inside, they sat at the kitchen table. Ma made peanut butter sandwiches and they talked about their day—griping about work, griping about being a kid, griping about St. Jude, there was always something to gripe about. Once the small talk was exhausted, Ma gathered the plates and stood up from the table with a sigh, telling Cinque without speaking that it was time to go to bed.

"My Pa's dead," he blurted out, the pressure finally too much.

She froze, her face considering and confused. Ma's eyes fell on the envelope as he pushed it across the table to her. She slouched back into the chair. Looked at the paperwork, but did not touch it.

"Just as soon as I'd put that man behind me, he finds one last way to turn up. Bad penny . . ."

"You never said much about him." Cinque's finger gently touched the manila corner.

"No. No, I didn't." Ma's eyes hadn't left the envelope.

"I always figured that if I needed to know him I could find him, maybe when I was older." Cinque waited for her to say something before speaking again. "But I guess that isn't gonna happen now, is it?"

She took in a deep breath. "No, I guess it's not." Looking up at last, she said, "I guess it's up to me now, huh?"

"I guess so . . ."

With voice reluctant, Olamide told Cinque how he came to be. "Fifteen years ago I was a freshman at the University of Chicago. One of the few who'd made it out of St. Jude the good way. Not in camouflage, not in a prison-blue and not with a tombstone, but with a scholarship.

"St. Jude is a tough little town but it was still a little town and I was eager to get out into the wide world. That's when I met Kelly Lee, an older man, a man of the world—a man with a colourful past.

"He was in and out of my life in a whirlwind two months,

a smooth talker with a lot of money for someone who didn't have a job. Worldly-wise. I always figured he was a con-man, though I never learned what kind of cons he ran, where he came from or where he was going. But a month after he was gone, I learned I was pregnant." She reached over, held Cinque's hand and smiled, "With you."

She sighed and Cinque saw the weight of those years settle on with the memory. "But that's when the tough times started. I had to drop out of school and move back here just as my sister Keisha came back with Darren. Keisha moved on weeks later, leaving behind Darren and a note saying motherhood wasn't her thing."

Cinque knew the rest of the story. For the next eleven years, Ma, Grandpa and Grandma struggled to make the time and money to raise the boys right. When Grandpa passed away his Ma had found herself working all over St. Jude in every miserable, low-paying, short-lived job the city had to offer. Once the mortgage was paid off last year there had finally been the time and money for Olamide to return to school.

He'd imagined a hundred different fathers over the years, but no one like this. Cinque had grown up thinking of his father in shades of betrayal, the source for all of his troubles. If the family had problems paying bills, it was because Pa wasn't around to support them. If Cinque didn't understand something about life, it was because Pa wasn't around to teach him. If he caught his Ma crying late at night when she thought everyone else was asleep, it was because Pa had broken her heart. His resentment was a complicated thing. Now the blame changed directions and for the first time in his life, he was angry with his Ma.

He pulled his hand out of hers and pushed up from the table. "You shoulda told him! He mighta come for me!"

"Cinque, don't pin your dreams on the man just 'cause you don't know him. That's what I did."

He pointed an accusing finger at her. "I shoulda been able to meet him!"

Olamide stood, shaking her head. "He never took responsibility for anything. . . ."

"He woulda come for me! He woulda taken me away from here! Away from you!"

Cinque knew he'd crossed a line. He didn't mean it. He loved his Ma, but he was too angry to take it back. His Ma had betrayed him. She'd kept his father from him and now there was no making it right. He'd never get to know his Pa, and it was her selfish fault.

Olamide tried to explain. "Cinque, please trust me. Trust my judgment. You are better off without him in your life. I know because I'd have been better off without . . ."

Her face suddenly fell, realizing what she almost said.

"You'd be better off without me?" Cinque trembled, his hands formed fists and his eyes welled up. "Is that whatcha saying?"

She reached out to hold him. "Oh baby, I love you and I thank God for every day that I have you."

"Shut up!" Cinque grabbed the letter off the table. "This says that his estate is waiting in Chicago. It says that only I can go get it. Me and me alone! I don't know what he's left me but I'm getting it."

"Cinque, you can't go to Chicago by yourself."

"Yeah, I can. I'm the only one who can. And I will." He turned to run upstairs.

"Cinque! You'd better stop this foolishness!" Now she was angry too. "Come back here and give me that letter."

Cinque looked back at her over his shoulder and yelled, "You stole my father." That ended her anger and the fight.

Cinque locked himself in his room, lay on the bed and wondered about his father's estate. It might not be much: personal items, some papers—adults always had important papers—maybe some cash. Odds were his father wasn't a rich man but he had to have a few hundred dollars to his name. Any cash would be more than Cinque ever had.

His fight with his Ma must have woken Grandma. He heard the two women talking downstairs. Cinque reckoned they were probably planning to take his letter and keep him from going to Chicago, to stop him from finishing his business with his father, from claiming his inheritance.

"Let 'em try."

Cinque drifted in and out of sleep all night, dreaming about his father, Kelly Lee, a blank outline of a man, until he realized there was something in the darkness. Cinque stared at it for a long, puzzled moment before turning on the little lamp by his bed. A tangle of black wire, about the size of a basketball hung in the air above him.

Unsure if this was real or dream, Cinque tried to slide out from under the strange sphere when it spoke in a man's voice chiselled out of hate: "Cinque." It pronounced his name correctly, "sink." Dread pinned the boy to the bed, as a fingerless hand whipped out from the ball and stabbed down into the boy's chest. It grabbed and pulled, tearing out the orange muscle of his heart.

A searing heat filled the hole in Cinque's chest while frost crystallized across the organ's surface as it hit the air. Had the hand burned into him? "The father shall be visited upon the son," the black wire hand hissed as it flipped the heart once and rolled back into the shape of a ball.

"No!" Cinque cried and grabbed at the ball, trying to pry it open and take back his heart. His fingernails snagged uselessly on the uneven but slick surface as the ball spun between his fingers. It turned and coiled smaller and smaller, taking his heart into oblivion. Desperate hands pressed hard against his ribcage but nothing stirred inside. Dazed, Cinque rolled over and fell out of bed, ribs twisting in agony. The little lamp, knocked off the table in the attack, illuminated the room as best it could from the floor. He was still in his room, not the afterlife, and it was as it always was, not much to see— just clothes, a few pieces of art he'd made in school, an old encyclopaedia set and a few books.

Sitting up, Cinque tried to breathe away the hot pain in his chest and wake himself up. The minutes ticked by in electric red numbers and he still burned inside without a pulse. The Black Wire Hand was no dream; he'd been struck by something strange. What was the Black Wire Hand? What did it say? "The father shall be visited?" And if it really took his heart how was he alive?

3

VISITED

Later that morning, on the corner of Belmont and Potts, Cinque's chest still burned, the rest of him didn't feel too good either. Tired, sore and stupefied, he was still thinking about last night. He still couldn't feel the beating of his heart. He waited across from a trash-filled alley opening while Darren bought alcohol, cigarettes or something worse from whoever lived back there, past the garbage. Yesterday he'd promised himself he wouldn't let Darren use him again but Cinque's head and body were still a hot mess from the abuse of the Black Wire Hand and he wasn't able to put up much of a fight.

He found himself staring at the red, white and blue pole outside the -arber Man. Today it was different. Something moved along its surface, a dark blue spot on the thick, white band. As the pole spun the spot moved, danced or walked along the white strip like an illuminated road. The stripe thickened and the spot grew and became defined: a dark man, an African man in an indigo robe. In a few seconds he wasn't walking on the white, spiral road anymore—maybe he never was—he was walking on the sidewalk in front of the -arber Man. He held a walking stick topped with a rough carving of a head in his knotted hands and kept his dusty feet in worn, leather sandals. The African stopped and somehow locked eyes with Cinque through mirrored sunglasses.

A Black Ball of Wire, a missing heart and now an African dancing down a barber pole into St. Jude. Was all this real or was he crazy? Which would be worse? The world started to spin, and Cinque barely managed to fall against a telephone pole instead of the sidewalk.

The African hadn't moved. A slight, pleased smile touched the man's lips. The sun reflected in the lenses though in St. Jude the sky was solid cloud.

Across the street Darren called at Cinque, "Come on, boy! Whatcha lookin' at?"

Cinque shook his head, and the dizzy spell passed. "I'm looking at that African," the boy said as he caught up.

Darren gave him back his bag. "Yeah? Well, wait till we get to school. Then there'll be a whole mess a Africans you can look at."

"They ain't Africans," Cinque corrected him. "They just black."

"Well, we as close to Africa as you ever gonna get."

At school Cinque tried to hide in the crowd. If no one noticed him they wouldn't notice he was going crazy. He was quiet and still, even for the boy who never spoke up. Even in his head, he tried to whisper, imagining and remembering images in subdued colours and blurred lines. It was too much for him to keep up and he had to ditch sixth period to hide in the boy's restroom.

By that time of day, the restroom had been used and abused, with no sign of the janitor. Cinque sat in a stall, cupped his hands over his nose and tried to breathe through his mouth. He heard voices from the next-door girls' room. He listened to take his mind off the smell. He couldn't make out the words, but it was strange—there were too many voices for a bathroom, and not just girls.

Curiosity pulled and the stench pushed Cinque out of the boys' room. He took a quick look to make sure no one was around before sneaking into the girls' room. Disoriented by the absence of urinals and the knowledge that this was a place he shouldn't be, Cinque crept ahead. The voices were louder now, so many that he could only make out bits and pieces.

"—all you could do wasn't—"

"—something in the—"

"—this isn't good enough!"

"You're not the one—"

"—called you fat."

There was no one in the stalls and no one in the room, but the sounds were too real to come from a radio. Cinque kept looking around until he noticed something through the mirror, an inconsistent texture on the ceiling, a large lumpy mass stuck up there and coloured to match the concrete.

He turned and glanced up as the lump turned blue and unfolded in a clump of mollusk arms, dropping on him and grappling with its suckers. Like the Black Wire Hand the monster took something out of him. Suddenly weak and exhausted, Cinque thought, "Not again!" as the weight of his backpack dragged him into a stall and to the floor. Panicking, he tried to stand to fight the monster and accidently slammed the door shut. The swinging door squeezed the thing out of the stall and off the boy. The creature was lighter than it appeared, almost cloudlike.

The voices jabbered on.

"Never fit in."

"You know what they said about you?"

"—called me fat."

"That guy right there? He's on to you."

Trapped in the stall, Cinque's chest flared with heat; twice now he'd been attacked by the maybe-real and that made

Cinque frustrated and angry. Using his anger and pain to get a second wind, he scrambled and scooted along the floor, his numb fingers slipping as he gripped and pulled on the partition. He fumbled through the stalls until he hit the wall at the end, wobbled up on his feet and staggered out into the open. Free from the stalls, free to run for the door.

Cinque wanted to believe that there was no creature, that he was imagining this, but as he hit the door he paused for a look back. The unnatural thing still hung in the air, translucent and illuminated, blue, mottled skin over its four-foot-long body, w-shaped pupils in its large, gold eyes on the top of its slope of a face, a set of eight octopus arms at the bottom with a tentacle to either side. A giant cuttlefish. He recognized the shape from the old World Book set he had at home. Real cuttlefish were six inches long and swam—this one was as big as Cinque. Instead of suction cups, the inner arms and the tips of its tentacles were lined with human mouths chattering in an idiot's chorus.

"Quick! Tick tock, tick—"

"—sigh . . ."

"Don't move! There's a bee!"

"I'm on to you—"

Its blue colour now spotted red. Horribly, Cinque felt a resonance with the thing, his energy flowed through its system, and knew it had a taste for him now. It gathered itself for a lunge, arms spreading out to envelop him.

Cinque stumbled out the door on flimsy legs, lungs gasping shallow breaths. He leaned against the wall, keeping an eye on the door, hoping that the Cuttlefish couldn't escape and swearing he'd never go into a girl's bathroom again. That thing, that Cuttlefish, its touch was like every bad thought he'd ever had, all at once.

He hobbled out of school, across the muddy field, through St. Jude to home. Climbing the stairs to his room took the last he had to give. He passed out face down on the floor, still dressed and wearing his backpack.

The next morning Cinque felt empty, tired and dull. He picked at breakfast. Grandma was saying something, but he didn't hear her words, he just had a vague sense of being spoken to. Incapable of forming or comprehending words, he responded in grunts that communicated nothing, but sounded like they did.

If Grandma and Darren didn't like it, Cinque didn't care. He went through the Friday motions. He drifted off to school, after Darren, out of the house, around the -arber Man and over the fence until something finally woke him up.

The Cuttlefish was in the athletic field. Floating closer to the ground than before, its tentacles passed back and forth over the dirt. Inhuman tongues from the human mouths extended to taste the grass. Its skin was a shade of red-brown, still flush with the energy it stole from him yesterday. It might even have been a little larger than before.

Cinque's chest blazed up again; he stopped and grabbed his head, trying to think. He'd hoped that the Cuttlefish lived in the girls' room, that it was trapped, that he'd never have to see it again. It must have oozed through the crack under the door, following his scent home. When it got there would it stop with him? Or would it suck the life out of his family too? How could Cinque protect them? He knew he couldn't just warn them, they'd never believe this. He grabbed his cousin's wrist, stopped and whispered, "Please."

The monster's voices jabbered.

"I know what you're missing and—"

"—just another bit, a little bit."

"If you know what's good for you!"

"—gotta sleep sometime—"

Darren jerked free, turning on the smaller boy. "What?"

"Please." Cinque mouthed the word at Darren without sound.

"Now you wake up?" Darren followed Cinque's gaze ahead and then slowly back to Cinque, "What 'Please'? Whatcha want?"

Cinque pushed the larger boy towards the sideline. Darren, confused, let him. Imposing himself between the monster and his cousin, Cinque kept one palm on Darren's chest and his eyes on the creature.

"Go."

He guided Darren to the space between the rotting buildings of the outer campus. Cinque ordered his cousin, "Take a different way home. I don't care how."

"Who'd you see back there? Was someone fittin' to jump us? Someone in the bleachers?"

"Just do it!"

The rest of the school day was hazy, an inside-the-head kind of hazy. Instead of being the quiet kid who was secretly listening, Cinque was the quiet kid who spent the day in his own world. Imani might have said something to him at some point during the day, but he was too deep in his troubled thoughts to hear. Chicago and his father were still on his mind but they took a back seat to his fear of the Cuttlefish.

Little things went wrong, were wrong. From the corner of his eye, or when he was too deep in thought, angles lined up incorrectly and left undefined space in between. Old buildings reeked of purpose just by being there. Shadows were especially treacherous, shifting without their owners and sometimes straining to break loose. At these anomalies, Cinque only looked out of habit. Let the world slip apart at the seams, he thought. He had bigger problems.

Again he ditched his last class, this time creeping back to the athletic field. Not taking the usual way, instead he came around the far side of the bleachers, from behind the old utility shed. He saw no surprises. He could see that the Cuttlefish had moved further down the field, away from the school. It was heading for where the fence had collapsed, tasting the ground as it went, slowly following his scent. One more night and it would be at his house, then in his house. And Cinque would have to sleep sooner or later.

Hustling back to the corner of Belmont and Potts he came across an African woman in a green head wrap and robe waiting on the bus stop bench, hands folded over the envelope in her lap. When she saw him she grinned a wide, nervous grin, stood up and waved him over. Too weary to be shy and beyond fear of consequence, Cinque walked up to the woman, his eyes fixed on the envelope and said, "Is that for me?" He was learning to expect the unlikely.

Through a nervous smile she began reciting an introduction, "Haloo. My name is Yetunde and I am here to help you find Pastor Akotun. He . . ."

Though she hadn't offered, Cinque took the envelope, interrupting her. He opened the letter and she began again from the top.

"Haloo. My name is Yetunde and I am . . ." Inside there were two hand-written pages, a pebble and a stick of strong smelling, soft wood.

"He wrote this for you, little boy. He saw you were special yester—"

Cinque held up a hand, silencing her distraction as he looked at the letter. He tried to comprehend but after the Black Wire Hand and the Cuttlefish had each taken a piece of him he couldn't concentrate on the letters and make them words. He looked up from the letter when she tried to continue, but Cinque cut her off, "This is from the African? From yesterday?"

She gave a long exhale and nodded, surrendering the conversation.

"You sayin' he real? An' he's like an . . ." he snapped his fingers trying to remember that book he read last year on African folktales, ". . . an African witchdoctor?"

She replied with a nod. "In Africa, we call them Hougans. And he wants to talk to you."

Cinque glanced at the letter one more time before folding it up and walking home, saying nothing to Yetunde as he left.

Cinque tried to read the African's letter again when he got home without any luck. Up in his room he could tell that Ma or Grandma had been looking for the Chicago letter. They thought that the piles and stacks in his room were the product of disorderly habit but there was a pattern. Cinque could feel it. When he put something away Cinque was careful to place it in the flow without making a ripple. It was obvious that unmindful hands had been searching in here. Their intrusion didn't bother him, Cinque kept his secrets in his head, or in his Place across town. He knew he had to bring the African's letter there now, the place where he'd hid the Chicago letter.

Cinque left and wandered east. Up, around, left, right, he let his feet set the course. He had important things to think about, and it was hard to get lost in St. Jude. This far east, he couldn't see the -arber Man anymore. Instead he used the dead smoke stacks of the old Armour meat packing factory up on the hill as a guide.

There was a family connection with the plant. Grandpa spent thirty years up there until Armour Meat Inc. moved out of St. Jude, closing the plant and laying-off Grandpa months before he was due to retire and collect his pension.

As Cinque walked he felt the little errors and little inconsistencies that he'd dismissed earlier now taunted him in the wider world.

The feeling of strangeness, of cracks in reality, was increasing. As unrealities became more real to Cinque some were more than phenomena, they were alive. Little monsters danced among St. Jude's overgrowth, turning tree branches into groping arms or tendrils. They scurried about the derelict homes and buildings, filling windows and doorways with inhuman faces and half-seen monstrous attackers. These visions were becoming more tenacious, persisting longer under scrutiny. He passed a derelict house filled with rats that were coloured stark black and white—no grays, living cartoons that watched him in rows from the broken windows. An empty set of baby's clothes ran away from Cinque. He knew it wasn't running in fear; it was running ahead to wait in ambush.

Cinque went the other way and came to the edge of a patch of grass filled with foot-long alligators moulded out of warped plastic. Painfully, they crawled towards the boy, mouths biting the air. More than once, Cinque caught a fox-headed figure about his size watching him from behind an old billboard or other signage.

Every few feet, Cinque crossed another monstrosity. Occasionally, he thought he saw the Cuttlefish among them, or in the blowing of a curtain, or on the oily surface of a puddle. These false sightings pushed Cinque further out of his malaise and into the feeling of being prey. The city was dangerous and full of predators.

He started to run to his place of safety on aching legs, swinging sore arms. His feet felt wrong in the mismatched sneakers, they made him list to the left. A branch bent down in his way. He ducked under it as it bowed under the weight of a dozen bright pink creatures, swinging out after him. He ran around a four-winged bat as it flopped on the ground and up the barren hill, right up to the Saint.

Every kid in St. Jude claimed one of the abandoned buildings as his own. Cinque had claimed the St. Jude Presbyterian Church. The twenty-foot tall, rough sculpture of the white man in front of St. Jude's was supposed to represent Jesus but it didn't look like the pictures of Jesus Cinque had ever seen. The eyes were too far apart, the face was too round and the beard too full. Years after the church had closed down people assumed that the statue on the lawn of St. Jude's Presbyterian Church was Saint Jude himself.

Being in the old church brought Cinque back to calm and clarity. He stood in the aisle, eyes closed, and for a long moment he let the outside world drain away.

The building used to be a church, but Cinque had never considered it such. Church was the Liberty Christian Church, closer to home and alive, where Grandma used to take the boys every Sunday. He used to enjoy church back when Brother Pearson was still around, always with a smile. Cinque was too young to understand most of his sermons, but he enjoyed the feeling of joy and solidarity. When Brother Pearson left, Brother Phelps took over, and church stopped being fun. Brother Phelps didn't like to sing and didn't like to smile. His wasn't a god of good news, but a god of punishment. Sermons were shouted instead of sung. His congregation wasn't his friends, they were sinners.

Brother Phelps's sermons scared Cinque and he carried that fear with him through the rest of the week. Darren, however, wasn't scared. Darren was angry. Brother Phelps spent an entire sermon railing against Darren's favourite rapper, Black Jesus. Darren had been passionately loyal to Black Jesus since getting his autograph in a record store in Chicago. That was Darren's last service. He used it as an excuse to quit going to church. After fighting about it for a week, Grandma let it go, and when she saw how fearful Brother Phelps' sermons made Cinque she left him at home as well.

Churches were supposed to be living places and although this place was dead, it was his dead place.

The large, stained glass window in front had fallen victim to a group of kids with too much free time and too many rocks. Open and cold, the city's numerous squatters weren't interested. Occasionally, someone would come sniffing around looking for something to steal, but the building was picked clean long before Cinque had gotten to it. What made the site so valuable to the boy was not shelter or loot, but the space below.

Cinque had only discovered the trapdoor by luck when he spied the lifting ring. Once, on a daytime talk show, he'd learned that witches sometimes held their covens in old churches, and he had been hoping that the trapdoor was a secret stairway down into a dark, candlelit cave or something like that. But he had discovered the trapdoor only covered a white, cubic baptismal with steps out to either side. It was a good place to keep things safe from his family or from looters. For good measure, Cinque covered the lid with a fallen bookcase.

Except for an extra padlock he kept here in case he needed to lock the church door behind him, the baptismal was empty. The last thing he kept in there was a pair of dirty magazines he'd found in the trash. He'd lost interest in them and passed them on to Darren who had been going to sell them for Cinque. Cinque had never gotten the money.

Being in the church—in his Place—made Cinque feel safer than he did at home, at ease enough to try reading the letter again.

Hello Little Boy!

I call you Little Boy because I do not know what you call yourself. I am Pastor Titun Akotun and I would like to help you.

You have been seeing things that were barely there, have you not? Did you not see me walking the world tree yesterday in your city of Saint Jude? I was not there, but you saw me anyway?

You have a sight more than sight. You can see things that are in this world, but not of this world. This is bad for you because there is no one in Saint Jude who can help you, no one who can teach you what to do. Where you stand there are only roads leading to madness.

But I can give you some help, even though I do not live in your city or even your country. I live in Africa.

On the next page there are instructions for opening up your dreams. I will try to visit your dreams every night for the next week. If your mind is open, I will see you there.

Pastor Titun Akotun

Written in the deliberate, irregular block letters of a first grader that contrasted with the message, the instructions looked pretty simple. He hoped that the African could help with the monsters. He pocketed the pebble and the stick, left the pages in the baptismal, sealed it back up and left his Place, replaying the ritual in his head. It was almost time for dinner. He wanted to avoid his family but the needs of his stomach won out over the needs of his pride.

He walked down to the street and as he passed the statue of St. Jude there he was again, the little man with the fox's face. He wasn't hiding or pretending to hide anymore, instead he sat, smiling and cross-legged, on the other curb. Cinque steadied himself on the statue as he faced down the creature across the street.

"That's someone you don't see everyday," the fox-faced figure said, chuckling. "A boy with a hole where is heart used to be."

Cinque cocked his head. "What do you know about it?"

The man-fox cocked his head the opposite way. "I know you'd better do something about it before it's too late. I gotta think why you're wandering around like it's nothing. How long you expect to live without an abstraction of a heart?"

The fox-faced man stretched and cracked his knuckles. "You do as you do, you. But first, you need to get a clue."

Cinque felt stupid. He knew he had to find his missing

heart and soon. How long could be live without it? "The only clue I got is the hand that took my heart said something about a visit from my father. But my pops is dead."

"If Pops won't go to Mohammed then Mohammed'll have to go to Pops." He stood up and brushed off his pants. "Either way I'm curious to see how this one plays out." He disappeared into the bushes behind him.

"Mohammed'll have to go Pops? How am I going to talk to a ghost?" Cinque shook his head to clear it but the thought wouldn't go away.

The family ate in silence, except for Darren. He assumed that everyone else just didn't have anything to say so he filled the air by talking about what interested him, which meant talking about Black Jesus.

". . . I don't need to be hearin' 'bout no East Coast versus West Coast, no Dirty South, it's about time we got some quality hip hop comin' outta Illinois. You know what I'm sayin'?"

Somewhere between the thug-chic of the West Coast's Tupac and the insanity of the East Coast's Old Dirty Bastard, Black Jesus was the only rapper Darren cared about anymore and he made sure everyone else knew it.

"He just rhymes so damn fast, you know? I gotta listen to everythin' twenty times before I start to get a picture of what he's laying out for us. Every song's a story and every story's a message. Black Jesus is like the white man's Jesus, except for us, you know? I wonder what kinda ride—"

Grandma pounded the table with her knife handle. "Darren. I don't want to hear any more about that man at this table. It's sacrilegious."

Cinque rolled his eyes. Here it came. Darren loved to proselytize for Black Jesus.

"That's just like they say. But you can't say that until you listen to his music."

"I'm not going to listen to that noise. There is but one way to God and that's through His son, the real Jesus. Not some scrawny, foul-mouthed rapper. You'll do good to learn that, Darren, the sooner the better."

"See? That's what I'm talking about. You don't know. Did you know that the real Jesus was black? That the white man been coverin' that up for centuries?" Darren pointed to the portrait of Jesus Grandma kept in the kitchen. "That ain't what Jesus looked like. That's the bastard son of the Pope. . . ."

Grandma slapped Darren across the face, her opinion on the matter clear and final. She glared at him across the table. Darren bit his lips in anger but that didn't stop his eyes from watering. He pushed away from the table and stormed upstairs to his room, acting like it was his idea to go.

"I don't know what's going to happen with that boy," Grandma said to no one in particular. "You try to raise a boy right and all that work is undone by some fool on the radio." She gave Cinque a sideways glance. "The boy doesn't understand that his family only wants what's best for him. That we just want him to live up to his potential."

Cinque didn't take the bait.

That night, in his room and in the darkness, Cinque waited for quiet. Afraid of the twitching shadows that might have been alive, that might be coming after him. Flashlight in hand, Cinque duelled with the creeping darkness. It was the perfect weapon, enough light to fight off the shadows, not enough to gather suspicions from the other side of the door.

Eventually Cinque heard Grandma order Darren to turn off his music and go to sleep, and soon after that Ma got home and saw herself to bed. Only then was it time to start.

Following the instructions in the letter, he took the stick and lit one end with a match. With a light puff of breath, Cinque blew out the flame, but the ember continued to produce its sharp, acrid smoke. Cinque carried the stick around the perimeter of the room three times before extinguishing it and picked up the pebble. It had once been half of a smooth, rounded stone, but was now bisected by a jagged flat side. He was supposed to sleep with the stone in his hand. He didn't want to risk dropping it in his sleep so he taped his fist closed around it.

Finally, he lay down and visualized the illustration on the bottom of the second page, a large oval with a smaller oval interrupting it at the top. He used the stray sparks and faint nebulous formations that formed in his head when he closed his eyes. He moulded the light, like clay, into the two ovals. When the light floated away, he gave it a mental push back into place. Gradually, the light took on a third dimension. The oval at the bottom became a dish and base, and the oval at the top formed into an uneven, gray sphere and with time and effort he shaped it into a rough approximation of a human head, with what appeared to be shells marking its eyes and mouth. Cinque looked past the clay sculpture.

The African was waiting.

4

PAST THE CLAY

Pastor Titun Akotun sat on a stool playing one of those African drums shaped like a giant mushroom.

"Oh little boy, you need to be collected," he said without looking up from his drumming.

They were outside, by a watering hole in a place that looked as if someone had tried to make Africa out of St. Jude parts. The ground rolled unevenly, like an African plain, but covered in Illinois grass and weeds. There were sparsely gathered pine trees with needles pushed up into a wide canopy at the top, the trunks given a twist. On the horizon, a pride of almost-lions fed on their kill. They were the shape and size of lions, but in the colours and fur of domestic cats, one with black and white spots, one solid black, a few calicos and a tabby. Nearby, large, bald pigeons with extended necks waited their turn.

The African's indigo robes gleamed in the twilight, and the man released his grip on his half of the pebble, the other half of the stick smouldering by his feet. He put the drum aside and picked up two lengths of hemp rope, one dripping wet—

somehow Cinque could tell it was cold—the other smouldering.

"Come close."

Cinque hesitated. Now that he'd crossed this line he didn't know what to expect or what the African wanted.

"You are drifting apart. This makes it difficult for you to understand, difficult to think. If we are going to talk we should not waste our time. I need you to be as one. Now come here, I anticipated this and prepared a remedy."

Cinque had to trust the African, at least this little bit, so he took a step closer and the African twisted the two ropes together, indicating that Cinque should raise his arms. As the braid wrapped around the boy's chest three times Cinque felt the desperate functions of his scattered mind interlace once again. The hot ache in his chest and the persistent anxiety were gone. As the ends were tied, he felt his ability to concentrate and a sense of self returning. He closed his eyes and stretched, he'd forgotten how good it felt to move without pain.

"It is so much better to be together, is it not?" Pastor Akotun's eyes returned Cinque's smile though his lips did not. "Now. Now we can talk. What is your name, little boy?"

"Cinque. Cinque Williams."

The African offered his hand, and Cinque took it. "It is nice to meet you, Cinque Williams." He paused, and when Cinque didn't say anything he continued, "You have many questions. You have been seeing things you have never seen before, such as myself?"

With Pastor Akotun's rope around his waist Cinque felt alive again. He was glad he'd trusted the African. It was good to know that with all the weirdness in his life these days, not all of it was trying to eat him. "Yeah, it seems like there be little monsters everywhere, in the corners, in the shadows. And there's a big monster that looks like a giant cuttlefish that's been following me to my home, its arms are covered in mouths—"

Pastor Akotun interrupted waving aside Cinque's words.

"Your American living has not prepared you for this. If you had been born in Africa and among those of us who maintain our traditions these things would not be so strange to you. Rare yes, but not unheard of." The African picked up his wooden staff and laid it across his lap. "An African would have known that these things are not the real you are used to, the real of Earth and Sun. You are not imagining these things."

Cinque tilted his head to one side and said, "Uh, how?" As soon as he opened his mouth Cinque wished he'd kept it shut— he seemed smarter that way. If Pastor Akotun thought less of him for this it didn't show. "How did I get this way?"

"Your eyes were opened. There are many ways that this could have happened. Most likely, you were touched by something of the spirit."

Cinque's hand went to his chest as the memories of the night he received his father's letter came to the surface. "Someone— something took my heart. It was orange and frozen. Is that what you mean?"

"Possibly. What does the frozen heart mean to you?"

"I don't know. I was hoping you'd tell me."

The African held his staff in one hand like a sceptre. "The orange, frozen heart was a symbol. It is a personal thing to be interpreted by you. If you were of my lands, I would be able to help but you come from a strange land with strange ideas. My help might be harmful. What the heart stands for and who took it is a riddle you will have to solve for yourself."

Cinque shook his head. "I don't have a lot of clues."

"There are many clues. If you don't know them for what they are then you don't know yourself."

"So then all this craziness I've been seeing—" Cinque caught himself looking at the pack of almost-lions when he said that and quickly looked back to the African. "—you say they're spirits?"

Pastor Akotun nodded. "They are spirits and signs of spirits, real, but not solid—at least not usually. You have a sight beyond sight. In Africa you would fall under the tutelage of myself or one of the other Hougan who would teach you the ways of Juju."

Cinque shook his head. "I can't go to Africa."

"Nor can I go to America, though I hope to one day, but that doesn't matter. In America the ways of Africa would be of limited use to you. Our principles would be the same, but the techniques would be of little value. You need American magic. A new magic.

"Your America has only small, trivial traditions of magic, at least so far. You live in the Black Man's America and the White Man's America, a gray America, over pressed stone and between sheets of chalk. Removed from the natural ways you will need to learn new ways."

Cinque's fingers twisted. "Then are you going to teach me?"

"No, I will not. I have already said that my teachings would do you little good."

"Whose magic am I supposed to use?"

The African opened his hands and said, "Why, your own, of course."

"I don't have any magic."

"Then you had better make some and make it soon. This is for the best. It is better to learn magic the hard way." He leaned forward and asked, "Do you trust me?"

In the distance, the cat-lions had finished with their kill and the pigeon-vultures moved in to pick at the bloody bones. Distracted, Cinque said, "I guess so."

"You do or you do not. I am not interested in guesses."

"Yes." He almost shouted in frustration.

"Yes what?"

"Yes. I trust you."

"You should not. Trust is to be earned, not given freely. Suspect those who ask for your trust and never trust those who demand it. I will never ask you to trust me," said the African. "Either you do, or you do not. I have done nothing to help you. In fact you will regret ever meeting me. But years from now, you should think back to this day and imagine what your life would have been like without me."

The words stung. Cinque's hands formed fists. His voice rose, "So I can't trust you and you won't be teaching me how to put up with this sight beyond sight! Then what good are you?"

The African looked down at him with that calm look of his and Cinque felt stupid for losing his cool.

"I will help you to know yourself. I will teach you about life." He picked up his drum again. "This is something you need far more help with. You cannot know Juju without knowing yourself. What I teach you, you should meditate upon, take the lessons apart, try them on, see if they fit, keep the ones that do.

"You have troubling times ahead. Few who touch the spirit world remain intact. Tonight I will tell you a story. Within my story is a lesson that will help you through the darkness."

The man sat down on his stool and picked up his drum. Cinque sat cross-legged on the ground. As the African began the first story he tapped the drum in time with his speech, and it was as if the drum was also telling the story in its own language.

The Farmer was desperate. There had been no rain for months. If it rained today it would be too late. The last of his cattle had died, his land was brown and dusty, his family gaunt and thirsty.

Again he knelt before the altar, a head he had formed from mud and clay with the various family heirlooms piled before it, anything from the past: a comb, a knife, a doll, a goad and a bowl. He made the act from himself. Again he cried to his ancestors for help as he had so often before. Only this time it was different. This time someone came. The Farmer heard the footsteps in the darkness, looked up at the approaching figure and, before it hobbled fully into the light, he recognized his mother's mother, dead some fifteen years. His rising heart sank again. She had been a demanding, unpleasant woman in life, like a dark cloud over the family. No one had been sad to see her go, least of all the Farmer.

"Beg for it," she sneered.

"Beg for what?" asked the Farmer. He knew what he was begging for, he was begging for help. He also knew she would lie to him so he needed to test her.

Ghosts knew secrets, secrets they did not know while alive. That is why the Farmer had called on his ancestors; he wanted one of these secrets.

He spoke to the ground, "Please, Grandmother, my family is starving."

"What matter is that to me? My bones lie in the graveyard, my spirit sleeps peacefully. Well, it did. You woke me from my long, deserved rest. You must make amends."

"I need money. Maybe some is buried and forgotten somewhere near? I was hoping—"

"I know why you are here. You are a failure, and you are desperate. You ask me for help because no one else would." She was the same in death as she was in life. "I am hungry," said the ghost. "It has been long since I have known the taste of honey. Go to your neighbour's house. He is not home. He has left his door unlocked. Find the jar with the three stripes and bring it here."

The Farmer went to his neighbour's house. The door was unlocked and the rooms dark. In the moonlight he found the one with three stripes and brought it back to his grandmother's ghost.

Again, she stepped out of the darkness. Without a word of thanks to her grandson, she dipped her hand into the jar and gorged herself on the honey.

When she had finally emptied the jar she spoke. "Now I

want some cigarettes to take with me. Being dead leaves one with a lot of time that could be better spent smoking."

"But I just got the honey for you! Now you have to tell me where to find the treasure!"

She sneered back at him, "The honey was payment for waking me. If you want my knowledge of hidden treasure it will cost you further!" She looked up idly at the moon. "The market in town—the shopkeeper is out and he's left his young daughter in the store. She's a foolish girl. If you tell her that you have come for the carton of cigarettes you paid for yesterday, she will believe you."

The Farmer fought down his rage. There was nothing he could do but give in. He stormed off to the market. The girl was there as his grandmother said. He told the girl the lie given to him by his grandmother, and she believed him, just as the old woman said.

He returned to the altar and laid the carton next to the empty jar. Out of the darkness his grandmother returned and slipped the carton among her burial robes, looked at him and said nothing.

The Farmer lost his patience. "Now! Where is the treasure?"

"You want to know what I know about buried treasure?" she said with an unfriendly smile.

"I've given you what you asked for—"

"What did I ask for?"

"The cigarettes! You asked for them, told me where to get them and I have brought them!"

"I never asked for anything, boy. I was only thinking out loud." She gave herself a satisfied chuckle. "We never made a deal.

"If you want to know what I know about buried treasure you're going to have to bring me a bottle of rum."

"What?" The Farmer's hands went to his hips.

"Wait in the bushes by the nearby road and arm yourself with a good, strong stick."

"I've given you your offerings. By Egungun, tell me where the treasure is!"

She continued as if he had not spoken at all. "Within the hour a man with a bottle will pass by."

"I have given you your offerings. By Egungun, tell me where the treasure is!"

"He has already finished off half the bottle, but I am feeling generous. . . ."

"I have given you your offerings. By Egungun, tell me where the treasure is!" the Farmer screamed, feeling his throat go raw.

His grandmother stopped her musings, her eyes glazed and against her will, she spoke, "This is what I know about buried treasure. . . . There is none within a thousand miles of here."

The Farmer dropped to his knees. "But . . . but you said—"

His grandmother's foul disposition snapped back, "I've given you what I said I would! I've given you what I knew! You were born a fool and now you will die a fool with your fool's family."

With a sneer she slid back into the darkness.

By the time the African completed his story the pigeon-vultures had finished with the carcass and had flown away.

"Who is Egungun?" asked Cinque.

"The Collective Dead. He is a ghost who had never lived. Every ghost is also Egungun."

"I don't understand."

"Are you a Christian?"

"Yeah, I guess."

"What good are your guesses?" Cinque winced and reminded himself to watch his mouth.

It had been a long time since Cinque had been to church,

but he had still thought of himself as a Christian. What he had seen of the world made the faith feel quaint, limited.

"I don't know anymore."

This answer satisfied the African. "I will use the god of the Believers as an example, the three who are one, Father, Son and Holy Spirit, though they are all spirits. Three beings but one god, they are aspects of one being, a collective. Change the name and you change the aspect."

"Would I be able to use Egungun to find my Pa's ghost?"

"Why would you want to do that?"

Cinque wasn't prepared for that question. "Everything's telling me to do it. The Black Wire Hand that stole my heart said something about a visit from my father. Then a little fox-faced guy told me I should look for my Pa. This is all after I got a letter saying he died. . . . Maybe this is all because I never got to meet him when he was alive."

"And by meeting his ghost . . . ?"

"I'll know where I came from, how I got to be and how I got to be where I am now."

"I will not tell you to do this thing, but I will say that it is better to know than to not know, especially to know yourself. The Farmer's magic was personal. If you are going to call on your ancestor then your magic should be too."

"Could my father help me find my missing heart? Maybe that's what this is all about. Maybe whatever stole my heart wanted me to find my father's ghost so he could help me." Cinque should have connected the theft of his heart with his father sooner. The Black Wire Hand *had* said, "The father shall be visited upon the son" as it left, but he hadn't connected his father with Juju. It seemed absurd. If this was part of a plan and his father was on his side in this plan, that made him feel better.

"Or," the African suggested, "Perhaps it was your enemies and they attempt to mislead you. Perhaps they strike at you out of vengeance toward your father. This black wire curse could be lethal. Perhaps your father is the one who stole your heart. You said yourself that you don't know the man." The African's voice faded and Cinque realized he was the one drifting away. He tried to fight it but that just woke him up.

When Cinque returned from the liminal dream-not-a-dream the clock by his bed read 3:14 AM. He sat up grateful that after everything that had happened to him over the last couple of days, he'd finally found someone who was on his side. He finally had hope. The curse of the Black Wire Hand was going to be the death of him if he didn't act fast. But he had to take care of the Cuttlefish first.

Inspired by the African's story he put a plan together as he threw on his clothes and dug into his hamper for bait: a light blue t-shirt with a ringer collar. It was once his favourite, but it was getting too small. He had worn it on the hottest day of last week, and it was rank. It was perfect.

A bit of himself to evoke himself, like when the Farmer used bits of his grandmother to evoke her ghost. With his t-shirt and a wire hanger from his closet he went to find the Cuttlefish.

In the darkness the Cuttlefish looked solid, floating listlessly in the moonlight. It had made it to the Belmont sidewalk, hovering just outside a chain link fence. It had pushed most of itself through one of the openings. One bloated limb hung behind it, slowly passing through the metal link. Sluggish, w-shaped pupils spied Cinque immediately, and its arms grasped toward the boy.

Cinque kept back, holding the t-shirt on the hanger between himself and the creature, edging around the monster in a circle to the left. It turned after him, tugging its arm free from the fence while Cinque moved the t-shirt up between them like a puppet. Agitated by the closeness of its prey the Cuttlefish grabbed at the shirt and Cinque stumbled backward, almost tripping with every step as the creature oozed after him barely beyond the reach of the gibbering mouths.

"—let me tell you about my mother—"

"Do you know how it feels to know you never cared?"

"I wouldn't have to go—"

"You'll never find your father—"

"—viously we're especially concerned about—"

Did it just say something about his father? Cinque almost stopped in his tracks, but with a mighty push of its arms the Cuttlefish shot at him. Cinque ran back, off the street, away from Loyston, among the ruined buildings that used to be St. Jude's business district. Twisting and circling, crossing his own trail more than once, he led the monster out into a nearby residential area that had been burned out for as long as he could remember. Then, he went up to the door of a one bedroom that had been decimated by fire. The Cuttlefish followed, moving in short fast rushes, drifting to a stop in between bursts of speed to pull its arms forward for another stroke.

Panting, Cinque stepped over the fallen doorway and into the building's remains, back behind the remaining walls, inside what might have been a bedroom. If family heirlooms can attract the Farmer's grandmother's ghost, he thought, if things taste of the people who owned them then the Cuttlefish should like the taste of *this*. He put himself into the shirt every way he could think of: he used it to wipe the sweat of his face before he took a deep breath and blew through the shirt, pushing a thought of himself out with it. Then he hooked the t-shirt and hanger on the deteriorating ceiling. He wrote his full name across the front of the shirt with a black magic marker. While writing, he called up his fear of the Cuttlefish. Concentrating, he pushed that fear down his arm, through his trembling hand, and into the shirt. He used his fear like the Farmer used his desperation.

He hoped no one he knew would find the shirt. He didn't want to explain what it was and what it was doing here.

His ritual over and his concentration fading, Cinque noticed a train of black ants encircling the room in a twisting line along the wall, running over the glass window and across the doors, including the door he'd just closed behind him. Just below the train of black ants another train, this one of red ants, rode up right next to the black train in the opposite direction, like traffic on the highway.

Careful to leave every ant uncrushed and undisturbed, he left the building through an open window, the ants running across the top half while Cinque slipped through the bottom. He ran a wide circle around town to make sure he wouldn't cross paths with the Cuttlefish on the way home.

Back in bed, Cinque slept hard through the rest of the morning and into the alarm clock's wail. He'd taken care of the Cuttlefish, at least for now, and the pain in his chest was gone. He felt good. So good that he forgot he was angry with his Ma until that afternoon, by then it didn't matter so much.

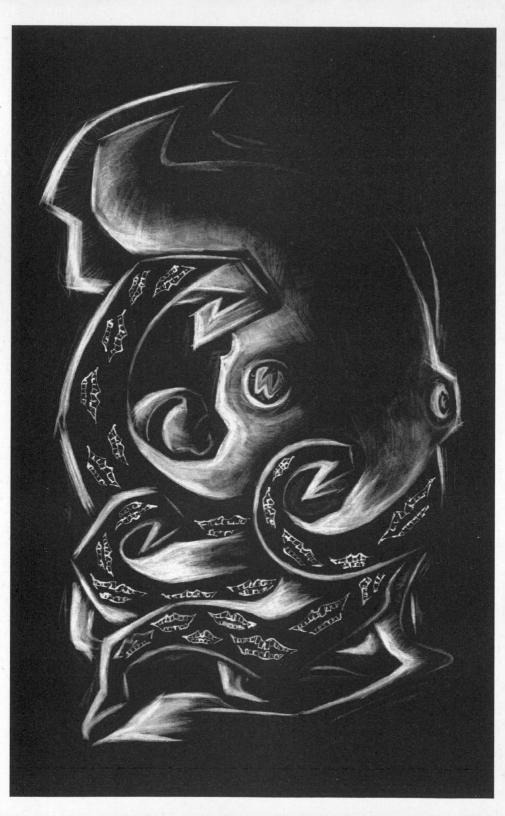

5

UNCRUSHED AND UNDISTURBED

That Saturday morning, flushed with success after his first, tentative foray into Juju, Cinque wanted to get to work looking for ghosts, but when he tried to leave the house, Darren followed his little cousin, pestering him with questions about his pending inheritance.

"A few hundred?" Darren said, "You think that's all? Naw, boy, ain't no grown up that broke. More like a couple thousand. Whatchu gonna do with it?"

Cinque stopped. "I don't know. I hadn't really thought about it. Maybe a computer, I don't know any kid in St. Jude who's got a computer."

"Whatcha need a computer for? Whatchu think you gonna be a scientist or somethin'? If you're gonna throw that money away you might as well give it to me, I'll show you what to do with it, what's important."

"Maybe." They turned the corner of Potts and Belmont. "Maybe it's more than just the money? Inheritance that is. You think it's important to know where you came from?"

"If you wanna get back home it is," was his cousin's sarcastic answer.

"Not where you live. Where you came from. Who your folks are. Remember Damarco and Jaric? And look at Aaron Dorsey, he been in juvie longer than he been in school. All of them, they all messed up and what do they all got in common? Nobody knows who their dads are—"

Darren sucker-punched Cinque in the back of the head, knocking him to the ground.

"What you tryin' to say, boy?"

Cinque rolled over on his side. Darren stepped on Cinque's hand, pinning it to the ground.

"You tellin' me that I'm fucked from birth?"

He had forgotten for a moment that Darren didn't know his father either. "Yeah, well you won't ever know also," his cousin yelled. "That government letter said your Pa was dead, so you fucked too."

Cinque squinted up at Darren silhouetted in the morning sun.

"I won't let that stop me from being what I want," Cinque said defiantly.

For some reason Darren relaxed.

"Me neither." He helped his little cousin up off the ground and left him alone.

The sun was somewhere overhead but Cinque couldn't find it in the flat gray sky. Searching, he lay stretched across the only bench left standing in the derelict Calico Cemetery which marked the grave of Mister Emmons, 1889-1925—"Mercy on his soul"—covered by a large, plain slab of granite. On the opposite side of the slab stood an ornate five-foot, old-fashioned headstone. An angel blew his trumpet down from clouds at the top. Along either side, a robed man and woman waited, in case Mister Emmons might someday need assistance, along the bottom, a row of five-petaled flowers. Mister Emmons' final residence was on the high ground, where the rich men's graves were kept. The wealthy living had long since abandoned St. Jude, leaving the wealthy dead behind, their graves now overrun by the same weeds as the poor folks down the hill.

The graveyard hadn't seen a keeper in a good long time. The woods were invading from the north, upending the fence with their roots. At the base of the rich man's hill grew a single, small pear tree, grown from the refuse of some long ago picnic. Cinque helped himself to the one pear ripe enough to eat.

The ground was an ankle-twisting hazard of rain ruts and roots hidden by the high grass. Shallow trenches, four inches deep, two feet wide and five feet long marked many of the older graves. At first Cinque thought that leaving graves unfilled was the custom back when the nineteenth century turned into the twentieth. Then he realized that these holes formed when the coffins below had collapsed, finally giving in to the rot and weight, stepping into a trench meant stepping into a grave.

The graveyard seemed like a good place for ghosts and good ghost weather—overcast, damp, and threatening rain—but the only spirits he saw were scurrying, little inhuman things. In this place, there were only a few of them and they kept their distance. The Pastor's fix of rope and smoke made Cinque feel like himself again, like before the Black Wire Hand took a piece of him. While he could still see the creatures that no one else could, he now knew they were some kind of real, which meant he wasn't crazy and he knew there were ways to handle them if they ever gave him any trouble.

As they became more familiar, Cinque ignored them and they rarely paid him any mind. Mostly, they flew about, pestering each other, making noise and then bolting off for parts unknown, like birds. If he looked closely, he could see other spirits sleeping in old buildings and trees. He had apologized to the spirit in the pear tree before taking its fruit.

He sat on the bench and ate his pear, core and all, despite its slightly earthy taste. "You had to walk before you could run." Grandma had said that one morning. He'd hoped he could get a feel for this ghost work by practicing on some wandering spectre who happened by. When he brought his Pa's spirit back from death, it wouldn't do if he choked. Better to choke in front of a stranger's spirit.

Besides, he was hardly prepared to meet his Pa. Not before his talk with Ma and certainly not now. On one side Cinque had all this weirdness telling him to find his father; on the other there was his mother telling him to leave it alone. He didn't know who to trust. His feelings still had to work themselves out but he still had some time to do it. *If* he could do it.

In the story, the Farmer built his shrine from his family's physical and emotional legacy. All Cinque had was a name and how many dead men named Kelly Lee were out there? Dozens? Hundreds? Why couldn't his mother have saved something instead of cutting all ties? Surely if his father had known he would have left his son a picture, a clue, someplace for him to start.

Cinque stood up, brushed himself off and headed home for lunch, careful not to step in or on any graves. He might have some success at midnight but to spend any more of the day here would be a waste of time. People rarely visited this graveyard, few even knew it was here, hidden by the encroaching forest. If there ever had been any ghosts in the Calico Yard, they had moved on to the next life out of loneliness. If this place of death wasn't haunted, then Cinque knew he had to try a place of dying.

Memorial Hospital was unpleasantly familiar ground. The concrete building was brown and streaks of rust dripped from the gutters. It wasn't any cheerier inside. Ma had brought Cinque here last month when she'd discovered his body taken by violent seizures, eyes rolled back in his head. All Cinque knew was that he woke up that morning in a hospital bed and had to spend all Saturday there waiting for test results. It had ruined his weekend, Darren's too, because Grandma dragged him along an hour later.

The air was cloyingly thick with the smell of flowers, contrasting with the dismal building and the dismal weather. Cinque didn't know much about plant life but he knew an early bloom in this gloomy weather was strange. But it was just one more thing to add to the list, and Cinque had other concerns.

An adult could bluff his way around the hospital but Cinque knew there was still one major rule of access: "ALL CHILDREN MUST BE ACCOMPANIED BY AN ADULT AT ALL TIMES." Signs saying so were posted in every hall.

But he had long ago learned a useful trick from Darren for getting around this particular hurdle. He waited out by the parking lot. It didn't take long before a group of three ladies waddled up from their car. They had everything he was looking for: they were of reasonable ages, they walked like they knew where they were going and were too interested in their own voices to notice much of anything else. Casually, he walked up behind them—close, but not too close.

Darren had taken the hospital's policy of limited movement for the under-aged as a personal challenge. He had always resented being called a child. Of course Darren knew he'd never be able to convince the hospital staff of his manhood, so he skirted the challenge by skirting the rule. The hospital was full of strangers, and when he drifted along behind someone else's family, he was treated as another bored, reluctant son dragged along to visit another sick relative in the eyes of the staff. Cinque affected the act: indifference with a faint touch of attention to where he was being led.

St. Jude being St. Jude, almost all the patients were black folks, as were the non-professional staff. The doctors and nurses were white. Cinque had never seen so many white folks in one place before. When he'd asked his Ma why that was, she answered, "These white folks got their reasons for being here. Some are here on government programs that paid their way though medical school, and now they're paying the government back by spending a few years among the poor, places that have a hard time attracting medical personnel. Some of them are here 'cause they think it's the right thing to do, they got a little of the white man's guilt." Saying that amused her. "And then there's those who couldn't cut it anywhere else, has-beens, never-bes and screw-ups."

"Don't anybody from St. Jude become a doctor?" he had asked.

"Sometimes, but you can't become a doctor here in this town. You gotta go to a real city, a better city, for medical school and when you've been out of St. Jude you don't ever wanna come back. You'll see."

Today Cinque walked behind the ladies he was using as cover, Cinque saw deaths pending all around. A shrivelled up, old woman in the wheelchair with an ethereal, discoloured lump clinging to the side of her neck. A hospital room full of smoke no one seemed to notice, the same blue tinted smoke that poured out of the smoke stacks of the chemical plant night and day. A gurney passed by, carrying a middle aged man. He had a purple, glossy scab over his heart that showed through his gown.

A woman caught his eye. There wasn't anything strange about her on the surface except that she was white and she wasn't a doctor. She was one of those weird white folks, dressed in black, patched hoodie and worn denim shorts. Her cheek bones were real thin and high and her skin was so pale he could barely tell where her scalp stopped and her bleach-blonde dreadlocks started. Her eyes hid behind dark circles of glass and a black messenger bag lay on the bench next to her, a large white flower embroidered on the flap. Years ago on a family trip to Chicago he and Darren saw a group of white kids dressed in tattered black clothes like this. Darren said they were devil worshipers.

Cinque passed by her without looking. She seemed like trouble. Even behind the shades, he still felt like her eyes were following him.

The three ladies arrived at their destination halfway down the first hall, forcing Cinque to find new cover folks.

Around a corner the hall extended for a few feet before terminating in a pair of well-scuffed doors, each fixed with a small red sign reading "HOSPITAL PERSONNEL ONLY BEYOND THIS POINT." Cinque pushed through the doors and found himself in a dark hallway that did double duty as a storage area. The walls and floors were an unfinished gray along both sides. The shelving was for cleaning supplies and baggy hampers of white cotton. Under the overpowering scent of flowers the room smelled like floor wax and bleach.

The door closed behind him, trapping Cinque in pitch black. Aware that the room had more than its fair share of clutter, he stood still, waiting for his eyes to adjust to the darkness—sightless, defenceless.

Cinque realized he wasn't alone. Somewhere in the dark, a boy softly cried.

It wasn't a cry for attention; it was too quiet. It wasn't a cry of pain; it was too unsteady. It was the cry of a child trying not to cry, trying to hide. A cry of terror.

"Hello?" Cinque knew he had to say something. "You okay?"

The hushed, steady sobbing stopped, leaving a momentary silence punctuated by an intake of breath. As his eyes adjusted, the crying stuttered on. Cinque was sure that it was coming from among the hampers in the room.

"You hurt? Whatcha crying for?" He wasn't sure what to do. Other people's emotions made Cinque uncomfortable, especially the emotions of strangers. "Whatcha need?"

Finally, a small voice asked, "He here? The Cloudy Man? You seen him?"

"I . . . don't . . ." Cinque looked around cautiously. "I don't know, but probably not."

The stark white bandage hung in the darkness. Gradually, the boy filled in behind it. His gray t-shirt was ruined by a dark stain running down from his neck and across an iron-on decal for something called The Herculoids. His hair was cut in a short, even fro, a style Cinque had only seen on old sitcoms. It made the boy's head look round as a ball. He sat on the floor, keeping close to the shadows. Cinque thought he would have disappeared through the wall if he could.

"He here. In the hospital."

"Who's here?"

"The man who killed my brothers and my mommy."

A chill ran down Cinque's spine. Something was wrong. The kid was too old to be using a word like "mommy" but then he was too young to have lost his family.

"Did he do that too?" Cinque asked, pointing to the bandage on his neck.

The boy nodded. "He thought he killed me too, but I just played dead until he left. He must have come back, saw I weren't there no more and came here to get me. That's why I ran in here. Why'd someone do this? We ain't never hurt nobody."

So this is what terror looks like, Cinque thought. Knuckles clenched, chin shaking, knees knocking. All the expressions were true, and it was contagious. Cinque felt his own fear rise in sympathy. He needed to get out of here. . . .

Forced himself to stay. "My name is Cinque."

The boy twitched as if someone had shot a gun. "What was that?"

Cinque cocked his head and listened, his own heart beating faster. "I didn't hear nothi—" Something came through a door. Not the door in the doorway, Cinque realized, but a second, phantom door attached to the same hinges. A man's dark silhouette held the door open, dressed in heavy work boots, jeans, thermal shirt and one of those old, padded ski vests. His free hand held a claw hammer, claw forward. Where his head should have been was a small, black cloud. Cinque's chest began to burn again.

The second froze for so long, Cinque thought time was broken.

The Cloudy Man stood motionless in the framing light, waiting. Cinque stopped, half turned towards the intruder, dully aware of something else happening in the room. Like an alarm clock's buzz drilling though the thick morning sleep, something was trying for his attention.

The boy was screaming.

The second ended.

The Cloudy Man rushed forward. The phantom door swung shut behind him, his body still outlined in a horrible, gray light. Three great steps brought him a few inches from Cinque. His instincts finally kicked in and he jumped back. The Cloudy Man ignored him, lifted the hammer and waited, listening. Cinque turned back to the boy and tried to grab his wrist and run back the way he'd come. When he touched the boy's skin his hand went numb—not the tingling of a sleeping limb or the pain of ice held too long. It was a plain, simple numbness that made him doubt his hold on the boy.

Cinque pulled anyway but the boy didn't move. Rooted, he stared up at the Cloudy Man, terrified.

Then Cinque grabbed his arm with his other hand, but felt the same icy numbness. He pulled with his whole weight but he couldn't move the smaller boy.

"Come on, man! Move!" He winced as he pulled. If the Cloudy Man wasn't deaf, Cinque had just given them away.

The hammer hung in the air, begging to come down hard on something.

The boy wasn't going to run, Cinque realized. Desperate, he turned to the Cloudy Man and, remembering the story of the Farmer, said, "By Egungun—" he stammered "—fuck off!"

Nothing. Cinque stepped between the Cloudy Man and the boy.

"By Egungun, fuck off! By Egungun, fuck off!"

The Cloudy Man turned towards the boys. The hammer was above them both and he was stepping forward toward the boy.

Then Cinque was on the floor, unsure of how, and the Cloudy Man was past him. A sound repeated behind him. Thunk and squish, thunk and squish . . . Cinque looked around the room dumbly to see the Cloudy Man lift the hammer and bring it down, claw first, with a thunk. The boy's remains shook from the impact. The Cloudy Man lifted the hammer again.

Before Cinque knew what he was doing, he burst through the hospital's front doors and ran across the grass. Free from the building, his legs dropped out from under him. He fell, face first, on the uneven lawn and lay there until his body stopped shaking and the heat in his chest faded.

6

A HORRIBLE, GRAY LIGHT

Cinque searched though old newspapers at the library later that afternoon, hoping to learn more about the dead boy in the hospital. Scanning the headlines was quick work, each a shadowy snapshot of St. Jude: corruption, drugs, murder and greed. He only had to read a few words of an article to taste fear, tragedy, loss or disappointment and sometimes, rarely, the sweet tang of hope. St. Jude always seemed to be getting worse, always someone there to rob the city of its cash or its dignity. Still, it staggered on.

The librarian asked if he was looking for something specific. He declined her help, believing the effort of finding was as important as the finding itself. Hours later, after Cinque talked himself out of giving up for the ninth time, something caught his eye: the boy from the hospital smiled out from the front page of September 6, 1969.

Residents of St. Jude are trying to understand why Shawn Bentley brutally killed his wife and children yesterday. The county truant officer attempted to contact Sandra Bentley when her three boys didn't show up to school. Their calls unanswered, the truant officer dispatched to the house discovered the door ajar and the body of one of the boys on the doorstep.

The police arrived on the scene and discovered Sandra and two more boys inside the house. The youngest boy, Michael Bentley, still alive but seriously injured, was brought to Memorial Hospital.

Shawn Bentley had gone into work that morning after attacking his family. Since he wasn't a suspect, police told him the location of his surviving son and was allowed to enter the hospital where he killed his remaining son.

Police Chief Yerby promised to investigate why Shawn Bentley was not placed immediately under police scrutiny.

A family portrait accompanied the article. Cinque recognized the smallest son as the boy from the hospital. The Cloudy Man had the build of his father.

Cinque slid the page out of the newspaper holder, folded it up, stuffed it in his pocket and left the library with purpose, a righteousness that made him feel good. And with a slightly selfish sense of satisfaction—he had proof that the hospital ghosts were real.

The feeling of purpose buoyed Cinque as he made his way back to the hospital. Armed with a newspaper clipping full of validation, he aimed to put this ghost to rest. He was reading the article for the fifth time as he walked when he heard the call, "Sin-Kay."

Cinque took another step along the cracked sidewalk.

He couldn't pretend that he hadn't heard. The setting sun cast long shadows across the yard of a single story building with peeling blue paint. Imani sat on the front steps, long legs stretched toward him from under her shorts. "Whatchu doing all the way over here, Sin-Kay? You know this ain't your neighbourhood."

Cinque tore his eyes up from her legs: "Um . . ."

"What's that?" She pointed to the newspaper clipping that he had tried to hide it behind his back. "You know if you don't tell me I'ma just take it."

Cinque looked at the scrap of newspaper in his hand. This was his life now and he'd have to share it with someone. Maybe it would earn her respect. Time to test the water. "It's about Michael Bentley and his dad, the ghosts of Memorial Hospital, but before they was ghosts."

Imani pulled her legs in and leaned forward, scrutinizing the boy, "How you know all that, Sin-Kay?"

"I seen 'em. In a back room, they've been relivin' the murder every night since. Michael forever the victim, his pop's the killer and Michael doesn't even know. Can you imagine that?" Already Cinque felt better. The secret wasn't pushing inside his skull anymore, trying to get out. It was hers now, she could do what she wanted to with it.

Imani studied Cinque, looking for signs of a joke. Even Cinque could tell that his talk of ghosts scared her, just a little. "I found this in the library. I'm going to find Michael's ghost and show him the newspaper. Maybe once he finds out who killed him he can go free."

"What for?"

"I guess, 'cause it's the right thing to do. Isn't it?"

"You bein' silly." She leaned back against the steps and tried to look bored.

Sneaking into the hospital in early evening was easier in some ways and harder in others. There were less staff present but there wasn't the crowd of visitors for him to lose himself in. After a few close calls, Cinque navigated his way back to the haunted store room. Waiting and concentrating on Michael Bentley, he pictured the boy in the corner where he'd seen him before. With the page in the newspaper in hand he said, "Michael Bentley. Come on out here, Michael Bentley. I'm here to help you." He was concentrating so hard that when the boy did appear Cinque wasn't sure if he wasn't fooling himself by calling up memories until the boy spoke.

"Who are you?"

"I'm Cinque, you remember me? From yesterday? I been here when—" he stopped mid-sentence not sure if reminding the ghost that he was re-enacting his own murder was a good idea.

"Whatcha talking about, man? I've never seen you before in my whole life." His voice was full of confusion. "And I don't care! Someone killed my family and he's here, the Cloudy Man is here, and he gonna kill me too!"

Cinque held out the page from the newspaper: "'Shawn Bentley had gone into work that morning after attacking his family. Since he wasn't a suspect, police told him the location of his surviving son and was allowed to enter the hospital where he killed his remaining son. . . .' Look, man, this is you! This is the paper from your tomorrow!"

"Wha—what are you talking about? Someone's gonna kill me!"

"Yeah, I know!" Cinque half-shouted. "Look at the paper, it'll tell you who he is!"

Michael pulled away. "He's gonna kill me!"

Frustrated, Cinque read the whole article aloud. "See? The Cloudy Man is your pa! It's your pa who's trying to kill you!"

"I ain't never seen him before, why did he do this?"

"Listen! 'Since he wasn't a suspect, police told him the location of his surviving son and was allowed to enter the hospital where he killed his remaining son.'" He smacked the page for emphasis. "You hear that, Michael? This is you, boy! You been dead for more than thirty years and you just keep on dying! You gotta face the truth, boy, there ain't no Cloudy Man, it was your pops that killed you an' your family. Can't ya' see?"

A slight shine of understanding was apparent in the kid's face. Had he finally gotten the boy's attention?

"Is you blind?"

Then it was gone. Michael repeated, "The Cloudy Man killed my ma. My brothers!"

The room filled with gray light. *Oh oh,* Cinque thought and turned slowly, expecting to facedown the ominous form of the ghost of a ghost. Instead the doorway filled with the biggest security guard he'd ever seen.

"Now I know you ain't supposed to be in here."

Cinque sat inside the security office, a little closet sized booth off to the side of the Emergency Room, waiting for Grandma to come get him. Sneaking around a hospital after dark might mean getting a whoopin'. Usually, Darren got whooped and Cinque got grounded, but if asked, tonight Cinque would opt for a whoopin', even if it hurt something fierce. He had things to do and places to go.

"So who's blind?" the security guard—Gus, one of the nurses called him—asked from the doorway.

Cinque hadn't said much, giving up his name and number easily. Since then the two of them had been waiting in uncomfortable silence, Cinque in the chair and Gus in the door sipping his coffee. The sudden attention caught Cinque off guard. He looked up at the man, not sure if he heard right.

"When you was back in the store room, in the dark, you was

waving that newspaper around and telling someone that they was blind. But it was just you in the room an' you can see just fine, so who's blind?"

"Michael Bentley."

"Who's Michael Bentley?"

Cinque pulled the page out of his pocket and handed it over. "Michael Bentley was killed in that room on September 6th, 1969. His pa caved in his head with a claw hammer."

Gus's eyes widened and his jaw dropped like he wanted to say something but didn't have the words.

"You know what I'm talking about, don't you?"

Gus folded up the page with unsteady hands and gave it back to the boy, "Yeah ... yeah I do. ... Where'd you hear about this? Your Ma know someone who works here or something?"

"Michael's been dying at his daddy's hand every day and night since he was killed the first time. I saw it happen yesterday." Cinque slouched in the chair and folded his arms. "I know enough to know what's goin' on but not enough to save him."

Gus looked at the boy with new eyes—respect and a little bit of fear. "Long as anyone can remember, there been something wrong about that room. Door swinging on its own, strange noises, and a chill in the air even in the heat of summer. Heard tell someone got killed back in there, a kid. Don't know more than that."

"He says it's the Cloudy Man that killed him. Killed his brothers and his ma too, but that's just 'cause he won't see his pa's face, even when the hammer comes down. I thought that maybe when I showed him the truth it'd set him free, like they say and all but he wouldn't listen. How do you get through to someone like that?"

Gus shook his head. "If someone don't wanna hear what they don't wanna hear, there ain't nothing you can do for them till they come around on their own. You know how God helps those who help themselves? That's 'cause he knows better than to waste his time on those who won't."

Another long silence. "Where is that smell coming from anyway? It's strong."

"The ditch out back fills up with water. They gotta dump chemicals in it every summer to kill the mosquitoes. They should drain the damn thing up but the county don't have the money to do it."

"At least it smells nice."

Gus twisted up his nose. "Smells nice? What does that smell like to you?"

"Smells like flowers to me."

"Boy, I don't know what kinda flowers you been smellin', but this place smells like it's always smelled. Like a swamp. Nasty."

Flowers only he could smell, ghosts only he could see. Cinque shook his head.

Then it clicked. It wasn't the hospital that smelled like flowers or even flowers that smelled like flowers, it was the ghosts.

When Grandma showed up, Gus had a talk with her on the other side of the ER, where Cinque couldn't hear. When she finally did come over, she asked Cinque for the newspaper page. She read it over and asked a few more questions about how Cinque came in possession of the paper. He could tell she didn't like the answers, but she didn't get angry like when Darren lied to her.

They drove home in heavy silence. Cinque was relieved that he wasn't in trouble, but also worried that he'd scared Grandma. He felt a little guilt and a lot of disbelief. Could a little thing like a ghost story shake her so? He'd rather she just get mad and hit him like she did with Darren. Then he'd feel like part of the family.

There was no whooping, no grounding. Nobody talked to

Cinque or Darren about what happened, though he was sure
the unspoken code of silence didn't apply to Ma and Grandma
behind closed doors. That didn't matter. Cinque had things to
do.

7

SMELLED LIKE FLOWERS

Cinque walked through St. Jude by the light of the setting sun. He wandered down a side street, passing by a huge pile of trash and a spirit wearing a flat, paper mask of George Washington as he looked on the dollar bill, flat and all whites and greens. George's mouth was torn away revealing lipless, shivering teeth beneath. A sickly yellow cloth tied around its neck concealed other deformities it might have. Its clawed hands clutched the broom stick it used to push through the layers of garbage, looking for something.

The creature saw Cinque and, startled, pointing the stick at Cinque defensively. "Back off, money bags!" It stabbed a few times Cinque's direction.

Cinque's hands went up and opened innocently. "Money bags? Who you calling money bags? I got less money than you got there on your face."

The little monster grunted and sniffed at Cinque over his stick. "You ain't got money in hand, but you got money a coming. Don't you think about usin' it on me!" It kicked a paper bag full of something soggy at Cinque. "That's how you do, I know, swingin' your heavy money sacks around all willy nilly, smackin' 'round the little guy like me who has no dough."

"What are you looking for in the trash?"

"Dough."

"You're looking for money, in the trash?"

"Where else am I gonna find it? Where'd you find yours?"

"I didn't find anything, but I am set to inherit my pops' estate. You saying there's a lot of money in there?"

"You smell like it. As if you need it . . . you with your fancy shoes that don't match. Just showin' off that you got two pair of shoes is all! Raghhhh!" It screamed, batting pieces of garbage at Cinque with its broomstick like a maniac.

Cinque ran out of range but the creature didn't follow. It just stood on top of its pile of garbage shaking its stick and screaming obscenities at him.

He kept walking along the street George Washington had chased him down until he came across a skinny brother, wearing last year's fashions, sitting on the hood of an abandoned Chrysler just outside downtown St. Jude. The man rocked back and forth and hugged his knees. Surrounded by concrete, spilled oil, and the ambient reek of the chemical plant side of town, he still smelled strongly of the familiar scent of flowers.

"Yo. I see you, man."

The strange man twitched. His head turned a little Cinque's way.

"I said I can see you, man, isn't that whatcha wanna hear?"

The man's head turned, slowly, unsure sure how to react. "Whatcha say?"

"You heard me. I can see you. I know you're there. An' I know why."

"Why?" The man's voice creaked.

"Why I can see you and no one else does. It's 'cause you been dead, ain't that right?"

He nodded, "Yeah. Yeah, I am. . . ."

Cinque was relieved. If a ghost didn't know he was a ghost Cinque wasn't sure he could convince him otherwise. "If you know you're dead then why are you here?"

"Someone's gotta keep a watch on Rikkia." The ghost looked down and shook his head. "She's got in bad since I left."

"What kinda bad she in?"

"Her new man. He don' treat her right. Someone's gotta stop all this. . . ." He looked up at Cinque. "Sorry, man, I ain't talked wit' nobody for . . . a long-ass time."

"How long's it been since you died?"

"Can't really say. Time's goin' faster now than it was. Maybe I'm just gettin' used to doin' nuttin'." The ghost pointed to the side of the house he had been watching. "That's where it happened, I remember that much. I remember wakin' up in the night, nigga breakin' in. Not for long though. I shot him, he shot me. He took off and I bled out on the living room floor. Least Rikkia made it through okay."

Cinque sat on the hood, next to the ghost. "You remember your name?"

The ghost looked at him like he was stupid, "Course I remember my name. I ain't that far gone, boy. I'm Willy Thompson, the people called me Willy T. You ever heard a me?"

"Naw, man, sorry I didn't."

The ghost was disappointed, "Guess no matter how big the player, when it game over, it over."

"My name is Cinque, Cinque Williams."

"An' whatcha want, Cinque Williams?"

"Who says I want somethin'?"

"Everybody wants somethin', an' people who gonna talk to a ghost, they must really want somethin'." Willy T smiled. "'Less you used to lookin' a fool."

Cinque was, but he didn't admit it. "I want to see my Pa."

"I don' know your pa."

"My Pa's dead."

"So? You think I know all the dead niggas in the world? We all chill at the Dead Nigga Club or somethin'? If that were true I'd be gettin' it on with Left Eye right now."

Willy T hacked out a dry laugh. "Ha Ha! Aw, man! Been a long-ass time since I had a laugh, little man, a long-ass time, been so long a little laugh is all I can take."

"I figure I got a better chance a findin' him with your help. I need a ghost to find a ghost, you know what I'm sayin'?"

"Yeah, I know whatcha sayin' an' I'm sayin' I ain't interested. You an' your Pa ain't got nothin' to do with me an' mine." He turned back to stare at the house across the street.

"That her house?"

Willy T said nothing.

"I bet that's her house, ain't it? I bet he's in there too, ain't he? Whatcha think he doin' in there? Whatcha think they—"

Willy T jumped off the hood, aiming a backhanded slap at Cinque, but Darren's little cousin was an old acquaintance of the cheap shot. He rolled back off the hood and onto his feet.

"Oh, now! What that about? Maybe you ain't got nothin' to do with me or my Pa, but you got somethin' goin' on in there, ain't ya?"

Furious, Willy T balled up his fists and came at him again. Compared to Darren, the man moved like cold molasses. Cinque had no problem dodging his punches.

"An' there's nothin' you can do about it, is there? Yo' ass can only sit out here in the cold and hate. Your hate's what's keeping you here, ain't it? Keepin' you on this corner, in this town, in this world, 'cause when you come down to it—" The swings kept coming, and Cinque kept ahead of them. "—you can't do anything about it, can you?"

The ghost threw a few more useless swings before he fell to his knees, out of humiliation, not exhaustion. "I couldn't hit ya anyway," the man said from the ground. "Can't touch nothin'."

"But I can. You a dead man who needs some help from the livin', and I'm alive and I need some help from the dead. I can help out your lady . . . if you help me first." Cinque had never tried to strike a deal with a stranger like this and he didn't like it. He might end up giving the ghost the help he needed only to have the ghost bolt. But promises were the only currency he had.

Willy T squinted up at the boy with one eye. "An' how am I supposed to do that?"

"You don't know?" Disappointment filled him. Cinque had figured that the ghost would have all the answers he needed, like the one in the Pastor's story.

"Naw, I don't know! You're all, 'Willy T, I need you to find my Pa.' And you ain't got no plan?" He chuckled. "Ain't that somethin'? Boy, you gotta think things through before you gonna make a play."

"I thought you ghosts knew about buried treasure and all that."

Willy T stood up. "Yeah? Well you thought wrong, boy. I don't know nothin' except that my woman needs me to look out for her!"

Cinque shook his hands, dismissing this little problem. "Alright, alright, gimme a second to break this down, I just gotta figure out what I know and then I'll be clear. It's just another problem, like in math. Start with whatcha know, and then figure out how to get to where you wanna be."

"You on your own there, boy, I ain't got no use for no math. That jack's for faggots."

Cinque thought about the Pastor's story of the Farmer and how he'd contacted the ghost of his mother's mother. "You been outta St. Jude at all?"

"Why would I wanna do that? I don't go nowhere that got nothin' to do with my girl."

"Man, don't you care about nothing else?" Cinque shook his head in disbelief.

"Naw, man, like you said, I'm made of smoke. What else do I need if I can't touch nothin'?"

"What about stuff you did together? Anything that means something to you 'cause of her?"

"Oh yeah, there's a picture of the two of us from back in the day. Them was some good times, when she an' I just started. Yeah, I think about that a lot."

"Where'd that picture get to?"

The ghost raised an unsteady hand and pointed. "It's still in that house . . . somewhere."

8

IN THAT HOUSE

Of the Williams boys, anyone would have picked Darren as the one who would break into a house, but in the early evening Cinque was clinging outside a second story apartment window, trespassing twice in as many days. His fingers pinched the sill, desperate to hold on. His toes barely dug into the rotten boards, as he waited for Willy to give him the all clear. He struggled and slipped, legs quivering and shaking. Cinque realized that Willy should have scoped out the apartment before he started climbing. But the fear of falling drove away the fear of capture. His doubts were telling him to climb back down while he had the chance.

Willy's head passed through the glass, looked down at the boy and said, "S'up, man? You just hangin' out? Ha!"

"Shut up, fool! I'm goin' in, clear or not!" Cinque straightened his legs, and pulled himself up onto the window sill.

"Lucky fo' you ain't none o' them home. See yo' inside!" Willy slipped back through the glass. Cinque pushed the window up in its track with his thumbs and into the house with his elbows. The latch came loose. He slid the window a little to the left and eased it back onto the track. Then pushing the window aside, he stepped through the frame and onto a dresser covered in glossy fashion magazines. His ankle twisted and he almost slipped, crumpling the top magazine's cover as he danced around the dresser top, looking for solid purchase. Stable again, he took a deep breath and slid down from the window sill into a space barely recognizable as a bedroom.

Cinque looked at the piles of clothing, the stacks of fashion and gossip magazines, the furniture shoved into corners and piled upon, the clutter of make-up bottles and he shook his head. "Man, there just ain't no way."

Willy just looked at him, uncomprehending.

"Look at this place, man! This is a sty! How we gonna find one picture in all this? And this is just one room!"

Willy just smiled. "She's a sloppy one, ain't she? I ain't been gone a year and ten times as much junk piled up in here. You know what that means, boy? That means what we're lookin' for is somewhere at the bottom of one of these piles."

"You say that like it's a good thing."

"That's 'cause we don't have to search the top of any of this." He waved at the mess.

Cinque glared around at the piles of clutter, he would have liked better news, "Well, I guess that's somethin'."

"An' since there ain't a lot of cleanin' goin' on around here, I'ma bet that it's still in this room. That good enough news for ya?"

Cinque shot the ghost a frustrated look. "That the best you got?"

"For now."

"Then it'll have to do. Let's get started."

"What do ya mean, 'let's'?" Willy passed his hand through the closest pile of junk.

With a resigned sigh, Cinque started to dig.

An hour later Cinque was shoving piles of junk out of his way. If they fell, he left them where they lay. He no longer cared if anyone knew that someone had been here. In this mess, he doubted that they would. He promised that when this was all over he'd clean his room and keep it clean.

Willy realized that pointing to things and saying, "How 'bout that one?" wasn't helping. He sat on the bed and tried to remember the last place he'd seen the picture. In one of the stacks Cinque found a fist full of bills and cancelled checks, utilities and credit cards, all in the name of Rikkia Mann with large outstanding balances all paid off as of five months ago. The payees and amounts on the checks corresponded to the bills, but had been signed by Darius Oates. "Hey, Willy. What'd you say that new guy's name was again?"

"Darryl, DeShawn or somethin'—"

"You mean Darius Oates?"

"Yeah that sound right. Why?"

"'Cause I don't think he's livin' offa your girl, man. It looks like he came in and paid all her bills."

"What?"

"Look at these numbers." Cinque held the paperwork out to Willy but he didn't look. Instead, the ghost tried to backslap them out of Cinque's grasp, but his hand passed through the papers futilely.

"I don' gotta look at nothin'! I'm tellin' you what I seen with my own eyes! He's been livin' off my girl. And I'm gonna stop it."

"Numbers don't lie."

"Yeah? Well people do! That nigga just fixed it to look like he's payin' his own way. Then she can't do nothin' 'bout it when she gets smart and kicks his goldbrickin' ass out."

Willy clenched his fists, daring Cinque to keep arguing. But the boy let it go, dropping the bills back on the pile where he found them. Out in the living room, the front door opened.

Wide-eyed, both trespassers stopped, each looking at the other for direction. Cinque dove under the pile of clothes by the closet. Willy hid behind the door.

Cinque could hear someone drop their keys and a heavy *thud* as something landed on the living room table. The floor creaked with footsteps and then a big arm pushed the door all the way open. It passed through where Willy stood and tossed a heavy jacket on the bed. The man went back out into the living room.

Cinque forced himself to breathe again and stuck one hand out from the pile. He shooed the ghost towards the bedroom door. It took a moment, but Willy caught on and stepped out into the hall, tip-toeing uselessly. From his hiding spot Cinque listened to the ghost's play-by-play: "That be Darius. Done got himself a pizza and beer with my girl's money."

There was a man's groan and a creak.

"He jus' sat his ass down."

Someone turned on the television.

"He's watching TV now."

Willy described every program Darius flipped past. Only when he resolved on a game show and settled in to enjoy his pizza did the ghost run out of minutia to report. Wandering back into the bedroom he shrugged at Cinque, and sat on the bed.

They waited though a commercial break or two, listening to the game show and the sounds of chewing and gulping from the living room. Cinque pulled free from his hiding place and, with his hands on his hips, shot a frustrated look at Willy.

"What am I supposed to do?" asked the ghost. Willy looked away from the boy and anxiously studied the room. It was getting dark but he was able to search by the doorway's light. Trapped, Cinque was too worried about making noise to continue the search.

He crept to the window and considered escape. Something caught his eye. The magazine cover he had mangled while coming through the window was now folded up. Inside the cover, an advertisement for car insurance had the picture of a stop sign. The angle of the picture and the angle of the crease combined, and the stop sign stood straight up. It was like the sign had been planted on the dresser top between him and the open window.

Cinque stared at the picture, stunned. He wondered what the odds were that he happened to mangle the magazine in just the right way so that this picture that just happened to be in the inside cover would be in this position. His skin crawled: there was no way he was climbing back out the window.

"Yo!"

Willy T snapped Cinque out of his daze. The ghost was pointing inside the closet at something on the top shelf.

"What?" Cinque whispered.

"That box up there! Get that down!"

"Is that where the picture is?"

"I feel like it is," Willy nodded.

"Do you feel? Or do you know?"

"What?" Willy threw his hands up in the air. "You wanna keep digging? If I'm right, I'm right. Right?"

Still unconvinced but lacking alternatives, Cinque climbed up a dresser. He used the open drawers as steps. Once he was high enough, he pushed his face into the darkness to let his eyes adjust.

"What am I looking for anyway?"

"Shoebox. Green."

Cinque found it at the bottom of a stack of shoeboxes. The edge facing him was split and bursting with photos. He could barely grab the thing with one hand as he leaned into the closet from his perch on the dresser. The weight of the boxes on top held it tight. Cinque had to work it back and forth until he was able to get his fingers under, tilting it up and sliding the other shoeboxes off. Just as the box was about to come free, the boy felt the dresser begin to tilt his way.

Cinque quickly pulled the green shoebox from the others and clutched it to his chest without thinking. He lost his grip on the dresser and fell, protecting the box with his body as he landed, painfully, on the pile of shoes at the bottom of the closet. The dresser dropped back into place with a dull *thud*.

Motionless, Cinque lay among the shoes, holding onto the box, holding his breath. Listening for signs of alarm from the living room, he could only hear the sound of his lungs working and a little of the television between breaths. A man's voice broke the silence. Cinque almost shouted.

"He didn't hear nuthin'," said Willy T.

Between clenched teeth, the boy whispered, "Don't creep up on me like that!"

Cinque struggled to stand up among the shoes, but the uneven surface wobbled underneath him. Giving up, he rolled off the pile onto a clear patch of floor where the standing was easier. He opened the shoebox and went through the pictures until he found it—the picture of a slightly younger and significantly more tangible Willy T tightly holding a girl from behind. A wide smile across his face, Willy's happiness was obvious though the girl's smile was less enthusiastic, maybe even forced, Cinque thought.

"This it?" he whispered.

The ghost stared at the picture over the boy's shoulder, transfixed. "Hells yeah that it."

Cinque put the picture in his back pocket. "How we gettin' past Darius out there?" The question snapped Willy T out of whatever daydream the picture had put him in. The ghost's expression went from enraptured to confused. He pointed back at the window. "Can't go that way."

"What? You scared of fallin'?"

"No." Cinque shook his head. "I just can't go that way."

"Why not?"

"Because of that stop sign." Cinque pointed to the dresser in front of the window.

"Huh?"

"On the magazine."

Willy T looked over at the magazine, the bad omen.

"Then I don't know what you're gonna do, 'cause Darius doesn't look like he's goin' nowhere an' you can't get out without passing by those wall-eyes o' his." That was true, Cinque realized with a sinking feeling in his chest. The television was a few feet from the front door and he didn't have a hope of sneaking past him in that chair. A thought came to him.

"You're gonna have to use that ghost trick on him." Cinque gripped his head with his ten fingers and shook his head in pantomime. "The one where you scramble a brother's brains all about."

The ghost looked at him like he was crazy. "Whachu talkin' 'bout?"

Cinque remembered the way his mind had been left a mess when the Cloudy Man had passed through him. Could the same thing work here? He hoped so. "Just make a fist and stick it in his head."

"An' if that don't work?"

"Then we's busted, so you best make it work! Get out there!"

Willy tip-toed back out into the living room, Cinque watched from the bedroom doorway while Willy passed his open hand through the man's head. No effect. There was none of the weakness and fear the Cloudy Man had made. Cinque bit his lip nervously.

Willy looked back at him and shrugged, his hand still passing through Darius's head. There must have been an extra trick to this, Cinque thought, trying to figure out how it all worked.

As Willy's hand pulled out of the man's head, Darius yawned. Maybe something was working? Cinque gestured for Willy to do it again.

Willy slowly passed his open palm through the man's head and he visibly nodded to the right. From where Cinque was it looked like he was nodding off. Willy T seemed to pick up on that and passed his hand thorough the man's head a few more times, slowly and gently like he was fanning a delicate flame. After a few passes, the man slouched in the chair, snoring. Willy T gave Cinque a proud smile.

Cinque crept out of the bedroom toward escape until Willy stepped in front of him, blocking the door as if he were tangible.

"We ain't done yet, little brother. You still gotta help me mess up this mutha fucka's life."

Cinque had been so focused on retrieving the picture, he had forgotten that it came second to earning the ghost's favour.

"Jack him." Willy pointed to Darius's wallet, lying on the coffee table between two empty beer cans. "You need the cash to get to Chicago and I need this fucka to suffer, somethin' for everyone."

Reluctantly, Cinque picked up the wallet, reaching in for the money.

"Naw man, the whole thing. I want him to lose it all. Credit cards, ID, the whole damn thing. It ain't much, but that'll set him back a few days and mess with his mind. Hate and discontent, boy, hate and discontent. Maybe he'll do something stupid so's Rikkia'll get a clue and kick his ass to the curb."

Cinque folded the wallet back up, stuck it in his back pocket. He promised he'd make it up to Darius Oates someday.

9

DO SOMETHING STUPID

It was early Monday morning. Cinque paced around the picnic table while Willy T stared at the picture, getting his fill. Tired of holding the picture for the ghost, Cinque had pinned it to the park table with a couple of good sized pebbles. Willy had wanted to stare at it all night long, but Cinque told him that he'd gone more than a year without it, and one more night wouldn't make a difference. The next day, Cinque had found Willy T waiting on the doorstep where he had left him, barely visible in the morning sun.

Cinque was using the trip to the park as an experiment. Willy said he had no memory of the place. He said he couldn't, or wouldn't, go any place that he didn't have some strong personal connection.

"How you feelin'?" he asked the ghost.

It took Willy a second to pull himself away from the picture, like someone watching the TV really hard. He turned and smiled a big old smile at the boy.

"One hundred and ten, little man. Like the fog's lifted, the light broke and the blind can see again! Hallelujah an' praise Jesus!" Willy wasn't just in a better mood: he was more solid, more real. Cinque could see the picture gave him an energy he'd been lacking. Like he'd been starving but couldn't die.

"Good thing too. I'm not sure how much good you'd be to me all cracked out like you was yesterday."

Willy T laughed, "See how cracked out you be after bein' dead fo' a year."

Cinque sat down at the table across from Willy T. Now was the time to start getting serious about *his* problem.

"You ever been to Chicago, Willy?"

"Oh, hells yeah! Gotta party somewhere, and there ain't no clubs around this town."

"Good. 'Cause you're takin' me there tomorrow."

At school later that day Cinque didn't have any homework to sneak into the teacher's mailboxes. He'd been too busy for homework. Still, Imani managed to intercept him anyway, walking right next to him on the way to their homeroom.

"No homework today, Sin-Kay?"

He noticed she had her old confidence back here on familiar ground.

"No." Cinque hesitated. "No homework today. I been too busy."

"How you been busy, Sin-Kay?" she said, sceptically. "We both know you ain't got no life."

"That's what I been busy doin'." Cinque chuckled. "Gettin' my life."

"How you doin' that?"

"By lookin' back." He pointed back, over his shoulder with a thumb. "I can't know where I'm goin' 'til I know where I been."

She looked behind them and joked, "You mean back there? In the field?"

"No. I mean I need to find what I can about my Pa."

She shook her head. "You ain't got no pa, boy."

"Everyone got a pa," he answered.

"Then you know where he at?"

"I do now." For a second he wondered if he should leave it at that but he felt the urge to tell her more. "I got a letter sayin' he died. He died up in Chicago and they holdin' his stuff for me."

They walked on in silence, then, in a serious voice that Cinque had never heard her use before, Imani asked "Whatcho expectin' to find? Anything that's worth somethin'?"

"I figure there's gotta be some cash, a few thousand dollars or more." Imani's eyes went wide at that. He'd never caught her interest like this before. He could feel the pendulum swing his way. It was refreshing. "But it's not just about the money, it's valuable like personal. I need to know where I stand so's I can take the next step, take a good step, no misstep. You know what I mean? An' who knows, maybe I'll step up to the man himself."

"Even though he dead. . . ." Her voice went from serious to shocked, another tone he'd never heard from her. "The other day when you was talkin' about ghosts? You was serious?"

For the first time Cinque was in control of a conversation with Imani. "Still am. That didn't go so well, back in the hospital, but I found another ghost and he gonna help me get up to Chicago. When I find my pop's ghost—" Cinque cut himself off, he didn't need to tell Imani about his missing heart. "Well . . . it's nice to have family, ain't it?"

Again, as it was on Saturday, in front of her house, the humour faded from her voice. "You shouldn't go, Sin-Kay. You should forget all this craziness before it's too late and you can't."

For the first time he spoke to her with confidence. "Too late, the craziness done got me. Now I gotta do this to learn how to deal."

Cinque caught the bus right after school, and by 3:00 PM he was at the end of the line, the last bus stop on the north side of town. It was also a highway rest stop and a carpool parking lot, normally a good place for a hitchhiker to catch a ride up the I-55 North. Cinque stood by the on-ramp, thumb out, three sandwiches and the letter from the City of Chicago in his backpack. The fifty-four dollars he'd stolen from Darius was still in his pocket, not enough for a bus ticket to Chicago. Besides, there wasn't a direct ride up there. The only way took a dozen transfers and there wasn't a train station in town. It was like everyone said: "You gotta get outta St. Jude to get outta St. Jude."

Yesterday, it had seemed to Cinque that he didn't stand a chance of getting to Chicago and back until Willy T pointed out that he only had to get there and get the goods. Then he could just turn himself in as a runaway and the trip back would handle itself. It wouldn't be nice but it would work. With his wits and charm recovered with the picture, the ghost had gone from annoying tagalong to useful partner overnight. Cinque liked the ghost. He wanted to have Willy with him for the trip.

Cinque kept the picture of Willy and his girl Rikkia in his backpack, so the ghost would follow, in time. On the street the ghost had no problem keeping up, but when Cinque had climbed on the first bus north, Willy disappeared. He thought the ghost had abandoned him but a few stops later, there he was, sitting next to the boy. The ghost had no recollection of disappearing, nor did he remember climbing on the bus.

They had transferred buses twice on their way to the rest stop, and both times Willy T disappeared as Cinque got off the bus and reappeared sometime later. The further they traveled from St. Jude the longer he was gone. Cinque had waited at the end of the line for half an hour before moving on, figuring sooner or later the ghost would turn up wherever the picture was. Besides, the weather was getting cold and cloudy and he wanted to be inside before it started to rain. He looked up just as the sun disappeared behind the thickening clouds.

The car pulled up in front of Cinque before he'd seen it, a metallic-gray four-door. The passenger window rolled down and a man's voice asked: "Where to?" It was too bright outside and too dark inside to see the driver except in silhouette.

"I'm headin' to Chicago."

"Then this is your lucky day. I'll have you there in four hours. Hop in!" As Cinque reached for the door a mechanical slide and click sound surprised him and he jerked back.

"It's just a power lock, kid, not a bear trap," said the man in the driver's seat.

Embarrassed, Cinque opened the door and climbed in. The car's interior had been recently detailed, the dash shined. The carpet was clean and it smelled powerfully of spray-on New Car Scent. There was a single document box in the back seat.

Inside, Cinque got a better look at the driver, a thin white man in a white button-down shirt, a dark blue tie and ugly wire-framed glasses. His hair plastered to his scalp and parted on the left with a few hairs out of place. His clothes were a little rumpled and it looked like he hadn't shaved in a couple of days. The stereo was playing a twangy rock song about the Twilight Zone.

The white man held out his hand. "Robbie Freegard, insurance sales. And you are?"

"Cinque Williams, uh . . . student runnin' an errand." Cinque took his hand and shook it firmly, like Darren said a man should.

"'Sink'? Like the kitchen sink?"

"Yeah, but spelled C—i—n—q—u—e."

"Welcome aboard, Cinque spelled C—i—n—q—u—e. Let's head on up to the second city, what do you say?" He pulled the car onto I-55 North. "From St. Jude to Chicago? That's more than an errand. What's in Chicago for ya, buddy?"

Robbie Freegard was more comfortable with Cinque than the boy felt with him but since it was his car Cinque figured he should try to hold up his end of the conversation. "My pa. Well, my pa's things, what he left behind."

"Ah, the estate and legacy of Mr. Williams."

"Mr. Lee, actually, Kelly Lee."

"Can't say I knew him, but here's to the late Kelly Lee." Robbie pantomimed taking a drink from a flask. "Lord have mercy." He wiped the imaginary drink from his lips on the back of his wrist and glanced over at Cinque. He grinned at the boy's confusion. "It's the spirit that counts. I, myself, am heading to the windy city with a box full of policies and a little bit of hope. Hope that I can sell enough to eat another day. You ever think of getting into sales, Cinque?"

"Naw." Cinque had only heard the last part. He'd been distracted by the car's steering column, the panel had been removed and some of the wires were hanging out in a knot. There was no key in the ignition.

"Keep it that way," Robbie nodded. "It's a hard life, living hand to mouth and out of your car."

Cinque looked back briefly at the document box. "Then why you do it?"

"I didn't have a choice."

"Huh?" Cinque thought Robbie was awfully cheery for someone who hated his job.

"I wouldn't call it destiny, because I hate that word. Destiny's a salesman's word. Piss-poor sales people use words like 'destiny' and 'legendary' to paint some importance on whatever they're selling. It's more like fate. Fate's a darker word, isn't it? Most of life is fate. Unavoidable . . . unfortunate."

"I don't know what you're talkin' about, man. I make my own fate."

"Why'd you just say that?" Without taking his eyes off the road Robbie leaned closer to Cinque, listening.

"Say what?"

"That right there." He pointed at Cinque. "I make my own fate. Why'd you just say that?"

"'Cause that's the truth."

Robbie shook his head a little when he said, "And you didn't feel like lying?"

"I don't lie."

"Even better." Robbie leaned back in his seat and slapped the steering wheel. "So there wasn't much chance of you agreeing with me at that moment, was there? You had to say something, those are the rules of conversation and it had to be contrary because you didn't agree with me, hence fate."

Cinque looked outside in time to see a passing billboard for the Illinois Lottery. "So what if I just flip a coin for everything?"

"Go ahead, fate's got that covered too. Everything is predetermined. When you work the system, the system works you."

Robbie's hand tried to illustrate his point with erratic waves and twists. "Your decision to let the coin make your choices? That was predetermined. When you flip that coin, roll those dice, pick that card . . . they were all set before you knew what was what. Chaos theory, man, nothing's random, it just looks that way."

Cinque frowned. "Doesn't that mean that life is pointless?"

"Totally. Totally and utterly pointless. It's a train ride from beginning to end, birth to death. For most people." Robbie changed lanes without signalling, cutting off a tow truck. "But I got a way to win the game."

"How's that?"

For the first time Robbie took his eyes off the road to look at Cinque. It was a look Cinque didn't like. "I play someone else's hand."

A familiar voice spoke up from the back seat, "Aw man, you

done messed up now. You shoulda waited for me to put my two cents in 'fore you took this ride."

Cinque turned to Willy T, now sitting in the back seat next to the document box and almost answered the ghost, but he shut his mouth and turned forward. Not in mixed company, he thought.

Robbie didn't seem to notice. He seemed to be finished talking, at least for now. From the backseat, Willy T picked up the slack. "I dunno about this cat, man. I mean, look at him, really look at him. He's tryin' hard to look weak n' harmless but it don't look natural on him. He jus' can't get it right. Ask him what he was doin' in St. Jude."

Cinque asked, "Did you make any sales in St. Jude?"

Robbie laughed. "Oh no. I didn't stop in St. Jude except for gas and to let go with the yellow flow. No offense, kid, but there's not a lot in St. Jude worth insuring. No, I'm driving up from Memphis. Now there's not a lot in Memphis worth insuring either, as far as I can see, but the people down there are of a different mind and if they're willing to pay the premiums then I will happily write up a policy for their trailer homes and pickup trucks . . . hound dogs . . . banjos. . . ."

Willy was still suspicious. "See how that all came out? Who talks like that? It's like he had all that on script. Naw, I don't like this dude. We should get lost when we get a chance, but for now just chill. If'n I'm right, an' he thinks you're on to him then this'll get serious with a quickness."

Cinque spent the next two hours keeping an eye on Robbie by staring out the window at the endless fields of corn and looking at the white man in the reflection. The pulse of the rows passing by the window eventually lulled Cinque into a hazy stupor until Robbie spoke up, breaking the silence, "Well, we haven't seen a rest stop in some time and I'm about to make my own gravy, so I'm going to have to pull off into this field and do a little irrigation."

He brought the car off on a dirt road by a water pump. He left the hotwired car running as he got out.

"I get a little gun-shy if you know what I mean. Get out and stretch your legs. I'll be a while."

Cinque relieved himself on a water pump and then walked rough circles around the car while he waited. Robbie's car had New Mexico plates. There was a small red flag stuck in the ground some surveyor had left behind. Willy T had disappeared some time ago, and Cinque found himself wishing the ghost was still around. The sun peeked out from beneath the clouds one last time before setting over the horizon. When Robbie returned he was tugging at his tie, glasses folded up in one hand. Something about the way he walked told the boy that Robbie wasn't doing any driving right away. That made him nervous.

"You know what's funny about identity, Cinque?" The salesman was speaking in his lecture voice again. "We place so much value on it, treat it as if who we are, who we think we are, had some sort of objective value. In actuality, when you think about it, concepts like 'me', 'you' and 'I' are constructs. Tools." He smiled. "So I ask you, what's the right tool for the job?"

He pulled back and tossed the glasses and tie into the corn field before he popped the trunk. Cinque said nothing.

"That's okay, it was a rhetorical question. The real issue at hand is this . . . since we make our personality, then why should we be satisfied with only having one? You ever heard the expression 'When your only tool is a hammer, everything looks like a nail?'"

He popped the trunk and walked around to the back of the car, rolling up his sleeves. "Well, what if your personality, the one you're born with, is the hammer? You could try and change the hammer, make it a screwdriver—" As he said this, he pulled an old, heavy, dirty screwdriver from the trunk and held it up for emphasis. "—but how well does that ever work?"

Cinque's eyes were on the screwdriver and he worried what Robbie intended to do with it. It was a thick, old tool with a Hazelwood handle. Its age and wear made it more serious, more real than if the man held one with a plain, plastic handle.

Pulling a pair of Michigan license plates from the trunk, he started to swap them out with the ones on the car. "What you've got to do is build a toolkit. Then when you need the hammer, you pick up the hammer. The same goes for the screwdriver. Why limit yourself to one identity? I make a new sentence every time I speak, right? I speak the words and toss them out. This is the same principle."

"What the hell are you talking 'bout, man?" Cinque was scared enough to curse. Willy was right, he'd got himself stuck in a bad place. He had to keep it together and think of some way out of here. For a moment, he considered kicking the man in the nuts, but remembered what Darren had told him in the bathroom, how that move had never worked for him.

Robbie finished replacing both plates. He tossed the originals into the corn and considered the screwdriver like he was going to throw that too. Instead he stuck it in his belt loop where it hung like a knife. Turning back towards Cinque he untucked and unbuttoned his shirt and rolled up the sleeves.

"I'm talking the hell about the fluid dynamics of identity." Robbie covered his right eye with his palm, his left eye locked on Cinque. "I'm talking about how you don't have to be you, you can be anything you want, within the physical constraints and limitations that is."

Cinque kicked at the dirt beneath him. "Why would I want to do that?"

"It keeps you hidden, keeps you safe."

"Safe from what?"

Robbie spread his arms and fingers wide. "Everything that's trying to find you. Don't act like you don't know."

"Man, I don't have to act. You crazy!"

"There's no such thing as crazy." He took a bottle of water from the truck and washed his hair with it while he sang, "Gonna wash that man right out of my hair. Outta my hair. Outta my hair," and laughed as if it was funny.

Freed from its chemical bonds his hair was surprisingly long and wavy. He tied it back to keep it out of his face. With these few alterations Cinque saw he'd radically changed his appearance from nerdy, uptight insurance salesman to wiry, shifty and dangerous drifter. He didn't even seem all white anymore. With that dark and wavy hair in his face he could pass for Mexican. There was something different about the way he moved too, like a panther, that made him seem dangerous in spite of the smile.

"You can feel it, can't ya?" Robbie shook his hands. "A different vibe, a new colour of vibology? Heh, but I'm just starting. Before the paint's done dryin', I'll be reworking the insides. Sounds backward I know, but backwards is how ya throw them off." The man drank the rest of the water and dropped the bottle. "You ready to play?"

"What if I ain't?"

"Then you'll be walking to Chicago."

They each took a seat on the layer of husks that covered the ground around the corn. The gray sky turned and raced above them. The man who was once Robbie Freegard said, "The first round is for the past," and dealt Cinque a hand of five cards.

"What game we playin'?" asked Cinque.

This amused the new man. "It don't need a name, *mi hijo.* You'll never play this game again and I got no reason to cheat."

"You know how someone's gonna screw ya over?" Willy T was back, leaning against the car. "When they say, 'Trust me.'"

Cinque used this. "How do I know you got no reason to cheat?"

"You don't, do ya?" The man who used to be Robbie Freegard

seemed disappointed by this. "Can't help ya there. But, if it makes you feel any better, you ain't got a choice."

"That don't make me feel better." Cinque's hand clenched, bending the cards.

"I figured it wouldn't. Draw," the man ordered.

Cinque drew a card. "What do I do with this?"

"Put it in your hand, and then get rid of the card you like the least."

"How am I supposed to know what cards is bad? You ain't told me the rules!"

"You don't need to know the damn rules! You ain't playin' to win." The man's voice, tinged with anger.

Willy sat next to Cinque on the ground. "Not playin' to win? How you s'possed to hustle a game like that?"

Cinque put the card in his hand and arbitrarily discarded the nine of diamonds. "How's that?" He snapped at the dealer.

"That's just fine. See? It's not so hard now, is it? Draw again."

Cinque rolled his eyes, drew the ace of diamonds, and tossed it straight out.

"And again."

Drawing the queen of spades this time, Cinque originally intended to throw this card out as well, but instead he added it to his hand and discarded the jack of spades.

"Now lay your hand out."

Cinque laid the five cards out in front of him and Robbie considered them carefully, "All upright, all good luck. Hope your future's the same. The ten of clubs, you're a good kid but not many friends. Six of spades, slow gradual change, eight of spades there's some jealousy round here, outward? inward? maybe both. The queen of spades—a strong woman who'd been knocked around and still kept goin'." He looked up at Cinque. "That's your mom."

Cinque was stunned. "Yeah . . ." He almost sighed the word.

"At your age couldn't be many others. Finally, we got the

five of diamonds, you're poor, course I could'a told that by looking at you, but being poor don't matter much."

"I won't be poor for long. Not after I get my inheritance." The fact that the man had read so much about him in the cards gave Cinque a chill. He tightened up, as if that would keep any other bits of knowledge about him from leaking out. "Is this a game or a fortune tellin'?"

"Neither. I told you what this was."

"No you di—" Cinque stopped himself. Arguing with a Crazy was pointless and as long as Cinque had no ideas of his own he should just play along.

The man looked at the cards one last time before shuffling them back in the deck. "Yeah, this hand shows you were the right choice."

"Choice? Choice for what?" Another chill ran through Cinque. Was this guy one of those kiddy killers? Didn't they only kill white girls?

"For this," the man said tracing a circle around the cards. "You think I pick up hitchhikers every day? The cards told me where to find you, the kid who was broken and cracked."

"What for?"

"For your fate. You've been damaged already. Taking your fate will be easy and you're fate is big, valuable. That's what the cards told me when they told me to come looking for you." He dealt the cards. "This round is for the future. This is the one that matters."

"Past and future. What about the now?" Cinque asked. "Ain't we gonna play for that?"

The man smirked in contempt. "You think I don't know what trouble you're in now?"

As the final hand was dealt, Willy spoke up. "I got's an idea. This bitch said he's hopin' your future'll be upright, so let's give him the other way. Flip 'em all around, nuttin' but bad luck."

As Willy spoke, something inside Cinque seemed to come up with the same idea. If this last round was so important, he had to take some control, push the "not-a-game" game in a bad direction.

As he picked up the hand, there were two cards already inverted. Keeping it subtle, Cinque turned one card over before drawing. The first and second draws were also inverted, so he just replaced the right-side-up cards and threw away the last draw.

The man who was once Robbie stared at the cards. The eight of hearts, the jack of hearts, the ace of diamonds, the ten of clubs and a joker, all inverted. What little good humour he'd been playing with washed away. With cold eyes, he looked up at the boy and said, "You expect me to believe that this is your hand?"

Cinque realized that he'd been wearing a satisfied smirk, confirming the man's suspicions. He dropped it for an apologetic stance, hands open and out. "Hey, man, this was your game—"

The man jumped to his feet, fists clinched, "A name."

"What?"

"I need a name. You've screwed me over, set up some hard time for me, but I'm a hard man. I'll pull through. Bad fate, bad fortune, bad deeds, I burn them all like fire. Burn away the silver cord and the karma trail. I can spin this, make it work for me. I'll take your hand of fate, I'll take your fixed game and I'll take a name, for the bastard you've made me become."

Cinque looked over at Willy.

"Go ahead, give him a name," the ghost whispered.

Without thinking, Cinque's voice created the name for him: "Ted. Ted Lopez."

"That's a lousy name. I underestimated you, kid. I should have left you back in St. Jude, you're bad luck—literally." He collected the five cards and put them in his shirt pocket. He considered Cinque again and asked, "What're you going to Chicago for?"

"I done told you. I'm getting my Pa's things."

"Like what?" Ted spat.

"I don't know. The letter just said that I had to come pick them up in person." Cinque said it like an excuse.

"You got this letter then?"

"In my bag." Cinque pointed to the car, hoping to draw Ted Lopez's attention away from him.

Ted pulled Cinque's backpack out of the car and the letter out of the bag, letting the rest fall to the ground. "Who are you really? How old are you? You look to be about twelve."

"I'm fourteen!" Cinque said protectively, embarrassed by how that sounded, like a four-year-old insisting that he was four and a half years old.

"How did this happen?" Ted asked himself, "I must be losing it. Just a kid and you're the first one to do some real damage."

Cinque stood up, quickly. "Man, I don't know what crazy-ass nonsense you're talkin' about, but I just wanna get to Chicago an' get my pa's things so I can talk to his ghost."

"You're gonna talk to your old man's ghost, huh?"

Cinque kicked himself for slipping. Not good, not with *this guy*.

"And how long'd you been talking to ghosts?"

Cinque clinched his jaw. "I . . ."

Willy jumped in between them. "Don' do it!"

Cinque said, "I been seein' ghosts an' other things for goin' on a week now." Willy cringed.

Ted responded with a suspicious shake of the head. "Don't mess with me, kid. I know you're after me for somethin'."

"Why you?"

"Why not?"

Ted was determined to see a conspiracy. Cinque was baffled. "What? If I was after you, shouldn't it be for something!"

"Who says?" Ted dropped the letter and walked back to the car.

Cinque ran up and collected his things. "So, what are we gonna do?"

"No, no, no." Ted shook his head. "There ain't no 'we', mi hijo. I'm drivin' on out of here alone. I don't know where, but it ain't going to be Chicago, not if that's where you want me to go. As for you, I don't know. But you're too dangerous to keep around." Robbie pointed straight down at the earth between them. "You're staying here. I'd wish you good luck, but that'd be bad luck for me."

"You can't leave me out here in the middle of nowhere, you crazy!" Cinque shouted.

Ted was suddenly stoic, calm. "I'm not crazy. I'm saner than sane."

The man opened the car door and Cinque got angry, the angriest he'd ever been, and he pulled a good sized rock out of the soft earth. Adrenaline raced through him, and before he had a chance to think about it, he had pitched it at Ted, striking him in the back of the head. The man dropped to his knees. Cinque gave him a kick between his legs, grabbed him by the hair and pulled him back, away from the car door.

Cinque had never driven before, so the getaway didn't go as smoothly as he would have liked. He made a seven point turn as he tried to pull the car around back towards the highway. By the time he was on his way, Ted had gotten to his feet and was staggering painfully after the car with no chance of catching up.

In anticipation of this moment, of a moment like this a few years down the line, with a car that wasn't stolen, he'd been watching his Ma drive and he got the gist of it. There was a close call with a pickup truck when they pulled on the highway, but from then on it was easy riding the rest of the way.

As he hit the Will County limit, he heard Willy laughing from the back seat, "Woo! Boy! That was some straight-up nigga shit! How's that bitch gonna explain this? Jacked by a kid! If somethin' like that happened to me I'd make up somethin' impossible jus' so no one would know!"

Willy's approval didn't make Cinque feel better about what

he'd done. Cinque didn't have a problem hitting back but he wasn't the sort to hit first or hit that hard. "What happened after I left?"

"He just stood there cryin' for awhile, then he got up and started walking back the way we came. I didn't see much else after that."

Ted was walking south. The only thing south on the I-55 was St. Jude. Cinque took a long look into the rear view mirror.

10

TOOK A LONG LOOK

They hit the Chicago city limit just before midnight. Cinque brought the car to an awkward stop in a supermarket parking lot just as the needle reached the bottom of the E. Driving was easy. His father probably had a car. When he got his estate he could just drive it back down to St. Jude. Cinque was sure that with the ten thousand or so dollars he'd have plenty for gas, enough to tip the guys at the gas stations to ignore the fact that a kid was driving a Lexus.

After the boy stretched his legs he lit the African's stick and walked around the car three times with the smoking ember. "You know . . . yo' business is yo' business an' all but, what you doin'?"

"I'm gonna check in with someone. The African."

"The African?" Willy was more surprised than Cinque would have guessed. "Who that?"

Cinque told him about Pastor Akotun and the *Illinois* planes that dreamed of Africa. While Cinque spoke it was clear, even to him, that Willy didn't like what he was hearing.

"An' how you know this mutha fucka from Africa?"

"He look African, at least to me. How you know he ain't?"

"Man, I don't know Africa, but I do know niggas and that nigga is settin' you up fo' a fall. You can't get somethin' fo' nothin'."

"He told me what I needed to know to get this far, didn't he? You'd still be haunting your girl's front yard if it weren't for him, so how bad can he be?"

Willy shot Cinque a look of contempt and rolled his eyes.

Cinque went back to work, tossing out Robbie's document box, which turned out to be empty. He laid out in the backseat and told Willy to keep watch. With the cracked side of the pebble held tight in his palm, once again he imagined the shapes that would take his mind half way to Africa.

The cat-lions had left since Cinque's last visit and a few herds of bovid had moved in to take a drink while they could. Antelope, gazelle and springbok were all remoulded white-tailed deer, the same familiar gray-brown winter coat and white undercoat and undertail on all of them, fuzzy antlers not branching but jutting out from their heads in straight or wavy forms.

The sudden appearance of the young man caused the herds to spook, running to the other side of the watering hole, stopping when Cinque didn't chase them but keeping a suspicious eye his way while they went back to their business.

Footsteps behind him belonged to Pastor Akotun with his iron staff in hand and his drum slung over one shoulder. He took a seat on a large rock as he deliberately laid out his things.

"Good evening to you, little boy. How goes your search for completeness? Completeness of family and completeness of body?"

"It's coming, at least the family stuff is, still hoping that the body stuff will follow." Cinque paused. "I wanted to ask you some things. I found a ghost that was haunting a hospital, called the Cloudy Man. I tried calling it Egungun to get it to stop but it didn't work. Are you sure that All-Ghost means American ghosts too?"

"Are you certain that this Cloudy Man is a ghost?"

"Sure, I gu—I think so. He was haunting this other ghost so why not?"

"It may act like a ghost, it may look like a ghost, it may even smell like a ghost. But only a ghost is a ghost."

Cinque folded his arms. "Mmm . . . it looked like a nail so I hit it with a hammer."

The African nodded. "After a fashion."

"That's my other question." Cinque told Pastor Akotun about his ride up the Chicago and the man named Robbie who became the man named Ted.

The African waited patiently until he was done. "And what would you like to know?"

"Uh . . . well, what was that all about? He claimed that he was looking for me. Could that be true?"

"Certainly. From what you've said the man has no small skill in Juju but he has done so much magic, held onto it so tightly that his hands have grown into it. He no longer uses magic; magic uses him. By wanting complete control he has lost control completely."

"Was he really making new people to be?"

"Oh, absolutely. But the people he makes are incomplete, obsessed with futures. He has abandoned the past. Moderation, little boy, is the way to a long life. This Shapeshifter you have told me about reminds me of a story." He began to play his drum.

No one wanted the Soldier. Though he had fought for his tribe since he could pick up a rifle, once he'd lost his good arm to a bullet and infection, he could fight for them no more. There was little enough use for a man with two arms, so no one bothered with the man with one. He sat in the market on the corner in the hot sun of the day, and watched his beggar's bowl collect a coin or two to buy food and fuel to keep him warm in the cold light of the moon.

The wars went on without him and they went badly. The Soldier liked to think that they went wrong because they needed him, even with one less arm. The tribe's fortunes turned and the coins became fewer and fewer and the nights became colder and colder.

Coinless for more nights than he could count, the Soldier huddled in the dark by a pile of sticks. He had hoped to find an unused match in the trash, but just as the charity was thinning, so was useful refuse. He could not bring himself to ask for someone's fire. Though he was a beggar, he never let himself beg. Though he had nothing, he never let himself steal. As he regretted what he'd become he clenched one of the bigger sticks in his hand with anger. He made the act from himself and felt a heat inside. A part of his soul was burning. When the burning inside ended a burning started in his hand; the wood cracked and his knuckles popped. The effort made his hand feel warm, so he held his grip. The Soldier smelled smoke and realized that the stick was burning. Where he had touched it, it was burnt in the shape of his hand.

The next day the Soldier went into town to prove his worth. At first, he went to the Captain of the Army thinking that with this power they might have a use for him again but the Captain said that wars were fought with guns and clubs: a man with a burning arm was less dangerous than a man with a burning stick. The Captain sent him away. He went to the Bread Maker, thinking that he might need a man to start his ovens but the Bread Maker was scared of the one-armed, raggedy man who could make things burn with his touch and sent him away, as did the Blacksmith and the Brick Maker.

While the Soldier searched, rumour had spread of the

beggar with the burning touch. The village priest thought he knew this man for a sorcerer and a threat. The Priest spread the news and gathered up the villagers. With sticks and rocks they chased the Soldier out of their village.

The Soldier stayed up in the hills. He did not eat or sleep. He just burned. Whatever he had lost, the part of his soul that burned up must have been what would have let him forgive. Instead he burned and burned until he stopped being a man who burned and became a Burning Man—a man of fire. He surrendered himself to the act.

The Burning Man returned to the village and he burned the Captain. He burned the Bread Maker and the Blacksmith and the Brick Maker and he burned the Priest. He burned the village and the villagers. He went to the next village and burned it as well, and the next, until he'd burned away his entire tribe.

"Don't you know any happy stories?"

The African put down his drum, stood and said, "Happy stories are lies. The worthwhile truths hide in darkness. Our time is at an end, Cinque Williams. My stories have provided you with the help that I promised. It is up to you to uncover it."

"Don't I have enough to think about?" Cinque could feel the car seat returning underneath his body.

"Easy things are worthless things." The Pastor's voice faded as dream descended into mundane sleep.

In the morning Cinque awoke to hear Willy hopping around the car and making fake-African calls like half-remembered songs from the Lion King. "Just tryin' to make you feel at home! Ha! I couldn't make you no teepee."

Cinque popped out of the car and shook out his dreads. "Teepees is for Indians, dummy."

"Like I care," Willy dismissed.

The ghost reminded him to wipe the car clean of his fingerprints. A thirty-two dollar cab ride took them to the Cook County Office of the Medical Examiner a few minutes before it was supposed to open. Willy had disappeared again.

Cinque expected one of the monolithic, old, granite buildings he knew from family trips to downtown Chicago. Instead, the office was in a bland industrial park on a tree-lined road. A short, thick wall ran along the front corner of the building. Someone strange and familiar waited.

The mysterious white woman in black, the one with the ivory dreads sat on the wall just like she had on the gurney at Memorial Hospital, without urgency. Eyes still hidden behind dark, round glasses, her messenger bag lay next to her, the embroidered flap facing up. For a second he suspected her of being in cahoots with Robbie but reminded himself that white people didn't all know each other. He sniffed the air but smelled no flowers so she wasn't a ghost, but he had a feeling that she wasn't human either. But here she was, far from Memorial Hospital, he had to ask.

"Are you . . . here?"

She smiled, patronizing and amused. "Does it look like I'm here?"

"I mean," he shook his head, "What are you doing here? Are you waiting to get in to see the coroner too?"

"No." She shifted her crossed legs. "I don't wait on dead people. They wait on me."

"Is that why you were in the hospital?" He put his hand to his forehead. "I don't know your name."

She put a hand on each knee and sat up straight. "I have a lot of names. For now you can call me 'Iku.' I like the brevity of it and I'll probably need to be Iku again soon, so we might as well get used to it now."

Cinque should have been frustrated and angry, but seeing a familiar face so far from home put him at ease. "Okay, Iku.

What are you doing here? Why were you hanging out in a hospital?"

"I'm not here to provide answers. I'm about making changes, transformations from one state to another."

Cinque cocked his head. "If you were straight with me and gave me some answers, I'd change."

"Clever, kid, but that's not going to work. I'm about making specific changes. Your change started when you were damaged."

Cinque knew this one this time. He tapped his chest. "The orange heart."

Iku nodded. "The orange heart. It's not going to end until you end it. You're missing a piece of yourself. You can let the wound fester, cut it out, or let it heal." She pointed up with her index fingers to each side of her face. "Two extremes and a middle path."

"Who took it from me and what did they take?"

She folded her hands in her lap again. "That's the question, isn't it?"

"You're not helping!" Cinque felt like kicking her messenger bag.

"No, I'm not helping. I'm here because you're changing." She swept a hand towards the front door of the building. "Before you cross that threshold you should prepare for what's in there."

"Because my Pa is in there?"

"Your Pa is inconsequential. It's the journey that matters. This is an important step on your journey."

"The only journeyin' I done was in a car with the crazy white guy with the cards and the screwdriver."

"Yes, the Shapeshifter. And what did he teach you?"

Cinque had been thinking about this all night. "That he can become other people, whole new people. That who I am ain't set in stone. But I think that guy's gotten carried away with it. I don't think he knows how to stop."

Cinque sat down next to Iku. "He said he stole my fate but I don't think that's such a bad thing, really. I got the feeling that there's some bad stuff coming up ahead. Maybe now I'm free to go my own way. Now he's out for payback and St. Jude's a small town. If I'm gonna butt heads with him again I better be ready or it'll go even worse."

"See what I mean? The journey is change."

Cinque tilted his head. "So if the Shapeshifter locked down everything that makes him him, then I guess the other side of that is a guy with no control at all. Am I gonna run up on someone like that next?"

"Maybe you will and maybe you won't. Either way I do what I do." Iku hopped off the wall just as Willy rematerialized.

"Well, hey, what's going on here? Who this white bitch? She from Africa too?"

Iku looked at Willy and said, "Speaking of a guy with no control at all."

Willy wasn't used to being looked at. "Who the hell are you? Do you know who you talkin' too?"

"William Thompson, born April 16th, 1984, died January 24th, 2008. Yes, I know who you are. You can run for a while, little ghost, but sooner or later you're going to have to pass on. They all do." She had stunned Willy into silence. She pulled a pack of gum out of her bag and offered it to Cinque, he didn't recognize the brand. The greenish-blue package proclaimed "Prickly Pear Gum! The Forgotten Fruit of the Desert."

Cinque looked at her without taking anything. "I've been warned about taking candy from strangers. And you pretty strange, lady."

She smirked at that. "It's all about trust, isn't it?"

"Why should he trust you?" Willy asked. Cinque thought he seemed nervous, like he was looking for a way out or a place to hide.

"He's made worse choices lately, hasn't he?" She asked the ghost before addressing the boy again, "Gum or no gum. This is your last chance."

Cinque cautiously took a stick out of the pack and then

slipped it into his hoodie pocket. "I'll save it for later."

Iku nodded. "Good call, kid. I'll leave you to your inheritance."

"Where you goin'?" Cinque asked, "There something else out there that needs changing?"

"Something's always changing, kid." She threw her messenger bag over her shoulder. "Right now it's you." She turned to walk away.

"And what happens when I'm done?" Cinque called after her.

"Then the new you will go on with your life and I'll go change something else," she said over her shoulder.

"Am I gonna see you again?"

She held her pointer finger up and kept walking. "Everyone sees me at least one more time."

The boy didn't like the sound of that, so he let it drop. Just then the lock on the Office of the Medical Examiner clicked open.

As he crossed the door into the office Cinque expected to have to fight for his inheritance. With so much valuable property at stake a kid who'd never even seen his father would surely have to jump through a few legal hoops. He would probably have to give a blood sample so they could compare DNA. When he'd finally proven himself there would be the paperwork. The titles had to be signed over, the car, bank accounts and probably a house too. With his new house in Chicago he'd have what his Ma had been trying for all her life, a way out of St. Jude. Of course he'd let his family move in with him, eventually, after they admitted that he'd been right to find his father. He hoped that there were enough bedrooms in the father's house for everyone. If not, Darren could live in the backyard.

But there was no fight, no hoops and no blood samples. With just a flash of his birth certificate and a few forms to fill out, the estate was his, both cardboard boxes of it.

"This is it?" Cinque asked the property clerk who just shrugged and nodded. "This is it. . . ." Cinque repeated. This time he was speaking right at the boxes, making his disappointment with them clear.

A couple of boxes could hold a lot of things, and Cinque started digging. They were full of old clothes, a few odds and ends, a dog-eared paperback book—*The Black Arts* by Richard Cavendish—and an unopened letter addressed to Kelly Lee in Ma's handwriting. No gold, money, bank books or important looking paperwork, nothing like that. Cinque sat cross-legged on the floor by the inheritance he'd spent so much time and effort on acquiring. A car? A house? Even if he put the boxes together they'd be too small for even Cinque to live in.

"I've been a fool," he announced to the world.

"I dunno about that," Willy said over his shoulder.

The boy shook his head. "What was I thinking? Runnin' off to Chicago like this? After my own dumb dream of easy money. . . . Yeah, Willy, I'm a fool."

"Naw, kid, you just lost track of what's important. 'Member, whatever it was that took your heart is what set you on this road and it still got yo' heart. I mean, yeah, this ain't no jackpot or nothin', but there's plenty here you can use to find yo' pops. And then yo' pops'll prolly help you get yo' heart back."

That got Cinque's attention. "Like what?"

Willy jabbed a thumb down at the boxes. "Like these. You got a bunch of his clothes here. That book must'a meant something to him, I'll let you figure that out on your own, an' you get a letter your moms wrote to him. That's all some pretty strong connections."

"Strong enough?"

"I dunno. But they got the strongest stuff of all—" Willy pointed down the hall, to the morgue. "—just through them doors. You came all this way to meet yo' pops, then you should meet yo' pops, you know what I'm sayin'?"

The remains clerk informed Cinque that normally the next of kin would be required to identify the deceased, but in this case since he had never met the man that would be waived. Cinque insisted on seeing the body anyway, to finally get a look at the man who was his father.

The clerk said he couldn't stop him from viewing the body if he wanted to, but he warned the boy that the body wasn't discovered for over a month after the estimated time of death, an unusually hot month. It was also unfortunate that Kelly Lee lived in a cheap apartment with ten times as many rats as tenants.

Still, Cinque insisted.

Willy and Cinque stood side by side in the cold chamber. The sheet-covered corpse of his father lay on its drawer before them. It had been a long moment since the coroner had left them alone. Willy broke the silence. "Well? Are you gonna do it?"

"I dunno if I have to. Or if I want to. I mean . . . there's a dead body under there."

"You come all this way and you ain't gonna have a look?"

Cinque squirmed in his mismatched shoes, conscious of their unlevel soles again. "Iku said I didn't really have to find my father, that it was the journey that'd make the difference."

Willy T walked around to the other side of the table. "You feelin' any different since you made your journey?"

"No."

Truthfully, Cinque was feeling scared. There was the corpse of his father under this sheet. There was a corpse under this sheet. A corpse that the coroner said was in a pretty grim state. Rats had gotten to it. Rats had . . .

"Well, do somethin'!" The ghost yelled. "I spent a year

wanderin' up and down the streets of St. Jude and in all that time I ain't never been this bored!"

Cinque reached out with cautious fingers and took a hold of the sheet, breathed in deep and slowly, pulled it back to reveal the hand, black with decay. Its knuckles bulged from thin fingers. He stared at the hand and couldn't bring himself to reveal any more of the body.

"You should take a piece," the ghost suggested.

Cinque turned on him in disgust. "What?"

"I said, you should take a piece. Look you ain't here to look at some mouldy old corpse. Sorry . . ." He apologized to the body. "You wanna get in touch with his spirit, right? Well I'm sure his ghost got some connection with his body. An' you can use that."

"You connected to your body?"

"It's at the Kumler Cemetery, six feet under. But I got a stronger connection to my girl. Always did."

Cinque wasn't sure if the ghost was right, but he'd never come this way again so if he was going to do this, he'd better do it now. He stepped over to the desk and grabbed a latex glove from the box. It was twice the size of his hand, which would work out just fine. He tried not to think as he grabbed the little finger of the corpse's hand and twisted. The decomposed flesh was soft and fell away like overcooked chicken but the tendons underneath wouldn't let go no matter how much Cinque pulled. He let go of the partially severed finger, went back to the desk and grabbed an aluminum clipboard. His frustration overwhelming his nausea, he returned to the glove and the finger, and he hacked and sawed away at the joint with the clipboard's edge until it came free. He then grabbed the glove at the wrist with his free hand and pulled it inside out capturing the dismembered digit inside. He tied the glove off at the open end and covered the remaining hand before wiping the clipboard clean and returning it to the desk.

Willy was still watching the boy, eyes agape.

"That . . . was some sick-ass jack."

"You was the one that thought of it," accused Cinque.

"But you was the one that done it."

He slipped the glove and finger into his backpack. Something about having a piece of his father just felt right, like they were finally together.

As he left the viewing room, Cinque signed a request that the remains of Kelly Lee be put to rest in the county plots.

Then came the hard part: from the lobby pay phone, he placed a collect call home. The phone picked up on the first ring. "Hello?" It was a woman's voice, a worried voice. It was so thick with emotion he couldn't tell if it was Ma or Grandma.

"It's me. I'm—" he was interrupted by a commotion on the other end. Whoever it was had just shouted something away from the phone, setting off a few other voices too. Cinque figured that it was the whole family, plus a few of Grandma's friends. From the sound of it the woman on the other end fought briefly over the phone with one of the other voices.

"Boy, do you know what you put your family through?" Ma had won the fight. There was no mistaking that voice, her angry voice. Cinque didn't get the angry voice often. "Tell me where you are so I can beat your ass!"

"I'm at the Cook County Coroner. Where'd you think I be?"

The cacophony of voices from the background filled the stunned pause Ma left open. "You . . . you in Chicago? How the hell did a skinny little thing like you get to Chicago?"

"I caught a ride."

"With who? Who you know with a car?"

"No one." Cinque shrugged.

"You got a ride with 'no one'? How's 'no one' gonna drive?"

Cinque started to squirm. "No. I don't know anyone with a car. I hitched a ride with a stranger."

"You what?"

Cinque realized he shouldn't answer any more questions.

"Boy, you better sit your narrow ass right down right there 'cause I'm heading up there to beat it all the way back home! God damn, boy, don't you realize that the city is four hours away? I'm gonna lose two days of work over this!"

Normally when Cinque made a mistake she'd play as if he'd have to fix it on his own, like telling him he had to walk home on his own. She didn't this time. Cinque realized she must have been really scared.

With the day to kill, Cinque took a seat in the lobby and investigated his inheritance, mostly clothes that would never fit him and a few odds and ends. The only items of interest in the boxes were the letter and the copy of *The Black Arts*, and the letter wasn't for him. Cinque could tell by the paperback's hideous blue and green cover that in this case "black" didn't mean "African-American." It meant things dark and arcane.

The book was all over the place, geographically and topically. It talked about people that he'd heard about, like the Egyptians, and people he'd have to read about later, like the Sumerians. The book left him with more questions than answers. It wasn't even clear about what the black arts were. On one page the witches of the Ozarks were having sex with the Devil and a page later it went on about a man named Hermes Trimegistus, an ancient Greek who built the pyramids. It said that witches used knots to place curses, curses that cut off the flow of good things. That made Cinque uneasy about the rope-fix the African had applied to him in his dream. The book also said that the great forces could not be described as good or evil, they just had good and evil sides. Magic was a tool, and just like any tool it wasn't any more good or evil than the arm that held it.

Maybe this was his inheritance. Not money, cars and houses. Not stuff, but knowledge and power. Maybe he didn't have to learn Juju from the African and his god. Maybe his father's ghost would teach him instead. Both Pastor Akotun and his father were strangers but his Pa was family and that had to count for something.

According to this book, many evil hands had held the tool of magic: Levi, Boullan, Huysmans, everyone involved with the Order of the Golden Dawn, especially Aleister Crowley. Maybe evil was too strong a word but they weren't nice. At best they were petty. They seemed to spend all their time fighting each other.

Hours later, Cinque looked over the top of his book and caught the faint outline of Willy T exploiting his invisibility by staring down the front of a woman's shirt. Cinque cleared his throat but the ghost just shrugged and said, "Hey man, just 'cause I be dead don't mean I be dead!"

Cinque snorted a laugh causing the woman to look up from the form she was filling out right into Cinque's eyes. The flush of guilt by association made the boy hide behind the book, embarrassed, like everyone in the room disapproved of him. Willy just laughed some more.

"Hey, boy, whatchu doin' with that book anyway? Only faggots read books. Is that *How to Be a Better Faggot in Thirty Days?* Ha!"

Cinque buried himself in the book but the ghost kept at him, passing his hand through the book, middle finger extended.

"Hey, boy? What yo' book say now? Ha!"

Cinque closed the book and turned his eyes to the ceiling. The ghost just leaned over him, pulling open one of his nostrils with his fingers he held it over the boy's face and asked, "See anything you like?"

Cinque jumped up and snapped, "Whatcha want, fool?" This might have earned him some stares from around the room but he didn't look around to make sure.

"Like I'm just gonna stand around, doin' nothin' till yo' moms show up?"

Cinque gathered up his boxes and went to wait on the short wall out front. He couldn't be around normal people with the ghost distracting him like this. As he left he mumbled to Willy, "What were you doin' when I met you? Walkin' around St. Jude talkin' to yourself, try that!"

"Boy, that was then. I been sleepwalkin', with half a brain. Now I'm mo' together. Now I'm kinda . . . anxious."

Cinque wasn't sure he liked where this was going.

"My girl be back in St. Jude and I be wastin' time here with yo' ass."

"You done forgot all about the other night, did ya? I did that for you, now you do this for me. Sorry, but you with me until I find my Pa." Cinque dropped his boxes outside and plopped on the wall where the White Woman had sat. "How long you gonna keep all up on her anyway? What if she lives to be a hundred?"

"Then I got a long job ahead a me 'cause I'm a be there when she crosses over, an' together we'll walk through them pearly gates. Till then I'm her guardian angel."

This was the first time a spirit had said something about Heaven. "You seen Heaven's gates?"

"Naw, not so much, but there been times and places I feel salvation be tuggin' on me, drawin' me in." Willy pantomimed being pulled by a rope at the chest. "But I can't go, I gots work to do here on the Earth, serious work, you know what I'm sayin'?"

Maybe God's salvation wasn't as picky as he used to think. Cinque kept that thought to himself.

Cinque was about a hundred pages into the book when his Ma showed up. It had been a difficult read and he often had to reread pages and passages while skipping over the chapter on something called Cabbala because it was complicated and the chapter on numerology because it was silly. He was so engrossed he hadn't noticed her pull up, but was suddenly taken up in her familiar, but intense embrace while she said, "Oh, my baby's alright, my baby's alright, my baby's alright."

Before he could hug her back, she pulled away, smacked him on the side of his head and shouted, "When did you become a damn fool? When did you become a damn fool? I'd have expected this nonsense from Darren! No, I wouldn't, because Darren knows that if his stupid-ass survived the trip up here and survived a day in this city, as soon as Grandma found out she'd a killed him! You lucky that she didn't come up here with me, she was about to! Get your ass in the car!" Cinque turned to pick up the boxes. "What do you think you're doing with that? Is that whatcha came up here for? Nuh-uh, that man's junk can stay right there!"

Cinque set a protective hand on top of the boxes. Filled with righteous indignation he looked up at his Ma as another obstacle to be overcome. "You don't know what it took to get here. It wasn't just that I was willing to come up to Chicago on my own to get this stuff. It was a lot more than that. So what do you think I'd be willing to do to keep hold of it?"

The boy's intensity stopped Olamide cold. She looked at Cinque and he could tell she saw a different boy under the layers of change, a hardened version of the boy she knew. Too surprised to be angry anymore she said, "Get in the car." They drove back to St. Jude in silence.

11

TO KEEP HOLD

Like his adventure in the hospital, the trip to Chicago earned him no punishment. Darren was surprised at what Cinque was able to get away with, Cinque was surprised that Darren wasn't jealous of his younger cousin's special treatment.

"That's 'cause I don't think you're off the hook, little man," Darren told him as they walked to school the next day. "I think you got them scared for you, but if you keep acting the fool ... they'll come down on you, hard. Once they figure out how."

"What do you think'll happen?"

"I think if you keep up this craziness they gonna tie you up in a straight jacket and mail you to the nuthouse."

"That's too bad." Cinque narrowed his eyes. "'Cause I'm just gettin' started."

"What you mean you just gettin' started? Your Pa be dead. That ain't a start, that a finish." Darren kicked a trashed plastic bottle into someone's yard.

"I don't think so." Then Cinque came to a realization aloud. "I think my Pa left me exactly what I needed, both the know-how and the means, to get in touch with him. Dead or not."

He felt Darren tense up next to him so he tried something. He looked his cousin in the eye and said, "Juju runs in his family."

Darren didn't say anything to that. He didn't have anything to say the rest of the way to school. Cinque had never heard his cousin so silent for so long.

After school, Cinque went to the St. Jude Public Library. Dark green plastic curtains held back the sunlight. The floor was polished, cracked concrete and the smell of old books was everywhere. Normally, Cinque's favourite spot was the hidden couch back by the historical records, the part of the library most people had no use for, but today he stood with the 158's (Applied Psychology) on his left and the 306's (Culture & Institutions) on his right. The picture of Willy and his girl was in the pack on his back. He put it out of his mind. He closed his eyes and thought of Willy T. Once he was satisfied that he couldn't call the ghost without the picture in hand, the real experiment began.

"By Egungun I call for Willy Thompson. By Egungun I call for Willy Thompson. By Egungun I call for Willy Thompson."

Then Willy T was there, in front of the boy. Wide eyed, the ghost fell on his butt and looked up at Cinque in shock, "What'd you just do, boy?"

This small success filled Cinque with hope. With all the Juju and witchcraft going on around him, maybe he had a chance of keeping ahead of the game. He smirked down at the ghost. "A little somethin' an African taught me. What'd it feel like?"

Willy T shook, and flopped around on the ground as he tried to stand before he gathered his balance. "Felt like someone pulled my leash, but without the leash, you know what I'm sayin'?" He stopped squirming. "It was like I was pulled here an' now. Not that I wanted to, it was more like fallin'."

Cinque said as he put the picture away, "I wasn't sure it'd work. It didn't work before on the Cloudy Man. . . ."

Willy leaned against the shelves. He looked at the books without comprehension. "Where the hell are we?"

"The library. Ever hear of it?"

"Why you bring me here?"

"'Cause I knew you never been here before."

"You got that right!" As he stood up, Willy scowled at the books to either side of him, like he was surrounded by enemies. "But what that got to do wit' anything?"

"Well, the African told me a story to teach me about ghosts, that they'll come when you use something of theirs to call them, like I just did with your picture." Cinque pulled a book off the shelf to his left and showed it to Willy to emphasize his point, *Needing Things*. Willy just scoffed and tried to knock the book away, the back of his hand passing through it with no effect. "And in the story ghosts like booze, cigarettes and food and stuff. They'll work for any of that."

"Ah, yeah!" Willy perked up when Cinque had mentioned alcohol. "I hate to agree with that African nigga but that's the ticket. I've been thirsty for I don' know how long now. Man, if I could get fit-shaced one more time . . ." Cinque walked around to the next shelf and Willy followed. "But, 'less things have changed in the last year, you too young to be buyin' no forties."

"I think I can figure something out. Last night I tried calling my Pa with his things and the name of the All-Ghost." Cinque pulled The Prodigal Father: Reuniting Fathers and their Children off the shelf to his right to taunt the ghost. Willy rolled his eyes.

"Course it didn't work, he's too far from this world and into the next, so I'm going to bring together everything I can think of and part of that is me taking a few steps closer to the afterlife. You said that there were places that felt closer to heaven. You mean like church?"

"Ha! You'd a thunk it wouldn't you? No, boy, not church, but I seen them in all kinds of other places, streets an' alleys, I saw a kid get hit by a car an' one opened up right there. I hadda get outta there or else it'a sucked me in.

"But I always felt a tug, a pullin' to go up there." Willy T pointed out the window, towards the smokestacks of the Armour Meatworks. Cinque figured it was time to talk to Grandma.

Cinque found his Grandma in the living room doing the ironing. Normally Cinque could talk to her about anything, anytime, but with all that he'd been up to lately he wasn't sure about his place in the family anymore. Unseen in the doorway, unsure how to go forward but reluctant to go back, Cinque stood, unable to decide.

Willy saw Cinque's hesitancy and gave him a push. "Okay, little man, if you let everyone know you got your eye on that place then they gonna know you're heading up there, especially after we just jetted up to Chicago. So we gonna ask about the meatworks without asking about the meatworks."

He made a circle in the air with his fingers.

"See what I'm sayin'? What's your angle? Your grandpa. Why'd you trip up north? Your pops. Ifin' you play like you just wanna talk about the old man then they'll be relieved that you ain't takin' things into your own hands again. Dig?"

Cinque nodded.

"Then let's do this. Don' worry if you get stuck. I'll help you out."

Cinque stepped into the living room. His Grandma didn't look up from the ironing. "Well, look who's home from school. How are you doing today, Cinque?"

"Okay. I guess."

"You guess?" She stopped and looked back at him over her shoulder. "That don't sound right. So how do you really feel?"

"Can you tell me about Grandpa?" Cinque walked around to the other side of the ironing board.

"Now why'd you want to know about him? Why now?"

"'Cause I need to know where I came from. Kids who know their pops don't turn out bad."

She went back to work, but kept talking. "Well, I hardly think you're going to turn out bad, Cinque. But you have been worrying us lately. I understand what you're doing but I don't like how you're doing it."

"I know. I'm sorry."

"So is that what this has all been about? Finding out where you came from?" She leaned forward, over the board. "Don't you know, boy, that where you're from isn't half as important as what you've done?"

Cinque didn't know what to say. She'd changed the topic so completely that he didn't know how to get back to what he wanted. Willy was pacing and thinking. "This is gonna be tough. Just tell her what she wants to know while I think of something."

"Things been goin' crazy for me, Grandma, like my life has missing pieces and I don't know where they went. I figure if I can find my Pa, then I got a chance at fixing all this."

Willy cringed. "You think that's what she wanted to hear?"

Grandma didn't like what she heard. "Your Pa is dead, Cinque. And I don't know enough about him to help you with that."

Cinque stood with a nervous twist. He hoped that Willy would think of something for him to say soon.

"Can you promise me something? Can you promise me you'll let this go?"

Cinque couldn't lie. "I can't do that, Grandma."

"Then I can't tell you about your Grandpa. Not because I don't want to. But because I don't want to encourage you down this path you're on."

Cinque felt guilty. If she'd told him about the meatworks and if something went wrong up there then she'd feel responsible. This was his burden and he had no right laying it on her.

As he turned to go without a word she called after him,

"Cinque?" He looked back to see her sad and worried, a pair of his jeans in her hands. "Be careful."

Walking through town to get to the meatworks they passed by an old building of blue brick, an abandoned beauty parlour called Wonderland. As they stepped up, the little fox-faced spirit stepped out, picking at his teeth in a broken hand mirror. He gave Cinque a wide, toothy smile and casually dropped the mirror, letting it shatter on the sidewalk.

"Hey, Donut!" It laughed at that. "Donut! I just thought that one up! 'Cause you got a hole in the middle, get it?"

Cinque gave it a single, unenthusiastic wave.

For once, Willy was the one who looked surprised. "You . . . know this little thing?"

"Yeah!" Fox Face interrupted, "Me and Donut go way back. Where you heading, Donut?"

"Don't call me Donut. We're heading up to the old meatworks. Willy here says that it feels funny to ghosts and I wanna check out why. Maybe it's something I can use."

"Heck and hack, kid, I can tell you that! It used to be a slaughter house. All that death, kinda . . . thinned the air between life and death up there. That's why Casper here is scared to go up in there, he might get sucked it."

"Casper?" Willy stepped forward, ready to fight. "Come here and say that again, see what happens."

The creature backed up, nervous. "I'm sorry, mister. I just wanted to tell Donut how disappointed I was in him."

Now Cinque was angry too, "Disappointed in what?"

"Disappointed that you're figuring it out. You're goin' up there to talk to your daddy, that's the right step. I was sure you'd never of figured out nothing on your own. I figured you'd just die slowly of a missing heart part." He went from fearful to disrespectful like the flip of a switch. "But I think you'll screw it up. I'll see you later, Donut, Casper." It ran back into the broken beauty shop.

"Oh, it's on!" Willy set to chase after it but Cinque stopped him.

"Forget that thing, Willy. Why you going to chase him when you don't even know if you can grab him?"

Willy paced up and down the blue brick wall. "I'd think of somethin' I could do to him."

Within the hour they were at the top of the hill, outside of the old Armour Meatworks. Inside the rusted chain link fence four mismatched buildings ran up next to each other surrounded by trees. A small black building was at the far end, in front of that a large dark brown building which was behind a white, open framework building. All of that was behind the closest building built of rusty red brick. The two brick smokestacks stuck out from the red building and at this distance Cinque could clearly make out the name "Armour" written on the right stack in fading white paint. Debris filled the yard, a stack of pipes over here, a pile of truck chassis over there, and right up front, by the gate, was what was left of a red three ton truck, its tires dry, rotten and flat. Here and there, other equipment rested and rusted, scattered among the overgrowth. The property was fenced in, but the gate hung wide open.

"This is as far as I go, an' dis a whole lot closer than I wanna be." On the walk up the ghost had lagged behind, and took any excuse to stop, claiming to be tired. Even Cinque didn't believe that one. Now that he could see the building, there was a weirdness about it. Not malicious or cruel, but wrong, the way the weather was wrong just before a storm.

"You feel that too?" The ghost had his arms crossed.

"Like the building's looking back at us?"

"Yeah." Willy was part scared and part hypnotized by whatever was up there.

"I'm going in to take a look." Cinque slung his backpack over both shoulders and started walking up the road.

"Hol' up!" Willy shouted suddenly. "Fo' you go. Why don' you leave my picture out here. With me?"

Even Cinque could tell that the ghost was nervous about something. "What's got into you?"

"Well . . . not that I don' think you comin' back or nuthin'." The ghost looked at the dirty ground and rubbed the back of his neck. "But if'n you don't come back, then my picture'll be stuck up there wit you. . . ."

"Yeah, I got you." Cinque pulled the picture out of his pocket and put it under a rock by the side of the road.

"What? You jus' gonna leave it there?" Willy asked, indignant.

"Sorry, man, but I gotta go. I was nervous before, now I'm straight up scared. If I wait any longer I ain't goin' in at all."

Willy still didn't like it but he let it go. "Yeah, well, have fun in there," and with a mischievous grin added, "Nice knowin' ya!"

"Don't jinx me!" Cinque snapped back as he turned to pass through the gate.

He climbed over a pile of decayed sandbags, their contents fused into a single massive dirt clod, and up onto a large, flat gravel lot that must have been a parking area. The double doors on this side were chained shut. The windows still had their glass—strange for St. Jude, a town with so many rocks and kids to throw them. Behind the dirty glass, grates barred the windows. The same was true on all sides of the plant. There was no one around to hear; he might have been able to smash in a window and look for a latch to open the grate but that didn't feel like the right way in.

Instead, Cinque went for the roof, using one of the trees that grew on the building's north side. Fourteen year old boys are the ideal size for climbing trees, and Cinque easily made it to the top. He scrambled along the big branch and dropped down onto the roof before realizing it was go down into the building or stay up here forever, because the branch was too high above the roof for him to grab.

Grass and vines overgrew the roof, as if someone had planted a garden up here. Cinque thought he saw the tops of trees from the other side of the building, but as he moved closer he could tell that a small group of trees was growing up here, roots bored in the roof itself. He plucked a leaf and put it in his mouth, tasting it to make sure they weren't figments.

No one had stood up here since the Meatworks closed, probably longer. Along the horizon, through the tree and buildings, Cinque could see the sunlight sparkle off the length of the Mississippi as it ran along the city's edge.

St. Jude was laid out between him and the Mississippi, buildings of white, black and gray popped up from the trees like bones. That's what St. Jude was: a skeleton with a few people pointlessly holding it together in the face of inevitable decay. He spotted the statue of St. Jude that stood outside his church. It made him happy to see it so small.

The vines poured down through a hole in the roof, crawling along the scaffolding of the vast space inside of the large brown block. On the ground were huge pieces of rusting machinery that looked like colossal, antique sewing machines. Suspended pipes of various sizes ran through the room. Invading green veins shot through the gray and red of concrete and rust.

Cinque descended into the pit, climbing from the vines to the scaffold and dropping onto a big machine with a large, flat top. From down here, the hole in the roof looked so small. If he hadn't just passed through it he wouldn't have thought it possible.

He slid down to the floor and explored. On the wall, by what might have been a generator, graffiti read, *Organ recital in progress. Please be quiet. Thank you—The management* and a rough cartoon of a smiling crocodile that was supposed to look friendly, but came off as sinister. There were other not-so-friendly cartoon crocodiles drawn in dark corners and behind machines, hiding in ambush.

Willy T was right: there was something about this place. Maybe the tens of thousands of animals killed here weakened the line between life and death. It was the right place to work some Juju.

Cinque walked over to the front room. Lockers lined the walls to either side. Cinque scanned the peeling, faded name tags until he found one labelled "J. Williams." Wondering if this was his grandpa's locker, he knocked the lock open with a worn, old boot, opened the locker and wondered no more. Inside the door was a picture of his Grandma with her arms wrapped around his Ma as she was in high school. It must have been about fifteen years old.

Other than a few sets of blood-stained coveralls, the locker was empty. Cinque imagined how the last day of Armour Meatworks had played out. The workers just showed up one day to discover the door chained and a company man outside passing out their last paycheques. Cinque put the picture in his backpack and explored on.

To the west the room emptied into a dark alcove, barren except for guardrails along the walls. On the far side was an even darker opening, pitch black, square and large enough to pass a van through. Above the black threshold, mounted like a crest at the top of the opening, was a large gear with five spokes. Cinque approached the opening and stared into the dark, forcing his eyes to adjust. There was no light from the other side of the gear, but there was sound, a slight rattle, a scrape, a moment of silence and then a regular click—click—click coming closer, until a medium-sized dog emerged from the darkness. It was a mutt, mostly terrier but with a shepherd's build, shaggy coat and floppy ears. Its fur was black with white spots, dirty and unkempt. Cinque smelled it coming before he saw it.

Cinque didn't get this close to a dog often. He held out a hand for the dog to smell. Grinning widely he called out, "Here, boy . . . or girl, maybe, I can't tell."

The stray just growled a deep, unfriendly growl. Cinque knew that once the dog got his scent he'd warm up. Dogs liked him. He slid closer and held his hand out further. Waving it a little to make sure the dog saw it.

The stray lunged at him, an explosion of noise and teeth. Cinque pulled his hand away. He tried to jump back but instead he tumbled and sat hard down with his legs all akimbo. The stray lunged again. Somehow Cinque managed to get his legs under him. He turned tail and ran back through the larger room, between the decrepit pieces of machinery. When outside, Cinque had seen a door with no handle, the one door that wasn't chained shut. He bolted for it with the stray at his heels.

Around a corner, in the white building, the door without a handle was right where Cinque figured. A sign above it declared "Emergency Exit" and "Do not block." Cinque hit the push bar with his hip. The door sprung open. Twisting in the air, Cinque hooked the door and spun, using his forward motion to slam the door shut. His feet slipped out from under him and he fell on his side in the dirty gravel, the stray barking at him from the other side.

"Ha! Missed me!" he yelled as he stood up and brushed himself off.

The stray charged around the left side of the building, running fast. It chased Cinque out the gate, back down the hill, past where Willy T was waiting. He stopped only when he heard the ghost call after him.

"Hey, boy! Whatcha runnin' from?"

12

BACK DOWN THE HILL

"At first I thought I heard a police car comin' there was this siren sound all, 'AAAAAAAAAAAAAA—' but it wasn't goin' up an' down like a siren's supposed to. Then I thought I saw a pair a headlights, but the funny thing 'bout them was they wasn't givin' off no light, see? And they was real close-like, comin' at me reeeal fast I thought it was one of them Japanese motorbikes, that's how fast this thing was comin' at me. But jus' as it be up on me I saw it wasn't a motorbike at all. Been your bug-eyed ass a screamin' and a tearin' down the road. Ha!"

Willy's teasing got Cinque mad enough to go back up the road and retrieve his picture from under the rock where he'd left it, an act of boldness that didn't make Willy quit. This was the third time Willy told the story. "An' where was your skinny ass at?" Cinque asked, trying to head off a fourth telling. "You didn't even come up there to see no dog, that empty building had you ready to piss yo self. Bet you would'a if you could'a."

"Well, when you a step away from Hell, take care which way you walk." The ghost muttered alongside Cinque as he walked to the market. From what the African had taught him and what he'd learned during his time with Willy, Cinque had pieced together a plan. Somewhere deep in his mind, a part of him was telling himself to hold off for a day, sleep on it, double check the facts but the rest of him was saying, if this was going to happen, it would have to happen tonight.

He carried that tingling feeling with him into the market as he walked over to the liquor store. Towers of boxes, bottles and cans loomed overhead, the shoppers dwarfed by their shadows. Unrenovated in its thirty years, almost half of the linoleum tiles were chipped or peeling, the plastic covers of the florescent lights were yellowing, and more than a few of the broken shelves were repaired with duct tape.

He walked back and forth in the aisles considering each bottle, focusing on how they made him feel. The gin bottles felt like hammers with painted handles, rum was a wide but toothless smile and the vodka felt like trying to write with a leaky pen. There were others, but as he circled the rows he kept coming back to a dusty bottle of dark brown liquid all alone on the bottom shelf. The indigo label read "Four Houses American Straight Whiskey" written around an old time prospector leading a mule. It felt right, a little more real than the rest.

He picked up the bottle and realized he was being watched, over by the registers. The lady without an apron, the one who bossed the other clerks around, had her eye on him. She was watching him in that deliberate way that old ladies do, a look that shot, "You'd better not do that" into his head. He deliberately set the bottle back on the shelf and went to leave. He told her, "I was just looking," as he walked past.

She hummed the same unconvinced "Um-hmm" that Grandma would give to Darren. Willy was waiting for him outside. Someone had dropped a still smouldering cigarette butt and the ghost was squatting over it, trying to inhale the fumes.

"Don't tell me you're getting something out of that."

"A little some-some," Willy said, the smoke trail passing through his face. "Or maybe it jus' helps me remember."

"Well, get up. You look a fool down there."

"So? Who's to know? You? Ha!" Willy said as he stood up. "If I make a good show you gonna put in a good word for me at the office? Ha!"

Cinque led them back to Loyston and Belmont, back downtown, to the mysterious alley where Darren got his liquor and cigarettes.

A figure stood at the edge of the alley, waiting for them. Three feet tall and stocky, its lumpy shape looked sculpted out of soggy puzzle pieces. It turned its blob of a head towards the two as they walked up and for a moment the three stood silently looking at each other until the puzzle-made man pointed down the alley with a fingerless hand.

"'Nother friend o' yours?" Willy asked.

"I never seen him before." Cinque didn't move. "You think that this means we're on the right track?"

"He ever lied to you before?"

"No." Cinque turned to face the dark alley. "I guess not."

Cinque had pictured a man in a large, baggy coat back here waiting for Darren. They'd make their deals while looking back and forth with shifty eyes. It was time to find that man and introduce himself. "You with me?" he asked the ghost.

"Yeah! Yeah, man. I'm wit' you! I ain't got nothin' to worry about, you know what I'm sayin'? No mugger's gonna give me no problems. Dunno 'bout you though."

"They know Darren in there. I'll be okay."

The two went down the alley. Like most of downtown, the plaster was chipping, and if the windows weren't broken, they were clouded with filth. Someone had dumped trash in the alley and vagrants had torn and picked their way through the bags. The scattered contents spread like undergrowth. An old water tower Cinque couldn't see from the street stood on the roof of the building to the left towards the back.

The alley was heavily haunted. The ambient spirits were far thicker here than anywhere he'd seen so far. A tangle of pale yellow yarn pulled itself along the ground with stringy pseudopods. A green Spider-Man mask, the cheap plastic kind, drifted on a breeze Cinque couldn't feel, the broken ends of its rubber band tasting the air like cilia. A faint, flat, white outline of a body dangled below it. A fish lay on the ground, its mouth gasping, pinned to the ground by the weight of a hundred gold chains.

Cinque tried to ignore the spirits.

The further into the alley he walked, the more he felt trapped. The alley clearly dead-ended a hundred feet in. As he walked down the alley, he was more and more surrounded by the spirits. As the only escape fell farther and farther behind, he became less and less sure that this was a good idea, but he didn't let it show. He hid his fear, something Darren had told him to do. Always act like you got crew to back you up, but know when you don't. Something he'd failed to do at the meatworks.

This time he did have crew. Willy was with him. He looked behind him. Willy T was a good distance behind him, dragging his feet.

"What am I doing up here? You the one that's dead! Get your ass up here and look around!" Cinque shouted.

"Whatcha want me to do?"

Cinque kicked a pile of trash and shouted, "Walk through some walls or something!"

"You knows I can't—"

"Walk through some doors then. Jump through some windows. I don't care!" He pointed further down the alley. "Just find out who's down here."

Cinque watched from the middle of the alley while Willy passed back and forth through the doorways. The ghost walked on tip-toes, steering clear of a large, dangerous looking spirit, a man-sized frog that lay along one of the walls. As Willy passed, it watched the ghost with lazy eyes. Every few feet he'd turn and shrug to show that he hadn't found anything until he passed behind a dumpster on the left and turned back quickly, arms waving.

"If this ain't it, I don' know what is."

Cinque caught up with Willy at the end of the alley and saw what he meant. Behind the dumpster was a door that was plastered with newspaper and magazine clippings, colourful pieces of plastic and other odds and ends. He stared at the display, trying to decipher a theme to the mess, but the door still managed a cheery feeling. It seemed to say "Welcome! Come on in!" The water tower on the roof above loomed over the door. Decayed and rusted, if it wasn't empty then, it was in danger of springing a leak any day now.

"What's inside?" Cinque asked.

"Jus' like whatcha see here 'cept . . . more."

Cinque gripped the gold-spraypainted door handle and gave it a tug. The door opened easily, rigged with a cheery shopkeeper's bell. Cinque looked uncertainly at Willy.

"Hey, man, it's the only thing down here," said Willy.

Cinque pushed through a thick yellow blanket that served as a curtain and went inside. From the ceiling's center hung a twelve inch light, the moon's craterous face drawn across its surface with gray crayon. In the bogus moonlight, the layout of the room suggested a storefront, but the display cases along the walls were piles of cardboard boxes and trash, covered with shiny and colourful pieces making it difficult to recognize. Cinque found just looking around was exhausting.

Every bit of open space, every crack and corner seethed with spirits: the figure of a man on a horse, stamped out of a single sheet of rusted sheet metal, rode violent circles around the room; a black puff of smoke with red malevolent eyes hung by the ceiling, orbited by a dozen small, blue, terrified pairs of eyes; a two-legged, elephantine figure with a hammer for a head pounded its face into the wall.

A group of spirits fluttered up from the floor and took orbit around Cinque's shoulders. They danced around Cinque's head. He could clearly hear their whispers. A green mailman said he was reading Cinque's mail for the CIA. A tangle of sparking electronic parts said it was installed in Cinque's brain when he was in the hospital. A four-armed monster draped in gun belts with a pistol in each hand urged Cinque to get a gun before they get to him, and a can of chilli just muttered, "Poison . . ." over and over.

"I seen some strange jack in my day." Willy said, "But nuthin' like this. I feel like we walked into a cartoon."

Cinque knew the feeling. The swirl of spirits made him feel caught up in a flow, out of control and strangely at home. It reminded him of his room.

Willy stayed by the door, looking ready to bolt.

From within the darkness and the clutter, a hoarse voice said, "You . . . see them?"

A man stepped out from the clutter, the whites of his eyes and his gray goatee the only parts of his face visible in the dark. The man wore a rumpled, red tuxedo jacket and on his head a paper grocery bag spraypainted black and curled up to form a brim.

"A mess of craz—strange little monsters flying all around me?" Cinque pointed around the room and the strange man nodded. "Yeah, I see them."

"I built this place for them. Nobody else knows that. I made bargains, to keep the good ones in and the bad ones out." The man attempted to single out examples. "But I don't think they're all so good anymore. You seen them before?"

Cinque tilted his head to the right. "Sometimes I do—" and to the left, "—sometimes I don't."

"I couldn't take that . . . the not knowin' when an' where an' what an' how. What'd be worse—if you could only see 'em some of the time or if they were there and you couldn't see 'em?"

They both looked suspiciously at the spirits around them. Cinque said, "Yeah. I'd rather they all go away or keep my eye on them."

"Then maybe you should." The man looked at his empty fist and unclenched it. "Who . . . who . . . who." He drifted off for a second, not as if he was falling asleep, more as if he had better things to think about. A sharp shudder ran through his body and he remembered he had company. "Who are you?"

"My name's Cinque," he answered, grabbing the straps of his backpack with both hands. "Cinque Williams. Darren's my cousin. You know Darren?"

For a moment the man stood still, his lips moved as if he was counting. When he was done he asked, "What's he do?"

Cinque didn't imagine that this man had so many visitors that he couldn't remember them all. "Uh. . . . He buys stuff off of you. Buys liquor and smokes."

"Oh, yeah. Greedy foolish fool. Sell his grandma for a dirty buck," he said turning and walking farther into the room to stand behind an office desk. The desk had been turned, length-wise up, and the man was using it as a short counter. Insulting his cousin should have made Cinque mad, but the bum wasn't far from right, and he knew Darren wouldn't care what his "business partner" thought about him as long as business continued. Since he wasn't going to introduce himself Cinque had to ask, "An' who are you?"

"I—umph—" He grunted as he sat on the stool, resting an arm on the desk. "—am Mr. Jaspers. And this is my Store of All Wants."

"You sell people what they want?"

"No." Mr. Jaspers leaned forward and pointed vaguely in Cinque's direction. "I buy their wants."

"What does that mean?"

"Desires, boy. I buy desires off people. I need them to

keep me going. To keep me alive." He slammed his fist on the counter with the frustration of having to explain himself.

"Your cousin's desires are simple, singular. He desires capital. That's common for his age. He doesn't understand the complexities and synchronicities of life. He cannot see past the bulge in his wallet and the bulge in his pants, for to him one will get him the other. Cash! Cash! Cash!" Mr. Jaspers flashed his hands with every word. "Get the green, the rest will follow. Am I right or am I right?"

"You're right, 'bout Darren that is."

"What? You don't want to be rich? Everybody wants to be rich. This is America. All twenty million of us want to be rich. Sell our souls, sell our pride, sell it all for the all mighty dollar. Am I right or am I right?"

"I'm sure there be more than twenty million—"

Mr. Jaspers covered his ears. "Don't argue details with me, boy. It makes my ass hurt."

Mr. Jaspers leaned back on the stool behind his counter, "So what do you want then?"

"I . . . I wanna be normal. I don't want to be crazy no more."

"Well, boy, I'll take that one off your hands for free."

He stepped out from behind the desk-turned counter, eyes locked on one of the tiny spirits. In one hand he held a bottle of green glass with no label. In the other he held a box of matches in his palm and a wooden match in his fingers, the match head pressed against the striking surface.

"You ain't never going to stop being crazy so you better just get used to it. The day I went mad, I mean really mad—you got to grab it with both hands and take it in." He brought his hands together as he closed in on his prey.

"You gotta make the madness all of you. Breathe it. Eat it. Drink it. Screw it!"

His stubby fingers deftly lit the match, dropped it into the bottle and pushed the rim up against his target, a floating cluster of small wooden boxes. As the air inside the bottle burned away, the spirit was sucked in. Mr. Jaspers sealed the bottleneck with the heel of his hand.

"You gotta try and screw the madness every. Single. Day. And it don't stop, cause let me tell you somethin' boy, madness got a lot going on! It's as much as anyone can imagine and a little more on top a that."

He dropped the matchbox and picked up a cap from the mess on the countertop; He screwed it on the bottle and placed the trapped demon on the upper shelf with dozens of other bottles, prison cells for spirits Mr. Jaspers had taken a disliking to.

Cinque didn't like Mr. Jaspers' advice so he changed the subject, "I need you to get me a bottle of whiskey."

"Whiskey?" Mr. Jaspers sounded genuinely surprised. "That a white man's drink. Whatcha want that for?"

Cinque didn't want to give the man any more information than he had to. In fact, Cinque wanted to get out of here as soon as possible. "What do you care? I'll pay you what Darren pays you."

Ms. Jaspers shook his head. "You can't."

"Yeah, I can," Cinque insisted. He had the money, though he wasn't sure how much he would need.

"No. You. Can't." Mr. Jaspers repeated. "You don't want money. I can see it in your eye. And if you don't want money then I don't want *your* money."

He stopped to let that sink in, but Cinque was still confused. "I buy wants. Darren wants dollars. I buy Darren's dollars with liquor. You don't want dollars. So neither do I."

"So what do you want then?"

"Aaaarr!" the man screamed in frustration. "I don't know what I want. But, you know what you want. And that's what I want. I can't make it any simpler."

"I . . . I want a bottle of whiskey." Cinque suggested.

Mr. Jaspers leaned forward, fists on his hips. "So you gonna give me a bottle of whiskey then?"

Cinque held his hands up and open. "I don't have bot—"

"No. You don't have a bottle of whiskey, so I can't buy a bottle of whiskey off a you then, can I?" Mr. Jaspers stood up and paced around the room. "Your cousin's the smart one, ain't he?"

That made Cinque mad. "Screw you!"

Mr. Jaspers laughed. "I done got my answer."

Meanwhile, Willy T had slipped around the other side and was poking around among the clutter. Occasionally one of the small, strange spirits would land on his head or try to climb up his leg and he'd shake it off.

Without turning, the ghost called out. "You gotta listen to what he's sayin', Cinque. An' you gotta remember this sucker's crazy. Look around, does it look like this brotha's playin' the same game as the rest? We playing Monopoly and he playin' Hungry Hungry Hippos."

Tired of nonsense, Cinque snapped at the ghost, "What do you know?"

Mr. Jaspers faced Willy T and asked, "Yes, ghosty. What do you know?"

Willy and Cinque froze. Cinque felt as dumb as he had all day. Of course Mr. Jaspers could see ghosts, he'd just bottled a spirit out of the air. Whether it was him or this place that he'd built, he'd probably known Willy was here from the start. "And what do you want? Ghosties always want something. That's what makes them ghosties."

Willy smiled like he hadn't been sneaking around. "What I got a want for, brotha? I can watch bitches in the shower any time I want."

"Just like a ghosty," he said turning back to Cinque as if they were sharing a joke. "They all about the wants, and it ain't ever something good." Mr. Jaspers tilted his head and stepped up to Willy T, inspecting him carefully. "You ain't all ghosty, are you?"

"Bitch, you livin' in a spaceman's zoo with a bunch of

imaginary friends. Whatchu know?" Willy turned and pretended to inspect the items on the shelf again.

Cinque thought about everything he wanted: a memory of his father, to get out of St. Jude, Imani—they were all too much to give up for just a bottle of liquor.

Mr. Jaspers was running out of patience. "Give me your want to be normal. It ain't gonna do you no good anyway."

Cinque protected his heart with one hand. "And then what?"

"Then you will be like him," said a new voice, a man's voice, a deep voice that came from all directions at once.

Cinque, Mr. Jaspers and the new figure were suddenly alone. The strange little spirits vanished, as if a great wind came through and blew out a hundred candles. Even Willy T was gone. The largest man Cinque had ever seen, seven feet tall or taller, had joined them. As broad as Cinque was tall, he wore a single breasted suit, red on one side and black on the other. Even his shirt and tie divided this way, and his bowler hat was either red with a black band or black with a red band. He carried a dark wooden cane, the silver head clenched in his giant hand. Cinque knew the kind of brother that dressed like that. Pimps.

As cluttered and as dark as this room was there had been no place where the giant could have been hiding. He'd stepped out of nowhere. Mr. Jaspers was even more shocked than Cinque was. His indignant shopkeeper act melting away, Mr. Jaspers was nothing but fear and uncertainty. "Wha—wha—what do you want here? What do you want with me?"

"From you, I want nothing." The man waved him away with one hand. "The time when you might have been useful is long past. Today you are just an obstacle." He pointed to Cinque with his cane. "He is the one that interests me."

"Me?" Cinque was both flattered and scared.

"Yes, you, boy. Cinque Williams." The big man looked down his nose at him. "I am Eshu Wara. And I am your god."

"Uhhh . . ." Cinque stammered. After a second he managed, "What?"

"I see we have a lot of work to do. Where to begin . . . ? Do you remember Pastor Akotun? You think of him as the African?"

Cinque nodded.

"He is one of mine. I charged him to spread my ministry here to the New World." He waved his hand dismissing objections neither of the mortals had the courage to make. "And yes, yes, I know that it's no longer called the New World by men, but it is still new to me."

He hooked Mr. Jaspers' counter with the top of his cane and gave it a pull. It fell with a bang, becoming a desk again. Again, he used his cane to move a sturdy looking box into position and took a seat behind the desk. The sight of such a large man behind the tiny, beaten desk should have been comical, but somehow, it enforced his authority.

"You are having a difficult time with Mr. Jaspers' offer because it's a bad deal, a swindle even." Mr. Jaspers shifted at the accusation, but didn't object. "He wants too much for his service. Because you don't care about something as gauche as money, and you are under such desperate circumstances, he is taking advantage of you. Instead of bargaining for the object of your desire he is making a play for your desire itself."

"Why? What good would my desires do for him?" Cinque asked, finally finding his voice.

Eshu Wara gave the boy a studying look. "Why is that your question? Why don't you ask 'How can he do this thing'?"

Cinque shrugged, "I dunno. I guess it isn't that hard to take out a piece of someone's soul. It's not like it's all locked up."

"No it is not, especially in your case." He looked at Mr. Jaspers as he continued, "To give up one's wants is to give up one's self. It's a man's desire that makes him what he is, defines him. I'll not see one of my worshipers damaged so." Mr. Jaspers couldn't make eye contact with Eshu Wara, and he flinched at the accusation. "I will mediate this transaction. My suggestion—Mr. Jaspers, you will go to the market and purchase one bottle of Four Houses American Straight Whiskey. They only have the one bottle: it's at the back of the middle row, on the bottom left."

Mr. Jaspers nervously glanced at his watch. "I can't go outside again until 3:13—"

"When you return you will receive this." He pulled a small, blue, square-shaped bottle from his coat. "One day of lucidity."

Mr. Jaspers gasped, his eyes growing wide. His hand moved towards the bottle.

"Because this," he turned the bottle in his fingers, "is Mr. Jaspers' want. Isn't it, Mr. Jaspers? What you gave up on so long ago."

"Only one day?" Mr. Jaspers asked. "Why just one day?"

Eshu Wara's voice shed its professional tone for something quite a few shades sterner, as if he was scolding a child. "Because it's only a bottle of cheap liquor that would be better used as paint thinner. I am being generous with you, Mr. Jaspers, but that does not mean I'm a fool. For a day you could think straight again. Remember that? Maybe if you had your head back right for a day you could discover a more permanent solution."

He returned the bottle to his coat, his voice again free of anger. "We both know you'll never find a better offer." Mr. Jaspers started to leave, but Eshu Wara stopped him. "Not so fast, Mr. Jaspers. You and I are only discussing price. The deal is between me and the boy."

All eyes turned to Cinque, Eshu Wara's with calm consideration and Mr. Jaspers' with the flare of insanity. "Mr. Jaspers and I have established my offer to him. Now, here is my offer to you. Commit yourself to me. Become my acolyte in this country. Believe in me and I will believe in you."

That sounded far too broad a commitment."What does that mean?"

"It means that I will teach you and you will learn but be warned—" Eshu Wara said, deathly serious, "—my lessons are harsh. There will be many times when you will regret this day. But I will make you strong. Stronger than you can imagine."

"Cows are strong too, but I don't want to be one of them. This doesn't sound so nice."

Eshu gave a short nod and almost winked. "It shouldn't. Cinque. I offer you hardship, sacrifice and suffering. This will be a most difficult life but nothing worth doing is ever easy. And don't forget—" He waved towards Mr. Jaspers. "—the alternative."

Cinque remembered what he'd come here for in the first place. "Can you help me find my pa?" the boy asked.

"Isn't that what I'm doing here?" His voice was too innocent to be taken seriously.

"I mean, like, take me right to him." Cinque pointed to the door as if he knew where his father might be. "So I don't have to go back up to the meatworks."

"No. I won't do this thing for you because it's the doing that's important." Iku, the White Woman, said the same thing. Cinque thought about bringing that up, but maybe Eshu didn't like her. They seemed cut from the same spiritual cloth. The big man continued, "I am not offering to solve your problems. I am offering to make you stronger, strong enough to solve your own problems."

Cinque pointed to Mr. Jaspers. "Ain't you solving my problem with him?"

"It seems that way, but I am only protecting you. When you wander close to the edge I will pull you back, but only as you start to fall."

He slid his hand down his cane so that his fingers wrapped around the neck and leaned it towards Cinque. The handle was a silver ant head, the wire antennae twitching.

The red and black of his suit, the-ant headed cane, they triggered something for Cinque. He remembered the ants that swarmed over the house back when he set up the decoy for the Cuttlefish. "Those ants were yours?"

"The ants were me." Eshu clarified. "That was a very dangerous thing you did, Cinque, for someone with one foot in the spirit to shed his sweat so carelessly. If I hadn't protected you, every predatory spirit in the area would have descended on you to take a piece. We wouldn't be having this conversation now. You may have never had another conversation again.

"But it would be a shame to waste such potential. That one was free. If you want me to intervene here with you and Mr. Jaspers, then someday there is going to be a price."

"What kind of price? Didn't you want me to worship you?"

"In time. This . . . this is just a favour to you and you'll owe me a favour in return. Consider the value of what I'll be giving to Mr. Jaspers," he patted the coat pocket where the small bottle was. "I'll ask nothing more than that and probably less."

"And when will you want me to worship you or become your priest or something like tha—?" Mr. Jaspers suddenly threw a fit.

"Stop asking stupid questions and do it!" Mr. Jaspers shouted from the door. He had one hand on the handle and was ready to run to the store for the whiskey.

The man's angry shout made Cinque jump in his skin, but Eshu Wara answered Cinque's question as if no one else had spoke. "Faith, worship, devotion, these must be earned. To force these things from you would be meaningless."

Cinque took one last moment to imagine an alternative and failed.

"Alright, I'll do it. I don't see as I have much choice."

Eshu Wara smiled for the first time. "There's always a choice. This time you made the right one." He spit into the palm of his hand and offered it to Cinque.

"To seal the deal."

Cinque looked at the hand, but kept his to himself. "Do we have to do this?"

"Yes," the big man answered. "Ritual is essential."

Cinque pulled up as much saliva as he could and spit into his own palm and took the man's hand, losing it in the giant fingers. As they shook, the squirming of their combined saliva made Cinque's stomach turn. Eshu Wara gave his hand three solid pumps and released it, slipping his hand behind his back. Cinque resisted the urge to wipe his hand on his sleeve and imagined the spidery mess the deal left behind, but the moist sensation was gone. His fingers explored the palm and discovered it dry.

Mr. Jaspers quickly pushed open the door. Even more quickly, Eshu Wara hooked the handle with his cane and pulled it back. For the moment, Mr. Jaspers' anger grew stronger than his fear: "What now? He signed the deal."

Without taking his eyes off Cinque, Eshu Wara replied, "And a package of three steaks . . . for the stray."

"Sure. Sure." Mr. Jaspers stammered. "Whatever you want." Eshu released the door and the man was gone, leaving Cinque and his giant benefactor alone.

"So what now?" Cinque asked. He was expecting some kind of special effects. A handshake and disappearing spit was a letdown.

"Now? Now you'll continue along the path you set for yourself when you decided that you needed to convene with your father."

"Will I? Am I going to find the ghost of my pa?"

"Maybe. Destiny is for the little people, people of small capability. Like plankton tossed about in the water, slaves to the tide and flow. Big people, people of large capability, they decide where they're going to go. They swim against the tide like whales. If you are going to be a person of large capacity, you'll have to learn how to swim. Learn fast, boy, lest you drown."

He set down his cane, and pulled the bottle of lucidity from his coat and set it on the desk, his right hand still hidden behind his back. "I am finished here. When Mr. Jaspers returns he'll only have eyes for this, so be on your toes." He tipped his bowler with his cane and gave Cinque a slight, cold smile. "Goodbye, Cinque Williams. I'll be watching you."

"Why do I feel like I just made a deal with the Devil?"

The big man laughed low and slow. "The Devil would have had you sign a contract."

It didn't take long for Mr. Jaspers to return. Sweat drenched his face and shirt, and his breath was ragged. When he burst through, he left the door open behind him, knocking the curtain down in his haste. The meagre sunlight seemed intense to eyes that had adjusted to the dark. Mr. Jaspers's head turned back and forth, until he spotted the vial left on the desk. He'd lost his paper bag hat somewhere on the way.

"Here!" He pushed the supermarket bag into Cinque's arms. The boy grabbed at it, pressing it against his thighs and barely saving it from the cement floor.

Uncaring, Mr. Jaspers grabbed the vial and fell to the ground. He leaned against the front of the desk, legs shot out in front of him. Cinque looked at the man's shoes for the first time, under the grime and the wear the beaten old sneakers were clearly mismatched, one was once a black high-top and the other was once a white tennis shoe.

"Why?" he asked, but Mr. Jaspers was distracted. He'd opened the vial and was breathing deeply from the lip. "Why don't your shoes match?" he shouted to get the man's attention, sounding more desperate than he wished.

Mr. Jaspers looked back at Cinque, surprised that the boy was still there. "Shoes? I don't know, can't keep a matched set. One's always walkin' off on its own. Now get out!"

He brought the bottle up to his lips and sucked it down while Cinque tried to think of a place he could get a new pair of shoes, cheap.

Outside, the alley was free of the spirits that had haunted it so thickly an hour ago. Even the giant frog-thing that looked too big to move was gone. Where the alley emptied out into the street, Willy T waited around the corner. "What happened?" the ghost asked. "That big nigga stepped into the room and it was like a tidal wave pushing me out. Next thing I know I'm on my ass, out on the street and can't get back."

"I think I met a god."

"You talked to God?"

"Not the big G, God, just a little g, god. Anyway, I got what we came for. I think I know how to find my pops." He gestured to his backpack with his thumb. "You ready?"

"Hey, man. I don't need to be ready, you the one pickin' up the ghost. Is you ready?"

Cinque looked back down the alley. Without the spirits in the way he saw what must have been one of Mr. Jaspers' murals, eight stars and a bird in a tree. "If I am or if I ain't, it don't matter. Tonight, everything's gonna work out fine."

13

IF I AIN'T

That night Cinque walked up the road to the meatworks alone, passed through the gate, climbed up the tree and down the vines to the top of the big square machine. Mr. Jaspers had bought him a three pack of chuck steaks that was on sale, old and turning gray. He took a steak out of the package, ready to sacrifice for passage past the dog or to buy time to escape. Meat in hand, he dropped from the machine and walked slowly back to the big, black doorway with the crest—the five spoke gear.

Sniffing and shuffling came from around the last corner. Cinque and the stray entered the alcove at the same time, Cinque from behind the machine, the stray from the shadows of the passageway with a low growl for the invading human.

"Here goes nothin' . . ." Cinque tossed the steak on the ground between them. The stray twitched when it landed, sniffed, and a moment later stepped slowly forward, eyes watching the boy. Cinque prepared to run, but the dog lowered its muzzle, grabbed the piece of meat by its edge, dragged it off to the side and began tearing away chunks and gulping them down. All the while it kept an untrusting eye on Cinque.

🐦 "Good boy. You just stay there and eat."

Cinque unloaded his bag, laying out the bottle of Four Houses, the unopened letter from his Ma to Kelly Lee, and the copy of *The Black Arts*. Finally, he took the dismembered finger out of his bag and lay it down in front of him, still wrapped in the rubber glove. He sat cross-legged in front of the dark passageway and flipped through the book for awhile, concentrating on what he was about to do. When he felt ready, he set the book aside, twisted open the bottle and poured some of it in front of him. He made the act from himself and spoke. Where the words came from he did not know.

"Let this not be.

Let there be no peace, no grace.

Don't bless him. Don't keep him.

Up from the dust, up from the ash,

Up from the earth,

End the rest for Kelly Lee."

Cold air passed through Cinque's throat, pushing the words out of his mouth and filling the alcove. The dog stopped eating, took the rest of its meat and left as a tapping sound faded in from the dark, hard leather footsteps on concrete. A man stepped out of the doorway, wearing dark boots with a zipper up the side, worn, straight-cut jeans, a red cotton button down shirt and a dark gray cowboy hat. The man was somewhere in his forties, but wore his years with ease. A thin man with brown eyes and black hair, fine features and a cocksure smile.

A white man.

He didn't smell like flowers, he smelled more like earth.

The stranger tipped his hat and said, "Hey now. Good work there."

Cinque stood up on unsure legs, "I'm . . . I think there's been a mistake."

"Oh?" the man said in a cheery voice. He stuck his thumbs in his pockets and asked, "An' how you figure that?"

"Well . . . Well I was trying to find my Pa. Well, the ghost of my Pa—"

"Oh yeah? Well what's he look like?" he said, like it was a joke.

Cinque couldn't say. He couldn't even shrug.

"Wasn't around much, was he? Say, what was his name? Maybe I know him." The man was still enjoying his joke.

"His name was—"

"—Kelly Lee." He interrupted, offering his hand. "Pleased to meet you, Cinque."

14

MEET YOU

The man pronounced his name correctly. Automatically, Cinque tried to return the handshake. Their hands failed to connect. Cinque tried again and watched his hand pass right through the white man's.

"I figured something like that would happen, but it'd be impolite not to offer," the man said.

Awkwardly, Cinque brought his hand back and took a careful look at the man's face. When he looked past the colour, he saw some resemblance in the chin and jaw. "I always figured my Pa was a light-skinned brother."

"Not this light, eh?" Kelly held his hand out showing the white skin on both sides. "Well, I'm not all white, you see, I'm one sixteenth Cherokee on my mother's side, and my father's full Welsh, which is about as close to black as you're gonna get north of Sicily, 'cept maybe the Irish, that is."

He seemed unnerved at Cinque's silence. "This isn't going to be a problem now, is it?"

Cinque realized that he must have come across as appalled

when he was just shocked. "No. No, a white dad's better than no dad, I guess."

Kelly smiled, "That's the spirit. Race is just habit anyway, am I right?"

Then Cinque asked, "Are you a cowboy?" His question made him feel stupid but it was the best he could think of.

Kelly took the hat off his head and shook the hat-shape out of his hair. "You mean this? Naw. This here is a Riverboat Gambler's Hat. I started wearing it as a way of holdin' on to my Southern heritage as I wandered the world."

Kelly twirled the hat on one finger.

"It's an affectation that became a habit that became a trademark. I tried to give it up a time or two, but no one recognized me without it."

Hat in his hands, Kelly's amused attitude fell to the side. "It's good to finally meet ya, son. I seen this coming since the day I died." He suddenly sounded sincere.

"Because the dead know things?" Cinque suggested, happy to know something himself.

"It sure is. See, when I was alive, I was unaware of your conception." He pointed to the envelope. "I never opened that letter. If I had I would a . . ." An embarrassed pause. "Your Ma, see well when we, she and I that is . . . When we was over she had a serious hate for me. I figured the right thing to do would be to just let her go. Give her a chance to forget about me. That'd be for the best. I never opened that letter 'cause I figured it'd be full a hate, accusations and other such venoms. Like she was the last time I seen her. But I couldn't toss it out either. Days turned to years, it fell in among my things and I forgot all about it, but it brought us together now, didn't it? Eventually it did."

"You want me to open it for you?"

He waved his hands dismissively.

"No. No, something like that . . . I can't see how what's in that letter could do any of us any good. Best we just let it lie.

'Sides, if we leave it in its unopened condition you can keep using it to get in touch with me. That was the kicker, you know. The finger helped but you can't do it all with just a body part. You need something special, something with intent. Like the letter, that and your little poem there." Kelly put his hat back on his head and cocked his head to the left. "That was pretty good. How long'd you work on that?"

"Didn't. The words, they just fell out of my mouth."

"That a fact?" He studied the alcove with suspicious eyes. "I figure you had some help with that, whether you know it or not." Kelly gave Cinque a warning look. "Thing is, there's a lot a wolves sniffin' round you, ain't there? Ever since things went all loco?"

"Yeah, everything started getting weird when I dreamed a hand made of wire tore out my—"

Kelly waved his hand, cutting him short and tapped his head with his thumb. "Ghost, remember? I know things."

"Oh yeah," Cinque sighed, relieved that he didn't have to tell his story again. "So then you can tell me what that was? The Black Wire Hand and all?"

"Yes I can." Kelly Lee hooked his thumbs in his pockets, looked away and looked back at his son. Even Cinque could tell that this was something that Kelly didn't want to talk about. "I'm sorry, son, but that was my fault. See, the doctors said my means of passing-on was a classic American heart attack, but things ain't what they seem. I made some enemies in my day, I was always good at making enemies, and lately, I've been getting better. Unfortunately, I've been getting worse at avoiding those enemies and they took advantage of my declining skills. I was laying low in a rat hole of an apartment, hiding out from their mojo. Well, I found out the hard way that I ain't as good at hiding as I used to be and half a dozen curses caught up to me all at once. Spells with names like the Fire of A Thousand Embers, Pain for Shame, and the Twenty-Seven Afflictions."

Those didn't sound pleasant and Cinque winced at the thought.

"It's not as bad as it sounds. Though I wouldn't want to do it again," he chuckled and got back to his story.

"What do you mean by mojo? Is that the same as Juju?"

"Pretty much, 'cept when I say mojo I don't rightly mean mojo. What I really mean is magick, with a 'k' at the end, western ritual magick. Mojo or Juju is more like voodoo. I know a bit about that, seen a bit of it time and again in the South. But I prefer my reliable rules and rituals."

"I guess I've been learning voodoo then, like I can smell ghosts. So far most of them smell like flowers, 'cept you, you smell like earth."

"Heh, well I figure that's because I'm further gone than any ghost you'll see haunting the earth. I spend most of my time under it."

"Is it okay if I keep learning voodoo? Or should I learn what you use instead?" Cinque asked.

"Learn all you can and use what works. That'd be my advice to you. You'll find that different kinds of magic have more in common than you'd think. But the most important magic ain't magic at all, it's how you present yourself. If you wanna do magic, act like you can do magic. Confidence. That's gotta come first.

"But I digress. The curse hit me when I stepped out of the apartment for a drink and came on all slow-like. I didn't see it coming, though lord knows I had it coming.

"As for you and your heart—" He thought a moment about how to proceed before he explained. "—some curses run off on their own and find their target, like a guided missile but a whole lot smarter. Since I was out of reach, being dead and all, that curse took to you instead. The sins of the father shall be visited upon the son."

Cinque shook his head in frustration. All he'd been through, because of a stray shot fired by strangers in another city?

Kelly Lee went on, "Uncalled for, if you ask me. I always kept family outta the picture when I been in a fight. . . . But here's the bright side, there is a way outta this. See, if I'd a been all the way dead then the Black Wire curse would a just evaporated." He pronounced the word *ee—vape—ore—ated*. "And if I can pass on to my final rest then you'll be off the hook, heart and whole like nothin' ever happened. Status quo." He smiled a hopeful smile.

"So why aren't you all the way dead?"

Kelly tilted his head forward, hiding his eyes behind the brim of his hat. "I did a lot of bad things in my life, son. What I done to your Ma and you's the worse of the lot. I wish I could make it all up, an' not just because of what them bad deeds done to me. Because after doin' all that wrong I should of done some right, by you and by your mother. I need to make that right before I can go on."

Kelly smiled again, a sad and cynical smile. "But the question is, the part I need your help with is, how. What am I gonna do to make up for treating her so bad and walking away all those years ago? With a dead man's . . . perspective, my sin's even heavier. Knowing that I didn't just abandon her, I abandoned you too." His hands fell to his sides. "How do you make it up when you're dead?"

"Sometimes the best you can do is say you're sorry."

"Heh. You know what? I hadn't thought a that." He pushed his hat back and sat on the floor. "But for someone in my situation," he pronounced the word with an "e" sound: *sit—ee—ation*. "—it can't just be 'sorry.' It's gotta be magick."

Cinque nodded, his excitement growing. "I'm just glad someone's finally talking straight about this stuff. What do we gotta do? Just tell me."

They sat on the floor together and as father and son, they planned what they were going to do to make it up to Olamide Williams.

The next day, in the afternoon, when Cinque came home, Willy T was waiting for him, sitting on the porch where they'd met, legs dangling over the edge.

"Where'd you go yesterday?" he asked the ghost.

Willy hadn't been waiting for him at the base of the meatworks road. He hadn't seen him all night long.

"I don't know if I went anywhere. I just wasn't there no more, not for awhile anyway. Sometimes I just go away and don't come back for hours or even days. Then I wake up outside my girl's house. Maybe that how us ghosts sleep. Or maybe I just been away from my girl for too long. Anyways, how'd it go? You find your pops?"

Cinque sat down next to him.

"Yeah, yeah I did. But he's got a problem. He's kinda stuck. Not like you are, hanging around because you feel you got work to do. With him, it's more like he won't let himself go, outta guilt."

"Guilt, huh? Never had much use for it myself."

"You don't feel guilty over nothing?"

"Guilt ain't ever changed nothin' so what good is it?"

"I always figured it was there to keep you from messing up the same way twice."

"An' you see how well that's worked out for your pops, huh?" He waved the idea away. "All o' that don' matter none to the job you got goin' on. Hell, I guess if it weren't for your pops' guilt you wouldn't a been able to talk to him these days. If'n he'd gone into the White you'd a prolly had no chance a catchin' him."

"Maybe. Sometimes these things happen for a reason."

"Boy, you'll go crazy thinking like that. Like a song they playin' on the radio is a special message sent to you by the CIA."

"Not everything. Just some things. I guess the hard part is knowing which is which."

A girl's voice interrupted. "Which which is which, Sin-kay?"

A jolt ran up Cinque's spine, the sensation of being caught doing exactly the wrong thing by exactly the wrong person. It only faded when Cinque remembered he didn't care anymore. He remembered what his father said, looked at Imani and pushed down any fear of doing the wrong thing and just did what came natural.

"Hey, Imani. I was just talking about how things happen for a reason. Like this here conversation."

"Yeah. The reason for this conversation is—I wanna know why you out here talking to yourself."

"Nope. That's wrong in three ways. One, this conversation started before you got here, so it's not up to you. Two, you don't wanna know why I'm talking to myself. You just wanna mess with me, but that's okay. Three, I wasn't talking to myself."

"Uh huh." She cocked her skinny hips in that way that she did. "And just who were you talking to, Sin-Kay?"

Cinque just pointed with his thumb. "Willy T here," he said, matter-of-factly.

Imani's head tilted to one side, "Willy T?"

"Yeah, he my friend, got killed a year back while protecting his girl. He's that ghost I told you about. Mostly he haunts St. Jude, but I brought him to Chicago with me, using this." He pulled the picture out of his pocket.

"Yo!" Willy T waved at the girl who couldn't see or hear him.

"And this conversation? Why is it happening? Well, it's happening so's I can test out some things my Pa told me."

"But you ain't got—"

"That's what everyone tells me, and it's true. He wasn't around while he was alive. But now that he's dead he's gonna make it up to me and my moms." Cinque told his story with total confidence. "I had to get my Pa's remains settled. That sent me on the road to getting in touch with his ghost. It's a long story, but tonight I'm a do it again so I can help him stop being a ghost and go on to being a regular dead guy."

He waited for her to ask another question, but she just stared at him, eyes bigger than normal.

"Willy is stuck as a ghost too, but he okay with that. He keeping an eye on his girl."

She tightened up, face frozen and smileless. A little grin crossed Cinque's face when he realized that he'd finally made her as uncomfortable and nervous as she'd always made him.

"Okay," she said suddenly and walked back the way she came.

"You know," Willy said, "that was funny and all, but you prolly just threw out any chance you mighta had of hittin' that. Don' talk too much, little man, you just let them talk and tell them how good they look until you hit it. Then quit out and find the next one. Ha!"

"Except Rikkia, right?"

That caught Willy off guard. He took a second to recompose himself. "Right. Right. Except her."

15

SMILELESS

Hours later, a fire truck, siren blaring, raced past Cinque and Willy as they walked through downtown. A foul burning smell tainted the air, getting stronger as they turned down Potts and saw Mr. Jaspers' alley was now a smouldering pile of charcoal and ash. Everything past the sidewalk was a blurry, black mess, and the spirits that had haunted the alley were gone.

"Yo, check it," Willy said, pointing past the crowd that had gathered across the street, and towards the White Woman. She stood at a distance from the other spectators as they watched the fire truck tear down the damaged water tower with a winch. The fire had eaten up the east side of the tank, leaving it a scorched, open wound.

"She do get around, don't she?" Cinque asked.

"Heh. You shoulda asked her for a ride back from Chicago," Willy joked.

"Let's see what she got to say." He walked over to the White Woman and the ghost followed.

"Iku."

"Cinque," she nodded.

"Is it changing? Or dying?"

She looked back at the water tower. "I'm not here for the tower. I'm here for the man within." She pointed to a man sitting on the curb further down the street. Cinque recognized Mr. Jaspers even without the paper bag top hat and the red tuxedo coat.

Willy huffed, "I guess sanity ain't all that."

"It is and it isn't. Go talk to him, Cinque, you'll see."

Cinque dragged his feet over to where Mr. Jaspers sat on the curb, his face in his hands. He didn't look quite so mysterious in the sunlight. Dark, stained sweatshirt and corduroy pants. Through his fingers, Mr. Jaspers watched the firemen tear his tower down.

Mr. Jaspers twitched when Cinque spoke.

"You look like you been beat down, Jaspers."

The man mumbled something through his hands.

"What?"

His hands dropped into his lap, his face turned to Cinque.

"So who done the beatin'? 'Cause I don't see no one here but us." Mr. Jaspers pulled the empty vial from his pocket and dropped it at Cinque's feet with disdain, when just yesterday he would have killed for it.

"You get what you wanted then, Jaspers?"

He shook his head with a pitying smirk.

"Only a little, just enough to hurt." He pushed himself to his feet with a grunt. "Just enough to see what a waste it's been, all of it. Best I can do now is try and hold on to a little bit of truth. Maybe I can keep that with me when the madness comes back. And my name ain't Mr. Jaspers, never was."

"Did you burn that place down?" Cinque asked.

Willy went "Pffft!" and shook his head.

"I surely did. Trying to keep myself from falling backwards." The man clenched and unclenched his fists a few times before punching them together. "Walk away, boy. Walk away now.

Walk away from the spirits and the ghosties and the gods, especially the gods. Go get yourself some help. At least pretend you don't see all the weird. It's better that way."

With that, he walked off to the west.

"I guess I should tell the firemen that Mr. Jaspers set that fire," Cinque said to Willy T as they watched the man disappear. The sun was getting close to the ground.

"Then why don't you?"

Cinque just looked at Mr. Jaspers' mismatched shoes. "It's getting late," he said. "Besides, nothing worth a damn was lost."

He shot a glance back at the White Woman and she tapped her temple with two fingers. He clearly read her lips. She was saying, "Think about it." Cinque watched the man walk away. The man who'd got what he wanted and was ruined for it.

Cinque got home an hour before sunset with Willy following along. Just as he came up to the yard, his Ma pulled up in her car, the motor knocked a few times while struggling not to stall. Olamide rolled down the window and ordered him to get in.

"Where are we going?" Cinque challenged. He had things to do this evening.

When his Ma was in a mood like this she never explained herself and she only repeated herself once.

"Get. In."

"Woo, boy, she got her mad on," Willy said with a whistle.

"You don't have to tell me," Cinque said to the ghost.

Thinking her son was speaking to her, Olamide's eyes flared in anger. Cinque jumped and ran around to the passenger side and got in.

As the car pulled away, Cinque could tell that Willy took great pleasure in his trouble. He waved after the car, a big smile across his face. "Yo! I'm a go check in on my girl while you gone. Hope she don't kill you fo' you get back!"

The little brown car creaked and shifted as it backed out of the driveway and took off down the road. Cinque never felt safe in the flimsy, aluminum thing. Especially after he'd spent time in Robbie-turned-Ted's new and sturdy four door. Today his Ma drove with both hands on the wheel and eyes locked on the road with an intensity that didn't make him feel safer. He wanted to know where they were going but knew better than to ask again so they rode in silence, across town until they came to the St. Jude Community College Center.

The facility didn't look like what he'd imagined. No sprawling, green campus of brick and ivy buildings, this was a single, three-story building with peeling paint and dirty, slatted windows, more like a factory than a school. Cinque found himself wondering how much worse it looked in the daylight.

Inside the building wasn't any more academic. The "classroom" was far too big, the ceiling was far too high and the temperature was far too cold. Cinque didn't take off his hoodie. Olamide didn't take off her jacket. It was weird seeing all those grown-ups sitting in the same old chair-desks that they had at his school. They all were too big for the furniture.

The teacher came in, a tired and haggard-looking white man, and got right into the lecture on logic. It didn't seem logical to Cinque, all the talk of "if A and if B then C as long as C doesn't contradict A and B," and he soon lost interest.

After class, Olamide lingered until the teacher and the other students left and she led her son down to the front of the building, stopping between the college and the car. "Neither of my parents ever went to college," she told Cinque. "And neither of their parents went to college either. My father's father was functionally illiterate and his parents were worse off than that.

"That means that when I got that college scholarship, back before you were born, that I was the first person in my family to go to college. In just two generations we'd come up

from high school dropouts to a full ride at the university, no
because we looked around and decided that we could do better

"You can decide to be what you want to be. If your father's
around or not it doesn't matter. It's up to you. Just you. If you
decide that not knowing your father is going to cripple you for
life, then it will.

"I'm showing this to you because I shouldn't be playing
catch-up at a community college. I should have had my
bachelor's ten years ago. I almost threw it all away the day that
man came into my life. I had to start all over again.

"I'm not putting all the blame on him. I did what I did and I
knew better but I am saying that we're better off without him.
Both of us.

"Cinque, you decide what becomes of you. You don't need
him in your life for you to be good."

Cinque wanted to tell her everything, from the Black Wire
Hand to finding his Pa's ghost but this wasn't like when he told
everything to Imani to mess with her head. This was his Ma.
Not only could she put serious obstacles in his way, but more
importantly, he just didn't want to hurt her. He didn't know
how she'd take it if he told her what he'd been up to.

"What if . . . what if he's changed? Or wants to change?"

"Baby, how he gonna change now?"

"I'm just saying . . ."

Olamide just shifted back and forth a bit, and for the first
time, his Ma didn't know what to say.

"Look, it don't matter anyway. I just gotta do this, and when
I'm done, I'll be done. We're almost done and then everything'll
be better, you'll see."

"Who's we?"

Cinque didn't know what to say. With one little word he let
slip everything he'd just decided to keep hidden from his Ma.

"Who is 'we', Cinque?" Olamide repeated, deliberately and
just a little nervously.

Cinque couldn't tell her, so he said nothing at all. Eventually his Ma softened, she probably realized that she didn't want to know who "we" was, and she told him to get in the car.

It was another silent drive home.

16

DIDN'T WANT TO KNOW

His bag packed with everything he'd need for tonight's ritual, Cinque snuck out after dinner. He left Willy's picture behind, safe in his room. He wouldn't need that ghost's help tonight.

Cinque didn't have to climb up the wall and through the roof of the meatworks this time. Yesterday he'd propped the door open with a broken broom handle. It was a lot easier to think ahead when he wasn't running from dogs. The stray lay in the middle of the alcove, waiting. It twitched its tail once, just short of a wag, and licked its chops.

"I guess we have an understanding now, huh?" Cinque asked, pulling the second steak from his backpack. "I won't be coming back this way again. But maybe, if my Ma lets me, maybe I can take you home with me?" He dropped the steak on the ground between them and tried to pet the dog again but the mutt pulled back with a scolding, "Woof!"

"Okay, okay." His hands up and open in innocence. "Too soon, I get it." The animal glared at him and wouldn't reach for the steak again until Cinque stepped back out of reach.

Taking its tithe in its mouth, the dog trotted back into

the darkness. He could hear the dog's sloppy, wet chomping while he prepared to bring his Pa forward. Again he placed the dismembered finger in front of him, poured from the bottle, spoke the poem, held the letter and the book, and the sound of the footsteps approached from within the portal. Once more, Kelly Lee stepped into the light.

"Evening, son," he said with a tip of his hat. "You ready?"

Cinque jumped to his feet. "Hell, yeah, I'm ready!"

"Ha! I guess I'm supposed to scold you for cussing, but damn me for a liar if I tried." Kelly walked past the boy and gestured for him to follow.

"Come on then."

Kelly strolled through the meatworks, pointing out a few things for Cinque to take with him, a length of thin plastic rope, a broomstick and a bucket of something dark and foul smelling.

"The actual goings on are gonna happen outside where there's more room and less interference," he said.

Following Kelly Lee's instructions, Cinque used the rope and a stake in the ground to trace two half circles, six feet wide and six feet apart, each with a one-foot gap in the middle. He then connected the four tips with two lines, making something like an eight in the dirt. "What we need this for anyway?" Cinque asked.

"Two reasons, son. One, to connect the two of us in a Möbius strip. It'll keep our identities in flow, bringing us closer for the ritual. Two, it's doing double duty as a circle of protection, though not a circle, per se. That'll keep us from all sorts of unfavourable interruptions."

"What kinda interruptions could happen?"

"Oh, all kinda things. Other ghosts . . . stray nature spirits . . . if you're having a real bad day, a demon or angel."

While he talked, Kelly traced a series of arcane symbols around the edge of the figure eight. Cinque followed his lead with the broomstick, dipping it into the dark fluid in the bucket and painting with the nasty smelling stuff while keeping the bucket as far from his face as he could.

Kelly smiled at that. "The magic we're gonna be doing will make metaphysical noise. It'll draw all kinds of attention. I'd like to make a circle around the whole hilltop, but that ain't possible. So we'll have to make do with a smaller one."

Cinque sniffed the stuff he was drawing with. "And what's this? Goat's blood or something?"

"This? Naw, that's just axle grease. It's the only thing I could find to paint with. Had to make do, you know?"

"You believe in all this?"

"That's the beauty of ritual magick, son. You don't have to believe in it. It just works."

He put a hand on Cinque's shoulder.

"We're ready."

It was dusk. In one half of the figure eight, Cinque placed a makeshift chair and desk fashioned out of cinderblocks and the rusted fender of some vehicle. The father he'd just discovered was going on to whatever was beyond. It made Cinque sad that they'd never meet again.

Kelly, on the other hand, seemed giddy. He rubbed his hands together, briskness in his step. Then he stepped through the gap in the half circle on his side and Cinque filled in the missing piece behind him.

"Alright, son, take your seat at the table." Cinque walked around the figure eight, passed through the gap on his side, and sealed it up behind him. He dropped his backpack beside the fender and dug out the paper and pen. For a moment, settling in behind a desk reminded him of school. The familiar feeling in this strange place made him smile.

"This design will channel my intentions through you while you write the letter as my proxy. There's no precedent for what we're about to do, so cross your fingers," Kelly Lee smiled. "Remember, do exactly as I say. Rhythm is key so it's important to keep up the pace." He took a deep breath and let it out slowly. "Here goes nothing."

"Let's hope it's something," Cinque countered. He took out the trappings of Kelly Lee, those he recovered in Chicago. "My name is Kelly Lee," Cinque said. "And I'm putting on my shirt."

He threaded a brown leather belt through the belt loops of his oversized shorts. "My name is Kelly Lee and I'm putting on my belt."

Finally, he strapped the chrome, windup watch to his wrist, and gave the knob a few turns. "My name is Kelly Lee and I'm winding my watch."

With each item Cinque felt a little older, a little taller and a little heavier. He sat behind the desk and, with pen and paper, waited for his father to dictate the letter.

"To Olamide, and anyone else who might hear me now or read this later, I'm sorry. I take full responsibility for all the bad things, the selfish things done in this world under the name of Kelly Lee. The lies are all mine, the sin is all mine and the responsibility is all mine. There's a lot I have to make up for, but it isn't going to happen now. When I return to the world, I will bear the load, the curses and obligations of the past. I will wear these chains of the past in hopes that time will wear them away."

Kelly stopped dictating. Then he said, "Now sign your name."

Cinque looked up from the letter, puzzled. Kelly spun his hand a few times, the gesture said hurry up.

The boy put pen to paper for a second, and then retracted it, leaving a single dot instead of a signature. He looked back at his father.

"Why am I signing my name? This is supposed to be your letter."

"Just do it," Kelly whispered. "I'll explain later. Remember the timing!"

But Cinque wanted his explanation now. "I don't understand this letter either. You ain't apologizing in it, you're just—"

"Just sign the letter, you little shit," someone shouted from the meatworks.

Cinque dropped the pen. Kelly shot a glare back at the building, towards whoever said that, his face red, hands curled up in fists he looked ready to use.

Cinque didn't know what was going on but he wanted out. He stood up, took off the watch and threw it to the ground. "By Egungun I command you back in the ground."

A nervous pleading quickly replaced Kelly's anger. "Look, son, I'll explain everything in a moment. But we gotta—"

Cinque pulled the belt free, tossing it out of the circle.

"By Egungun I command you back in the ground."

"—finish what we started. When a man says he's gonna do something he follows though. Especially, when it's for kin."

Cinque pulled the shirt over his head and dropped it.

"By Egungun I command you back in the ground."

Evoking the All-Ghost had no effect on Kelly Lee. He just slumped his shoulders and sighed. "So much for doing this the easy way. . . . Come and get him, boys!"

From behind every tree, every stack of debris, every derelict vehicle, monsters poured out into the open—small, monstrous caricatures of men. They ranged from the size of cats to a few inches larger than Cinque. The mob smelled the same strong, earthy smell as his father. Some Cinque had seen before: the creature in the dirty, yellow robe with the George Washington mask that was looking for money in the trash was here, the man moulded from soggy puzzle pieces that had pointed him in Mr. Jaspers' direction and the one that called him Donut, with the fox's face, its eyes smug and knowing.

Some held hammers or screwdrivers like weapons, but sharp sticks were their weapons of choice. Their circle closed around the boy, poking and jeering in their chattering speech.

Terrified, Cinque tried to escape, but something solid and hard hit his shoulder, sending a spasm of dull pain through his body.

"Watch it!" Kelly Lee warned the creatures, "He's no good if he can't sign his name!" If the creatures heard him order them around, they didn't seem to care. They held the circle, but by the malice in their eyes, Cinque could tell that they were looking to cause some pain.

Kelly, again the calm, smooth talker, said, "Now Cinque, please, have a seat. Sign the paper. And I'll let you go back to St. Jude and we'll forget all this ugliness."

"And if I don't?"

"Then you get to stay up here with us." Sinister giggles ran through the crowd of monsters.

"Ma was right. I'm better off without you." Cinque was angry. If only he had listened!

"Ha ha ha . . . oh . . . Boy, you still don't get it, do you?" He picked his hat off his head, slowly brought it to his chest. As the hat passed by his face he became a caricature of a man. His face became a flat, blurry driver's license photo wrapped around a rough, cork cylinder the size of a man's head. His clothing grew stiff and coarse. The pockets and seams were no longer stitching, but were sloppily painted in black ink. His boots became moulded black plastic. His hands were no longer flesh but bundles of black wire.

Black Wire Hands.

In one of those fingerless mittens the bizarre mannequin who called himself Kelly Lee held the frozen, orange heart—Cinque's heart. The boy felt that hot, empty hole in his chest, powerless in terror as Kelly Lee leaned into his and whispered, "Your Pa ain't dead!"

17

POWERLESS

Cinque pushed the hideous mannequin, shoving himself back among the misshapen mob of spirits. They swarmed over the boy, grabbing at his dreads and punching him in the face. He pulled his legs up to his chest and tried to cover his face with his arms. Through the violence, Cinque heard the one that called itself Kelly Lee order, "Quit it!" They neither slowed or stopped their assault. Then there was a sickening crunch, and a scream and the mannequin shouted again, "I said, quit it!"

This time they pulled back from Cinque, leaving him on the ground in their circle. The crowd parted for the demon that claimed to be his father. He held the broken, twitching form of one of the smaller creatures in his hand. He tossed it away and said, "I need that head in one piece!"

Kelly grabbed Cinque not by his pants, but by a smoky brown line around his chest, the cord belt the African had created for him. He pulled at the cord with both hands and a grunt, lifting Cinque off the ground. The cord snapped and faded away, leaving Cinque to tumble to the ground like a ragdoll.

"You should be ashamed of yourself for wearing it in the

first place," said the thing with a photo for a face. "Honestly, I'm doing you a favour by takin' it. Heal yourself, boy, don't hobble around on a crutch."

With the African's charm gone, the hot ache in his chest rushed in to mingle with the pain of the beating he'd just gotten.

"Why should I believe you?" Cinque stood, refusing to kneel in front of this thing. "You ain't gonna help me. I don't know what you want but all you given me is lies!"

It cocked its head and the picture on its face changed. The smile was patronizing now. "Figured that out, did ya?" He turned to the other monsters. "Here it comes, watch this . . ." With fake innocence, he asked, "Who am I then? Did I lie about that, son?"

"You ain't Kelly Lee!"

It spun around sharply, almost pouncing on the boy. "Wrong! I am Kelly Lee! That's why we're in this mess." The mob cheered and laughed at a joke that Cinque wasn't in on.

Kelly sighed. "You see, boy, you just fell into a trap your Pa set almost twenty years ago. I'm that trap. I'm a Sin Catcher, like a backwards voodoo doll. You heard the expression 'What goes around comes around'? Well there's some truth to that. Your Pa liked to send it around, but he didn't like it when it came around, if you know what I mean. So he made me, wove me out of his own hair." The creature tapped his head, and the face in the photo smiled with condescension. "A model of himself made from little bits of his life. Gave me his name and set me up to catch everything he had coming for all his bad deeds. All of his lies, his indulgences, his sins—I pay for them."

Cinque folded his arms. "I ain't buyin' it!"

George Washington laughed at that. "Why not? You got the money for it!"

"But I ain't done sellin'. Kelly came back to Chicago a year ago, which was a bad idea because some of the folks he'd pissed off ten years prior still held a grudge, but he had his reasons. Anyway, he gets seen, push comes to shove and before you know it, a dozen or so of Chicago's finest and pettiest magicians, witchdoctors and sorcerers are in a race to see who can kill your Pa first.

"And what does a guy like Kelly Lee do in this situation? He locates himself a hobo and tricks the universe into thinking that this bum is your pa, one of Kelly Lee's favourite spells. Then he skips town, leaving the poor sucker behind in an empty apartment with a case of liquor. All the curses that had been fired after your Pa zeroed in on the hobo leaving him a few short, painful hours of life."

Alone and in pain in a dirty hole, Cinque thought. His father could do that to another human being?

"That ain't the biggest sin I carry for your Pa. I used to be tiny, a doll." Kelly Lee held his palms six inches apart. "But his sins kept pilin' on and I accommodated, like a bubble."

Cinque looked at his tormenter harder: the rough feel of the clothes, the pockets that seemed painted on, the thickness of the hair, the moulded plastic cowboy boots, all small materials scaled up. He shuddered.

"A bubble? Ain't you worried you'll pop?"

"No, I worked that out a while ago. What I'm worried about is what'll happen when he dies." The picture now held a nervous smile. "If I catch all his sins in this life, will I catch them in the next? I don't know, I don't wanna find out the hard way and I ain't going to Hell for that man.

"I'm a spirit. I can't be forgiven because I can't be judged. As far as the cosmic balance is concerned I can't work off any bad karma. I'm stuck with this burden unless I can get someone to take it from me."

"So you were tryin' to trick me into taking my Pa's sins off of you?" Cinque demanded.

"It has a certain poetry to it, don't it? Sins of the father shall be visited upon the sons an' all that? Remember?"

Cinque remembered. His chest still burned.

"And you're not just his son. You're the seventh son of the seventh son."

"Wait! I don't have no bro—oh . . ." Cinque was learning too much about his father.

"What can I say?" The creature gave an almost apologetic shrug. "Papa was a rolling stone."

"And if I got six half-brothers out there, you picked me because I was the seventh? Why does that matter?"

Fox Face sang into an imaginary microphone, "Here they stand, brothers them all! All the sons divided they'd fall!"

The little creatures thought that was hilarious, but the Sin Catcher ignored his henchmen. "The English say the seventh son of the seventh son is born with magical powers. Does it matter? I don't know. Probably not, you wasn't born with magical anything until I came along, but the other six are all morons and losers. You're the only one that was smart enough to fall for this kinda scheme."

That made Cinque feel better for a second before he resentfully pushed the feeling away. "You took my heart, an' you the one behind all the craziness that's been goin' on? The Cuttlefish, the African, the Shapeshifter an' the Pimp?"

Kelly tilted his head and crossed his arms. "No, that's all my bad luck comin' at me. The Cuttlefish is a *qliphoth*, just looking for a meal, but that don't mean it ain't dangerous. I won't lie to ya—I'd be scared of that thing too and it's got a taste for you, son. That wasn't part of the plan but after I gave you the spirit touch, took a piece of you, brought you over, I set you on the road to become a shaman or a madman and to the Cuttlefish that's good eatin'.

"The African's some jackass that's in the right place at the wrong time. Ignore him. He's a folk magic fool, same for the clay guy from the highway, in a different way. But I don't know who this 'pimp' is that you're talking about. Who's he?"

"Man, I ain't tellin' you nothing! You wanna hear about what I been through? You let me go home!"

Kelly Lee chuckled, "You wanna go home? Then you take up this curse."

Cinque stomped his foot. "I ain't takin' no curse from nobody! By Egungun I command you!"

"There he goes again!" One of the creatures laughed.

Kelly tried to interrupt, "We're not going through this again, are we?"

"By Egungun I command—" The Sin Catcher smacked Cinque across the mouth with one hand and held the frozen heart forward with the other, like he'd pulled it out of his back pocket. He squeezed, the frost cracking around his thumb. Every snap of the ice resonated down Cinque's spine like a handful of broken glass. The sight of his heart in the Black Wire Hand took him back to that helpless night when he was torn open. His white shoe wanted to run, his black shoe wanted to hide. His legs could only wobble and twitch as the hot, empty feeling opened his chest.

"I don't mean to be violent, son, but that's just bein' ignorant. I ain't a ghost, so how is your little spell gonna work on me?" Kelly Lee shook his head in fatherly disappointment. "Show some sense."

The Sin Catcher turned the heart back and forth. "You know what this is?" Kelly Lee asked. "It's your bravery, your courage. It's what you need to get things done when you're afraid.

"I tore it outta ya, that's why you're different. Touched by a spirit an' all that. 'Cept I did more than touch, didn't I?" He knelt in front of the boy. "I needed you to be able to converse with me and I needed some leverage, a backup plan if you weren't willing to help me out. With this—" He waved the heart in Cinque's face. "—I got you where I want you. I just give this here organ a little squeeze and you can't get it together to face down nothing, especially not me."

Kelly stood up again and held the heart behind him. "But I gotta be careful. Too much playing with my new toy and I could break it, then your real one'll go too. I need you alive.

"Take the curse, son, and I'll throw the heart in for free. Now that's a bargain."

Cinque regained some control. "Don't call me 'son'," he spat.

The crowd went, "Oooo!" in fake amazement.

Kelly waved his hands, conceding the point. "When you're right, you're right. I apologize, force of habit, I ain't your father . . . I'm your brother. Your father made us, and left us behind without a care."

"My father didn't know I was born."

"You think so? You think that letter in your bag was the only letter your Ma ever wrote?"

His Pa knew, and didn't care?

"I took that sin too. As the one who catches all his sins, I know them well. Very well. He knows you exist. He just doesn't care."

Cinque's legs wobbled, unsteady. He sat and stared at the ground between his splayed legs. Nothing the Sin Catcher had done to him—the betrayal, the violence and the threats—none of it, hurt as much as this theft of hope.

"Sorry I had to be the one to tell ya."

Cinque just glared back at him.

"But that's why you're gonna help me," the creature said as it shook his head. "Not because you're trapped, though you are. Not because you could die, though you might. You're gonna help me, so I can get back at him. I'm gonna get him, Cinque. I'm gonna make him pay for what he done to us. We are going to make him pay for what he done to us."

"If you needed my help," Cinque said, "you shoulda tried askin' for it. Now all you done is make me mad. I ain't gonna help you. I'll get out of this mess and then I'll come to ends with my pops in my own way." He shoved his hands in his hoodie pocket and looked away, pretending that the conversation was his to end.

"Think so, do ya?" Kelly signalled to the other monsters. "Then let's take this to the next level—a level down."

Someone kicked Cinque in the back of the leg and he came down hard on his knee. Hands grabbed him by his hair and arms, pushing him face-first into the ground, grinding his face in the dirt as he was kicked in the ribs. As quick as the mob took him down they picked him off the ground, by twisted handfuls of his clothes, arms and legs they pulled, trying to pop something in him out of joint.

The crowd cheered as they carried him through the meatworks. Every few steps, they slammed him into the wall, and slapped and punched at his exposed face and legs. Stunned, sore, breathless, and disoriented, Cinque didn't realize the monsters had dropped him until he was rolling along the pavement. He curled up, protecting his face with his arms from further beatings that didn't come. Slowly he peeked between his fingers. He was at the bottom of a trench of dark brown concrete. Gutters on either side of the trench emptied into drains at the edges of a four foot pit. The ceiling above was a tangle of chains, hooks and grates. The small creatures smiled cruelly down at him from the lip of the trench. Some held flashlights, the only light in the room. They cast a crazy dance of shadows along the walls. The Sin Catcher stood in the hole with him, Cinque's backpack hung over his shoulder, the copy of The Black Arts tucked in its waistband. It came at the boy fast and pinned him to the floor with his knee while he grabbed something from the ground above Cinque's head.

"With this fetter, I do tether, my dear brother, Cinque Joseph Williams," Kelly said as he jammed something into Cinque's head. The sensation was warm and surprisingly painless.

"Go ahead." The Sin Catcher stood. "Go ahead and get belligerent. Talk tough. Act the hero. Play the martyr. Get it outta your system, because you ain't getting out of there. Not until you're ready to deal. I waited fourteen years for this. I can wait another night or two."

The Sin Catcher left the room. The rest of them followed

him out, closing the door and leaving Cinque in the cold dark. He reached to the thing the Sin Catcher had stuck in his head and discovered a large hook attached to a thick chain attached to a loop in the floor. The hook and chain were heavy and hard like iron but smooth like plastic. On touch he could tell the restraint was alive in some alien way.

He tried to pull the hook from his skull it wouldn't budge but he kept on until, exhausted from trying, he slumped to the floor and let himself cry.

18

IN THE COLD DARK

Cinque spent hours curled up on the cell floor wishing he was back home, missing his Ma, his grandma, even Darren. Trying to wish himself back home and regretting. Regretting every decision he made since the Black Wire Hand had snatched his heart. They'd all led him here.

After the adrenaline faded, the aches and pains of the beating joined forces with the heat in his chest that the African's rope charm had kept at bay. He was unable to sit, lay or stand without offending a bruise somewhere on his body. Occasionally, he'd feel around in the dark, but there was nothing down here with him except for the package of raw beef, concrete and whatever that coarse, sticky substance was that caked the bottom of the trenches. It smelled like iron and it nauseated Cinque. This was a slaughterhouse and whatever was in the runoff couldn't be good.

It was minutes, or maybe hours, later when the door opened with a metal-on-metal shriek that scared Cinque out of his exhausted stupor. The light of a flashlight cut into his eyes. Shielding them with his hand, he tried to see who was holding it. The figure of one of the little monsters was outlined in the doorway. The light twitched as whoever walked behind him shuffled closer. There was the sloshing sound of water in a bucket.

"Wakey wakey! Hands off snakey!" It was that little fox-faced man.

"Got some water for you, got to keep you alive and all." Using a long stick with a hook at the end it lowered the bucket, but Cinque didn't move. "Aw, don't be like that. So you got conned, that's past and forgotten. It's a brand new day, ain't it?"

Cinque glared at the spirit. "It was an hour ago!"

The fox man looked puzzled for a second and then nodded. "So it is, so it be. I get carried away with time sometimes. Well, hey, we just gave you what you wanted. You wanted to think you had money coming, we gave you that. You wanted to think you had power coming, we gave you that. You wanted to know your pops we gave you that."

"He ain't my pops!"

"He's close enough. He's all the pops you need to know. You might say that we couldn't of done it without you. If you do and if you don't, is up to you. Either way, you need water to drink and I got water to give. What you say?"

Cinque, thirst winning out over caution, came forward to receive the bucket. Once it was close enough to smell, revulsion overwhelmed his thirst. The water stank of turpentine.

The fox man smiled at his discomfort. "Bottled, bucketed, what's the difference?"

He let the bucket go, leaving it on the hook. The creature took it back. "Seriously though, you should take the curse, you know. It's a terrible offer, bad and horrible, but it's the only way left to you now."

Touching the bucket left a greasy feeling on his fingertips. Cinque wiped his hands on the front of his pants. "If my real father made Kelly Lee his Sin Catcher, then who made you?"

The fox-like head cocked in surprise. "Good question, kid.

Well, we're an . . . overflow. It's not like once Big Kelly made Little Kelly that he was gonna stop sinning. Sin after sin the Little Kelly grew, but came a day when the sins stacked up too high for the Sin Catcher to hold. They started to . . . spill over."

"So you're the Sin Catcher's sin catchers?" Cinque was stunned. How bad a man was his father? The entity he created to carry his penance for him had to create its own entities to help bear the load.

The creature nodded. "In a ways. We've all taken to calling ourselves 'Fibs', since most of us were born of lies. We are part of a larger whole, the Sin Catcher himself. That's why we lack individual names—we have only roles. Roles rolls."

"And y'all are helping Kelly Lee move his curse onto me because that'll be good for you too?"

"We don't know. This is strange territory we walk, but walk it we must for there is no point in standing still." He gripped the staff with both hands and pushed himself up. "We help the Sin Catcher because we are the Sin Catcher, that's our purpose. Just as he still carries your father's sins, that's his purpose."

"Why don't he go find a new purpose and leave me alone?"

"He is. Only with your help." Fox-face stepped up to the door. "Help us, we help you. Help you back to your heart so's you don't die. Simple and plain," the Fib said back as it left the improvised cell.

More minutes or hours in the dark followed. Cinque wished he'd gotten a good look around the room by the fox-faced Fib's flashlight. From what he had seen, there was only one way in: the big iron door. There might be another way out, but he'd never find it in the dark.

But he did have one way out. Pulling the cracked pebble and stick out of his back pack he burned the stick, clutched the rock and again dreamed himself to Africa.

When Cinque opened his eyes he was face to face with a lizard of familiar colours but strange shape. Its jowls pulsed twice and it scampered away, behind the rock where it had been sunning itself.

No cat-lions this time, no deer-antelope either. Tonight the watering hole had been taken over by a troop of baboons. Baboons with dark fur around their eyes like bandit masks and ringed tails. "Raccoon-baboon," Cinque liked the sound of that but the raccoon-baboons didn't like the sight of him. They started to hiss and posture. The boy ignored them and looked for the African. Turning his head he felt the hook still embedded in his skull. The chain dangled down to the ground and ran over the horizon.

Pastor Akotun was already there, sitting in his traditional place but this time he was not alone. At his feet sat two African women, the one who had handed Cinque the letter at the bus stop and one he'd never seen before. All three of them looked up at the sudden appearance of the boy. The women looked surprised. Pastor Akotun just looked.

"Ah, little boy, this is unexpected."

Cinque stepped closer, but something jerked at his forehead. The chain hooked in his head wasn't there exactly but somehow it still stopped him. "I'm in trouble," he pleaded.

Pastor Akotun studied him for a second and said, "Yes. Yes you are," and dismissed the two women. They gathered up their sitting mats and walked off into the landscape. When they were alone Pastor Akotun said, "I see my charm has been removed by force. I will prepare another one for your next visit but that will take a day's time. Tell me what happened."

Cinque told the African all about the meatworks, the Sin Catcher, the Fibs and the hook in his head. Pastor Akotun listened patiently, "This is quite a story. It reminds me of a story of my own." He picked up his drum.

"Story? I don't have time for another story. I'm trapped and I got a hook in my head here! Can't you help me?"

The African kept his cool in the face of Cinque's anger. "I can only help you to help yourself," and he played.

The others thought of the Fool as a lazy and useless man. When it rained, he sat outside. When it was time to work, he went to sleep. When it was time for him to find a wife, he stayed in his mother's house. He was not respected or even liked. The others in his village avoided him on their best days and called him names or threw rocks at him on their worst. He wasn't lazy. He just never did as he was supposed to. Was he useless? Mostly, yes.

Until the night the Hyenas came.

The town was overrun with Hyenas. They filled the courts and blocked the roads.

"Come out! Come out and meet your new masters!"

The villagers were afraid. They gathered in the street, holding on to each other, fearful of the teeth and claws.

Except for the Fool. He did not want to get out of bed.

Outside the Hyenas laid down their laws. "You have no names. We have taken them away from you," the Hyenas said. "Names are for the free and you are now our slaves.

"No speaking at all unless we command you to. We have taken your voices. Don't raise your head unless we command you to. No motion unless we command you to!

"Now, bring us your lion skins! All of them! Bring us your lion bones, teeth and claws. Any part of a lion that you have, we want!"

When the villagers had gathered all of these things the Hyenas told them to build a fire and throw them in, so the villagers burned anything that was of the lion, except for the Fool. He had heard the Hyenas, but he was not going to give up his prized lion skull. He had found it when a child and kept it ever since, despite his mother's nagging demands to get rid of it.

When the burning was done, the Hyena called for the cattle.

"We are hungry!" they said. "Bring it all to us, every head, every hank, every morsel! Feed us! Or else we will feed on you!"

So the villagers brought all their beef and livestock to the Hyenas for them to gorge themselves, except the piece that the Fool kept for himself. He liked to keep a dried hank around, in case he got hungry in the night.

Once the Hyenas gorged themselves on the beef and the cattle they ordered the villagers to put themselves in one of the empty cattle pens. "Try to escape if you like," the Hyenas joked, "if we catch you outside we will eat you and two from the pen."

The Fool waited until he was sure that the Hyenas were all asleep. Now that no one was demanding that he leave his house, he wanted to go out. He liked the village this way, quiet and barren of people, no one to order him about. It would have been perfect, except for the sleeping Hyenas laying all about.

When the Fool found the cattle pen that held the villagers he laughed. They looked so comical, behind the fence, staring at him in terror. Quietly, he walked over to them to gloat about his freedom.

"Quickly! Quietly!" they whispered, "Get in the pen with us. If they wake up they will eat you!"

"No," the Fool said, "I prefer to sleep in my house instead of that dirty old cattle pen."

"If they see you outside they will eat two of us as well!"

"That would be your problem. You've never had much use for me so why should I care for you? Look how free I am without you!"

"How free are you? You are only outside because they are asleep. When they wake up you will be a prisoner, unable to leave your house. Who will feed you, if not us? We may not live through this enslavement, but you will certainly starve out there, alone."

The Fool considered this. "I do not like either of these options. I am going to go home to think.

"But if I do free you, I will be a hero and I expect to be treated as such."

So the Fool went home and thought. In his thinking it occurred to him that it was rather strange that the Hyenas demanded all of their lion skins, bones and teeth. There had to be a reason for such demands. They didn't want to just build a fire. He considered the Hyenas' other demands: names, parts of lions, voices, pride and cattle, removed perhaps because they were a threat. Perhaps he could combine them with magic to chase the Hyenas out of the village.

The Fool did not know any magic but he had watched the occasional traveling witch doctor. It didn't seem so hard. He took out the lion skull and the hank of beef he'd been hiding. He had everything he needed right here .He just had to think of a name. He decided on "E Rú"—which meant "slave"—to steer his spell in the right direction.

All day he spent in the room with the skull, envisioning the spirit of the lion, offering the sacrifice, and calling it E Rú in the manner of the hougan. He made the act from himself.

When the sun set, E Rú finally came, stepping out of the darkness, he appeared as a male lion seven-feet high at the shoulder and a transparent, misty shade of gray. The Fool could not see the spirit itself, only the moon light that glistened off its fur. The spirit walked up towards the Fool and bowed its head, saying, "You called, I came. What would you have of me, master?"

The Fool was delirious with his success and exhausted by the ritual.

"You are E Rú, right?"

"As you have named me, master," answered the lion.

"And you must obey my commands?"

"As I have been constructed, master."

Already the Fool was thinking beyond the Hyenas, thinking of ways that E Rú could make his life easier, so much easier.

"E Rú, for your first order, my village is overrun with Hyenas. I want you to chase them away."

The spirit bowed again. "Gladly, master," and bounded through the wall of the building without touching it.

Before the Fool could rush outside he heard the cries of the Hyenas, "A lion! A lion is among is!" as E Rú ran them down. Within seconds the Hyenas scattered and fled from the village.

His task done, E Rú returned to his master's side and followed the Fool to the cattle pen to gloat. But the villagers were as afraid of E Rú and the Fool as they were of the Hyenas.

"We are not coming out with that lion here!" they cried, "We are no safer than we were with the Hyenas!"

The Fool turned to E Rú and said, "E Rú, see these villagers?"

"Yes, master."

"I order you. Do not eat any of them."

"As is your command, master"

But the villagers were not convinced. "If you are this monster's master you can change your order. We cannot trust it because we cannot trust you. We are afraid of your power."

"All right," the Fool was getting frustrated. Again he turned to E Rú.

"E Rú! Do something to make these cowards fear me no longer!"

The lion asked, "How should I do that, master?"

The Fool rolled his eyes and said, "I don't care how. Do it your way."

So the lion knocked the man down, pinning him to the ground with a massive paw against his chest and bit the Fool's head off at his shoulders.

The story ended and Pastor Akotun put his drum aside. Cinque leaned back on his hands and kicked at the dirt. His anger had faded but he still resented the African for not taking his problem seriously. "E Rú was a lousy slave," he muttered.

"Why do you say that?"

Cinque leaned forward, trying to imitate The African's authoritative manner. "'Cause he killed his master."

"What is the nature of a slave?"

"To do as it's told."

"Is that all? Do not some slaves live to be free? Why am I telling you about slavery?"

Cinque dismissed the question with a shake of his hand. "That's all long in the past. I ain't ever been a slave."

"You have missed the point, but found your own."

"Can you do that? Make a lion out of thin air?"

"The Fool didn't make the lion. He made a grou-grou, a spirit bound to a physical object." The African stroked the drumhead. Cinque guessed that the drum was an example. "A grou-grou can be made from thin air but they are stronger if you use a spirit. Spirits can be asked into a grou-grou or forced. Which is better? That depends on the spirit."

"Can you make a grou-grou then?"

"Of course, any fool can do it."

Cinque woke up saying, "How was that supposed to help?"

Before tonight, he used to wonder how it felt to be homeless, curled up in a doorway or sheltered in an alley. He'd thought about spending the night in the driveway, just to try it. When a wet gust of air blew across his face and that's where he thought he was: the driveway at home. He pushed the hood back and didn't see stars, moon or a cloudy sky lit from the city lights below as he remembered. When he tried to sit up, his face bumped into something cold and wet. He stopped, listened and heard something breathing. Close, right next to him. His hands shot out in the dark towards the sound of the breath. He got two handfuls of muscle and fur. He said, "What—?" before it bit his arm.

He let go and there was a scurrying sound of nails on floor. Cinque grabbed the arm where he'd been bitten, but the teeth hadn't penetrated the sleeve of his hoodie. That thing was somewhere out there. Maybe the fox-faced Fib came back, he thought. Then he smelled his hand. It smelled of dog—the Dog who chased him from the meatworks. "Whatcha doing in here?" he asked into the darkness.

"Grouph," the dog replied, whatever that meant. It must have followed him here looking for more steak. If the Fibs caught the dog . . . Cinque assumed the worst. The dog might have been mean to him, but he didn't want it getting it hurt.

"It's okay, I'll figure out how to get you out of here."

Just then, the door latch opened with a determined jerk. The tall, lanky outline of the Sin Catcher stood framed in light. The dog woofed a warning.

"What—" The Sin Catcher pointed into the room, "—is that doing in here?"

A goat-like Fib in a trucker's cap peaked around from behind Kelly's legs. "Wha—? Aw, damn! How the hell did that get in here?"

Kelly knocked the Fib to the ground. "That's what I just asked you!" He punctuated this with a hard kick into the fallen Fib's side. It screamed like a beaten child.

"Quit your crying!" Kelly kicked him again. "You're making us look bad." Sin Catcher picked up a ball-peen hammer from somewhere behind the door.

The dog growled. As Kelly Lee stepped up to the edge of the pit, it barked, glanced sideways at Cinque quickly, and backed away.

Kelly swaggered slowly towards the dog, swinging the hammer so that boy and dog could see it. The dog jumped forward, let out three of its loudest barks, and just when Cinque thought it was going to attack, Kelly feinted forward. The dog turned. Kelly threw the hammer and Cinque dove as far as the chain would allow, grunting as he blocked the hammer with his chest. Pain spread across the web of bruises Kelly's creatures had beat into his body when the hammer hit the boy. The dog jumped up out of the pit and escaped out through the same unseen passageway it had taken in.

"Damn pest," Kelly muttered past the boy before looking down at Cinque. "Son, you got your own problems and a dog is just a dog." It stepped forward and retrieved the hammer. "I'll get it next time." Its picture-face smiled confidently. It cocked its head and considered Cinque. "How ya doin'?"

"What do you care? Why you even askin'? Just use my frozen heart and make me do what you need to. If you can."

"Ah, come on now . . . don't be like that." Kelly took a seat on the edge of the hole, legs dangling over the edge and completely at ease. "Just because we found ourselves in these unfortunate circumstances don't mean we can't be civil. Remember, I ain't the reason you're here and you ain't the reason I'm here. Your Pa is the reason we're both here. That's the fact of it."

That wasn't the fact, as Cinque saw it. But he didn't see the point of splitting hairs right now, so he let it slide. Not without giving the spirit a glare that said *I'm hearing you, but I ain't listening.*

"Well," Kelly looked away. "I can see you haven't come around to my way of thinking yet, but you will. And not just 'cause I'm strong-arming you into it with all this." He pointed up and down the length of the chain.

"It's 'cause I'm right and he's wrong. Your Pa was wrong to make me like this. He was wrong to make you and leave you behind. As long as I'm still his sin catcher, then he can go on being wrong. He'll get away with it too. Now I ask you, where is the justice in that?"

While Kelly talked, Cinque took a seat, folding his legs

under him and picked at the ground. He was missing a piece of himself and far away from home, desperate, like the Soldier from the African's story. "Whose justice?"

Kelly cocked his head, the smile losing some of its certainty. "What do you mean?"

"It ain't my justice. You ain't called the cops or nothing like that. So is it your justice? If it is, then doesn't that make this revenge, not justice?"

Kelly nodded, understanding. "Ah. I see what you're getting at." He crossed his legs and leaned back on his hands. "You caught me. I don't believe in justice. I was just using that, invoking the cosmic balance, because I thought you might. The only justice you'll get in this world is the justice you make. Anyone who tells you otherwise is either a sucker or looking to screw you over. So what do you say you let me go make some justice, go get some revenge, for the both of us?"

Cinque turned away.

"Think about it. You'll come around."

With that, Kelly left the room, but just before he closed the door he said, "I almost forgot, seen a friend of yours heading this way. You remember it—lots of arms, lots of mouths, talks too much. . . . It's pretty determined to get back in touch with you, if you know what I mean, and you're just sittin' here. Waitin'. Think on that."

The handle turned shut with a clang.

Cinque lay down again, this time he couldn't sleep.

19

FRIEND OF YOURS

Alone, Cinque lay in the dark pit for minutes or hours, time blurred without context, until he felt something else in the cell, something huge. He jumped up and listened hard, heard nothing but his own breath but the sense of looming remained. He looked around three times before noticing that one side of the room, everything to the left of the door, floor, walls, every surface was a deep red colour, while to the right everything was pitch black. He realized that the surfaces glittered, sparkled not with light, but with a personal deepness, so real they didn't need light to be seen. The room rippled with movement, covered in ants, red ants on the left and black ants on the right, swarming the room, ceiling, walls and floor, up to a rough circle around his feet.

The ants spoke, a million little voices in chorus: "Again, I find you on the edge. Will you always keep me so busy, Cinque Williams? This is good, the further you explore, the more you experiment, the faster you will learn."

The sound was strange but he recognized the unique diction of the pimp in the red and black suit.

"Eshu Waru? How . . . how'd you find me here?"

A wave of motion rippled across the line of ants as if they were whispering to each other. "I can always find my followers, no matter how far they wander."

"But the Sin Catcher—it look like the meatworks is his, like he a god in this place."

The chorus of ants filled the room with laughter. The voice came from every direction at once, disorienting. "That little construct? A god? Oh my boy, he is nothing compared to me. With the flick of an eyelash, I could pop him like a soap bubble."

Cinque found himself turning in slow circles. He pointed to where the chain was bolted to the floor, the only surface free of ants.

"You're steering clear of his chain."

"Please, boy, it's not because the white man's magic can threaten me."

Cinque thought of something, maybe he could be slick like Darren would. "Then why don't—"

"—I prove it? You cannot trick a trickster. Or at least, you cannot trick the Trickster. I once fooled an entire village into tearing each other apart just by walking down the middle of it. Any angle you can think of was old to me millennia ago."

So much for being sneaky, Cinque thought. He would play it straight from now on. He was glad he hadn't angered the god.

"Remember what I said the first time we met? I will help you help yourself, but only when it makes you a stronger servant. I won't break this chain for you, but I might show you how to break it yourself."

"That all I get? Unhooked? How about this? How about you get rid of that scarecrow, the Sin Catcher?"

"No. There will be no easy escapes for you. The Sin Catcher is an enemy, and enemies are to be destroyed. I will not help you become a coward and a weakling, dependent on my help at every turn. I will make you strong and you will use that strength for me someday. You will see. I will show you how to walk free of this leash. From there you only have your wits to escape the rest."

Cinque said nothing. Eshu Wara's tone was clear: they both knew he would accept whatever help the god offered.

"In exchange, I will require another sacrifice from you, just as we sealed the deal for my services as mediator with the lapsed wizard."

"Um," Cinque looked down at his palm. "How are we going to shake on it if you don't have any hands?"

"I've had your sacrifice of spit, this time I want more. This time I want blood."

He balked, but he wasn't in any position to deal. Getting further in debt to the god felt like a walk down a dark road, but it was better than sitting in this cell. "How much?"

"Five drops. Leave them on the floor. I'll take them after you've gone."

"How?"

"You have teeth, don't you? Don't forget your animal capacity just because you call yourself civilized."

Cinque looked at his hands. They seemed the most likely place to draw blood from, the easiest part to bring up to his mouth.

He used his upper incisors to saw at the thin skin at the base of his thumb and away from his palm, tracing jagged scratches across the back of his hand. After the third attempt a drop of red finally blossomed where the three lines of ruined skin intersected. He squeezed out a drop with his other hand. As it hit the ground there was a wave of motion and a sound among the ants radiating out from where he stood, like the ripples in a pool or the excitement of a crowd. The god's exuberance over the sacrifice worried Cinque. He didn't like being the subject of such gluttonous desire.

"Do you feel like you are on the menu?" the ants laughed. "Do not fear for the blood in your veins, at least not from me.

Lesser spirits take what they can get, but my tastes are far more refined. It's the act of sacrifice that I find sweet."

Cinque wasn't convinced, but continued to make his offerings. With each drop he turned a little to the right, careful to keep them from falling on each other. When he was done he realized he had inadvertently placed the drops at even intervals in a circle with him in the center. He licked the wound and applied pressure to it with his thumb to stop the bleeding.

"Your sacrifice is accepted," the ants said in chorus.

"So how do I get off this hook?"

"You think yourself off of it. What is the hook for?"

"To keep me from escaping."

"Be more specific." The ants stirred in a clockwise motion.

"To keep me attached to the chain and to the floor."

"Anything else?"

Cinque couldn't think of anything else.

"What did he say?"

"He said my name. My full name. Which is weird, 'cause I didn't think he knew my middle name."

"What does that imply?"

"That this chain isn't meant to keep down anything but me—just me."

The ants shuffled clockwise again. "And if this leash is designed to imprison you, to restrain you and no other, then how should you escape it?"

"Do I change the hook?" Cinque asked. "Change it so it'll trap someone else?"

"Not while it's inside your skull you won't. Imbedded, its strongest connection is to you."

Cinque tried to picture the scene from above, outside of his body. Looking down there were three elements: the chain, the concrete floor and himself. Eshu Wara had already ruled out affecting the chain, at least from the inside. There wasn't much he could do about the concrete floor. He made a list of what he had to work with: the meatworks, the cell, the floor, the chain, the hook. . . .

"The only thing I can change is . . . me?"

"And what about yourself are you going to change?"

Cinque fingered the chain dangling from his scalp. "What's the hook using to hold me in?"

"You tell me."

"I can't change into someone else. Can I?"

Could he? He'd seen it happen on the way to Chicago, hadn't he?

Cinque looked into the black substance of the chain, its darkness deeper than its thickness. "How does the hook know who I am?"

He paused but there was only a grim rustling from the ants.

"Does it see me? Does it taste me? Does it know me? I don't know much about Juju, but everything seems to want my spit or some other part of me."

Eshu Wara spoke: "This isn't Juju, but the principles are similar."

"So if it's not holding on to my body, is it holding on to my mind?" Cinque tugged at the chain. The hook in his head hurt less than it should have.

"Why your mind? Why isn't it holding on to your soul or desire? Or your dignity? Who forged the hook and chain? And how well did he know your mind?"

"I guess he couldn't know me very well. We never met but all he knew was my name. Is that it? My name?" Cinque remembered reading in *The Black Arts* that spirits could be controlled by knowing their true name. This time, he was the spirit.

"Names are powerful things."

"How do I change my name?"

"Are you prepared to reinvent yourself?"

"If it'll get me out of here I am."

When the ants laughed they flowed like ripples in the water. "Oh I wasn't asking if you are willing to try. I was asking if you were capable. Can you take yourself apart, removing a piece of yourself and leave it behind?"

"I'm already in pieces, aren't I? I get the feeling that I'm halfway there."

"So you are . . . but you'll still have to peel off your identity and leave it on the hook."

"What if the hook was made out of my spit or blood?"

The ants rippled outward. "Then you would be in some real trouble."

"At least there's that then. So how do I do this?"

"Disassociate yourself with your name. Make it a strange thing. Let the sound of it lose its familiarity until it is gone."

He'd seen a man named Robbie turn into the man named Ted, exchanging identities with a pack of cards but Cinque didn't have a pack of cards so he did what he did best. He thought about it. He sat, cross-legged with his face in his hands until he felt his pulse in his cheeks and jaw. He followed this sensation, keeping the warmth and the movement for himself and distancing himself from the surface he touched. He made the act from himself.

He thought about the burning hands of the Soldier from the African's story and the thing in his hands took on a polished wood-like substance. His body began to rock back and forth of its own volition and his hands slid up and down the wood surface on the front of his head, fingernails turned inwards, scraping the surface. The wood covering his face gave way under his nails and he tore at the smooth, polished surface until it became a rough, splintered mask.

Robbie Freegard had cast away his own identity when he cast away his glasses. At his temples Cinque discovered matching knots and a string that wrapped around the back of his head, connected to the wooden mask though holes on its edge which ran along his jaw, up the sides of his head and across his forehead, just under his hairline. The Sin Catcher's hook was embedded though the mask at his forehead but the mask was too tight for him to tell if it also ran through his head.

Carefully, slowly, he used his fingernails to write his name, Cinque Joseph Williams, across the mask, just over the eyes. And once he finished the final "s" the mask loosened. Now he could get his fingertips between its wooden surface and himself and he could tell that the hook was only penetrating the mask, not his flesh.

The string was too strong to snap so the boy pulled it up over the top of his head, dropping the mask and the attached hook on the ground in front of him. He ran his fingers over the front of his head finding only smooth skin.

He came to his feet as the ants chimed in, "Excellent! But now the real challenge—what will a nameless, confused boy do when the Sin Catcher catches him?"

"The Sin Catcher?" The boy's memories, like his body, felt distant, like he was looking down on them. "Oh yeah, I remember him."

"You had better. He may be a small fish, but this is a smaller pond."

"Why can't I remember what the Sin Catcher looks like? Like he was in a movie—no, more than that—it's like he was in a book I read a long time ago."

"Because these are not your memories, they belong to Cinque Joseph Williams. Though you stand in his skin you are just a visitor."

"So I'm nobody?"

"No, you are a boy without a name. And if you don't find one soon you'll have nothing at all. Now go."

"Where?"

"Away."

With that the ants were gone. The boy stepped carefully to

the wall and then to the door until he gripped the latch. With a little feel and prod, he opened the mechanism.

In the hall a small goat-like figure slept in the middle of the hall. A backpack lay against the far wall. He automatically threw the bag over his shoulder, and picked his way through the building and outside, stepping carefully around ruined machinery and over sleeping Fibs. The dull grey morning sky peeked though the broken windows in places. Mindlessly, he let his feet carry him through the building, the yard and the gate. His head, just a passenger, let them do their work.

20

THE MECHANISM

"C—I—N—Q—U—E spells 'Sink'." The nameless boy said to himself, unconvinced. He read the name off the library card he found in the backpack. Trying to make a connection with the boy he used to be, or maybe the boy he replaced. He wasn't sure what the relationship was yet. He'd also found a picture of an older man and a teenaged girl and had stared at her for a long time. The boy thought he should try to find her. Maybe she could help him understand who Cinque was.

Love you, daddy! – Olamide was written on the back of the picture. "Cinque. Olamide. Doesn't anyone have normal names around here?"

The boy found himself under the bridge that ran over the Millsdale Expressway, the road which used to be the main thoroughfare from downtown St. Jude to the northern edge of town, the chemical plants and their jobs. The paper plants moved out and the chemical plants moved in a long time ago, grandfathering themselves into the weaker environmental laws of the riverside. Millsdale Expressway hadn't seen much traffic since the chemical plants quickly automated, and the lanes were covered in dust and trash.

A suspicious dripping sound echoed under the bridge, suspicious because it hadn't rained in weeks. Back when commuters spent at least five minutes twice a day passing under the bridge, an emerging hip hop group had used the bridge's blank surface as a billboard. A spray paint mural covered the underside to the east, picturing four young brothers in gold chains, tracksuits and weave caps. The band's name in an orange, block-letter banner ran across the bottom of the mural. After a careful study, the boy decided that they must have been the "Cold Money Crew." It had taken him a long time to read the name past all the taggers and other graffiti that had covered the bottom half of the mural over the years.

Half the members of the Cold Money Crew, the two on the top, had managed to survive unscarred. Being eight feet above the ground saved them from the mutilations inflicted upon their lower band mates. Blacked eyes, blackened teeth and tags sprayed across their foreheads, cheeks and chins. The guy on the right suffered the further indignity of a green paint penis spraying an endless stream of blue urine onto his face.

The boy sat by the road, on an empty shopping cart lying on its side. Where the cart came from was a mystery. There wasn't a supermarket for miles. Staring at what was left of the mural, he considered the Cold Money Crew and where they were now. Probably not making music, he thought

Their names ran along the side of each of their faces. The lower two were illegible but the faces above were untouched. The boy read the names aloud, "Dru Trip and MC Groove EEE of the Cold Money Crew—"

"—how do we do?" MC Groove EEE interrupted, smiling. "I can't say we doin' good. There gots to be better walls to be stuck to."

Dru Trip spoke up too. "'Cause our bodies be in lockdown, our minds can't roam free. If'in I get loose I'd be running things in a week."

Their faces remained flat as they spoke, confined to the surface of the wall and bound by the black border painted around them.

"But we's been painted in these cells. What you doin' down here, little man?" MC Groove EEE asked the boy.

"And what yo' name, if'in it ain't 'little man', little man?" asked Dru Trip.

The boy brushed a dreadlock out of his face and said, "I don't rightly know."

MC Groove EEE looked concerned, "You don' know what you doin' down here or you don' know yo name?"

"Both I guess. I just wandered down here, but I can't say why 'cause I ain't never been down here before."

Dru Trip didn't look concerned. He looked amused.

The boy's face twisted up with the effort it took to remember. "I think—oh yeah, I done left it behind. But now I'm not so sure that was a good idea, 'cause I don't know how I'm a get it back."

MC Groove EEE asked, "What was yo' name then?"

"I dunno." The boy shrugged. "I left it on the floor of the meatworks, up there on the hill," he pointed in the wrong direction.

"An that be where yo face went too then, huh?" asked Groove EEE.

The boy felt the smooth featureless surface on the front of his head. "Yeah, I forgot that's still that way."

Dru Trip and MC Groove EEE exchanged a knowing glance.

"You know," Dru Trip started, "There more than one road fo' yo' to go down now."

MC Groove EEE nervously glared at Dru Trip and added, "You can make yo'self a new name."

"Or take on another brother's name. A better brother than yo'self," Dru Trip snapped, as much to MC Groove EE as to the boy. "You a boy without a face, I'm a face without a body. Don' you think we could work somethin' out?"

"Or maybe we can work somethin' out. You an' me," MC Groove EEE added. "With me—we can be you, you know what I'm sayin'?"

"No." The boy answered frankly.

"I can be you, you jus' have to tell me how. I just be a face for yo' face. That's all. I'll be there fo' you." MC Groove EEE was practically pleading.

Dru Trip cut in. "Why be you when you can be something better? You can be me. Boy, when I was walkin' them streets I had all the money an all the honeys. You go with me, and you will be too!"

"Or, or," MC Groove EEE tried to look sure of himself. "You a smart kid, kid. You gotta be smarter than that. Yo, this fool right here just wanna take you down the same roads he was headin' down."

"You mean, headin' up! My star was risin'! F and F, boy! Fame and fortune!"

"You look real familiar, man," the boy said to Dru Trip.

"See?" Dru Trip asked MC Groove EEE. "I'm still out there. This kid remembers me even if my last album was cut before he was born."

"You mean our last album. An' so he prolly remembers me too, just not as good. You was always stickin' yo' big, dumb face in any camera." MC Groove EEE sniffed. "Daaaaamn . . . is that how you gonna treat this boy? Shovin' your face into his life, standin' in front of him? How that gonna be a life?" He looked back at the boy. "I just wanna be a small part of you. You know, help you out. 'Cause I can tell you gonna be a star, all on you own. An' we don't want this sucker takin' all the credit."

"Who you mean 'we'?" the boy asked.

"Yeah." Dru Trip added. "Who the hell is 'we'? You ain't part of nobody, as long as you ain't got no body."

"I's just in the habit," MC Groove EEE explained. "Back in the day it was always we, me and the sorry souls you see below me, against him."

MC Groove EEE appeared to lean forward towards the boy, as much as the wall would allow. "See, we learnt the hard way that there's no teamin' up with this fool."

Dru Trip rolled his eyes. "Dats cause we wasn't no team. Y'all was my back ups, y'alls was my Pips and I'm Gladys Knight."

"He do like to wear dresses." MC Groove EEE kept talking to the boy. "But that's as far as that goes. This sucker took all the credit an' all the money, took all the songs too."

"Bitch, you never wrote no song!" Dru Trip defended himself.

"I wrote 'Hypnotize them Eyez', an' you done stole it."

The boy didn't understand. "How did you get a song stolen?"

MC Groove EEE nodded with every syllable. "Wit a contract."

The boy looked back at Dru Trip. "Is dat true?"

Dru's face twisted up like he smelled something bad. "Like I know contracts?"

The two spray painted rappers argued some over each other about who had mistreated who and record deals for records no one listened to anymore.

While they fought the boy watched Dru Trip, and then it clicked. "You Black Jesus!" The rappers stopped fighting and cast stunned looks at the boy. "That's where I know you from. You is Black Jesus before he hit, ain't ya?" He looked around, committing the place under the bridge to memory. "I gotta bring my cousin . . . what's his name . . . Well I gotta bring him down here to see."

MC Groove EEE gave Dru Trip a sceptical look. "What's he talkin' about, Dru?"

"Yo. I don' know."

The boy explained, "Dru Trip . . . Well, the real, 3D Dru Trip that is . . . he went on. Now he calls himself Black Jesus an' he rolls solo, no crew." He cocked his head to one side. "Y'all didn't know this?"

"We . . . don't get out much." MC Groove EEE smiled nervously.

"What kinda ride he got?" Dru Trip asked.

"I dunno." The boy said. "Ain't all rappers rich? He prolly has more than one."

"That's what I'm talkin' about." Dru Trip smiled and nodded.

MC Groove EEE looked sideways at Dru Trip and asked, "What you all happy about? All your plans? All you been dreamin' 'bout down here under this here bridge? It all been done and the real Dru Trip was the one who done it. Even if'n he call himself Black Jesus now."

Dru Trip didn't like that. "Yo! Forget about B.J.! I make my own name, with his old name. Old school, you know? 'Cause the old days was the good old days!"

"The old days are over," said the faceless boy.

That gave MC Groove EEE a big smile. "You got that right boy. See? Not only would this dude try to make you into him, him been done. Him ain't no good. But me? I just wanna be you. I can help you."

The boy shook his head. "I don't need either of you."

"How far you think you gonna get in life with no name? No face?"

"Probably not far," he said, pointing at Dru Trip. "But if this clown can remake himself, rename himself so that his own old name don't know where he went . . . then I can do the same." The boy stood up and threw his backpack over his shoulder. "Now I'ma go figure this all out, someplace with less distractions."

"Distractions?" MC Groove EEE sounded angry. "You callin' me a distraction? I been tryin' to help you out!"

"You was tryin' to help yo'self. You ain't no better than that one." He nodded toward Dru Trip. "You just have a different way about you."

"Boy! You don't know me!" Dru Trip shouted.

"Me neither! But if you don't want my help then I don't know what'll become of you out there."

"What'll become of me is what I want to become," was the last thing the boy said to the faces as he climbed on top of the bridge. He was still brushing the dust from his hands when a little, two-tone brown and primer car pulled up next to him and the girl from the picture, older by a decade or so, leaned out to say.

"Get your skinny butt in the car."

21

SOMEPLACE WITH
LESS DISTRACTIONS

Olamide drove the boy to her home, through the morning light and in silence. He went along without complaint, didn't have any place better to be. She seemed tired and angry about something. The boy didn't know what that could be so he kept his mouth shut and studied the inside of the car, the broken vent, the sun-worn dashboard and the carpet that needed a good vacuuming. The backpack was stuffed between his feet. The gray, dusty train tracks of the southern switchyard looked like a sloppy, frosted-over spider web. They passed by rundown buildings on the edge of town with paint peeling like dead skin. Had the KLJK radio tower always twisted the air like that? He couldn't remember.

The boy touched his face to see if it was still missing, trying to find some crease or node but there was nothing. The front of his head was entirely smooth and flat. It seemed like she would be able to tell him what to do about his condition, but since Olamide didn't seem to notice he just let it lie.

When they pulled into the driveway the boy didn't notice

that the car had stopped. He had drifted off into his own world, and sat staring at the back of his hand until Olamide opened the car door.

"Well? Are you going to come in or what?"

Inside, an older woman waited in the living room. She was probably Cinque's grandma, so his cousin Darren should be here too. She had been sorting and wrapping coins from the spare change jar, the coins and sleeves spread out all over the coffee table. She must have abandoned them when she heard the door open. Arms crossed, she glared her sternest look at the boy.

"Sit down," Olamide ordered.

The boy wandered over to the couch while Olamide and her mother conferred in the kitchen. Lacking anything else to keep his attention, the boy took up wrapping stacks of coins from where his grandmother left off.

Darren came down the stairs, wearing his pyjama pants. He rubbed the sleep from his face with one hand.

"Damn, boy, you got up this early? For what?"

"I ain't just got up," the boy said while folding the end of a roll of dimes. "I just got in."

Darren's eyes went wide with surprise and then he heard the women talking in the kitchen. "Ohhhh. . . . Damn. I wish you'd a told me you was planning to pull something like this."

"Why?"

"'Cause I'd a got up to somethin' of my own. They's gonna be so busy beatin' yo ass, they'd be too tired to be beatin' mine." Darren smiled.

"You didn't know Cin—um—*I* was gone?" the boy asked.

"I know I didn't. I don't know about them." Darren jabbed a thumb at the kitchen. "The school's not gonna call in a missing kid until it's been five days, you know that. And you so quiet, how someone gonna know if you here or not? Where'd you go anyway?"

"The old meatworks. Up on the hill."

Darren shook his head, "Why you wanna go there for?"

"He was hoping to find his pops, Cinque that is." He confided in the older boy, Darren felt like the sort who would keep a secret. "I know I look like him, but I'm not. Not right now at least but I'ma try and bring Cinque back soon."

Darren nodded knowingly. "You know that don't make no kinda sense, right?"

The boy fed another tube full of nickels. "Yeah, I guess not."

"What you s'possed to do with that craziness? Like disappearing shoes?"

"Keep it to myself?"

"Keep it to yo'self."

The women emerged from the kitchen. With a snap and a point Grandma ordered Darren upstairs.

"But I ain't had no breakfast yet," he protested. That earned him no sympathy and the older boy angrily stormed up the stairs.

His mother and his grandmother stood across the coffee table from the boy, both with arms sternly crossed. The boy didn't notice that he was the center of attention. He continued to put coins in tubes.

Olamide called his name. If the boy heard, he showed no sign, so she called his name again. "Cinque!" she said, and snapped her fingers three times. He looked up at her hand and then her face.

"What's wrong with you, boy?"

"Where do you want to start?" he asked, calmly.

His grandmother spoke up. "Let's start with where you were all night."

". . . the meatworks? I'm pretty sure I was there all night, but . . . it ain't the meatworks that you'd of figured. It's haunted."

Olamide was appalled. "What were you doing up in that dirty, old place?"

"I think I know." Her mother interrupted. "Cinque was

asking about your father the other day. I didn't tell him anything because I didn't want to encourage him, lot of good that did."

"Oh yeah," Cinque said. "That reminds me." He fished around in his backpack and presented them with the picture. "I think this is for you."

"Oh my goodness," his grandmother said. Breathlessly she took the picture with gentle fingers. "He really was up there."

Olamide's eyes went wide. "I remember that. . . ."

The picture stunned the two of them for a moment. Olamide's mother came out of it first. "This doesn't change anything. He's still in trouble."

"Of course." Olamide turned back to the boy. "What are you looking for, Cinque?"

It took the boy a second before he realized she was talking to him. "Was."

Olamide just blinked.

"Was looking for. It's been found, kinda. Anyway the days of looking for Kelly Lee are over. You was right, he wasn't no good but Cin—I had to see for myself."

"Well you got that right." His grandmother put the picture on the mantle. "That was a foolish thing you've done, Cinque. Running around in that dangerous old slaughterhouse at night! What if you got hurt up there? Nobody would have known to go looking for you. You could have died."

The boy looked straight ahead at nothing. "True that."

His grandmother continued talking as if he hadn't said anything. "And for what? You didn't go up there to find no picture. What does the meatworks have to do with your father anyway? It was your grandfather that worked up there. And that was a long, long time ago."

Olamide spoke up. "He might be getting them confused. Reaching out to any father figures he can find and running them all together." She didn't seem angry anymore. She seemed sad instead. "What do you want, Cinque? What can we give you to make you happy again?"

"What?" her mother cried out, shocked and appalled. "He runs away and you're gonna give him something for it? The only thing you should be giving the boy is a whoopin'."

Darren shouted from upstairs. "Yo! If you givin' him something for bein' a fool then y'all owe me! An' I ain't talkin' bout no whoopin'. I had plenty of those already!"

Grandma shouted back. "I told you to get in your room."

"No, you didn't. You tol' me to get upstairs."

"Well, now I'm telling you to get in your room. Get in your room."

"And I still ain't had no breakfast!" Darren slammed his door shut.

Grandma turned back on Olamide. "Just when did you lose your mind?"

"I haven't. The boy is looking for a father figure. How am I going to punish him for that?"

"With a belt," Grandma said as she planted her fists on her ample hips. "That's how."

"I don't see how that's going to do any good."

"It worked all right on you."

"Did it?"

Something was exchanged between the two women, something the boy didn't understand. No one said anything for a long, tense moment until the boy spoke up.

"Should I go to my room then?"

Hours later, the boy wasn't grounded, not officially, but he was pretty sure that he wasn't supposed to go anywhere for a long time so he poked around the bedroom, trying to get a feel for Cinque Williams, what he was like. There wasn't much—just clothes, a few pieces of art he'd made in school, an old encyclopaedia set and a few books. He found a picture of a man and woman sharing an uncomfortable moment and stared at it for a while before realizing that this must be Willy T's picture and putting it back.

Eventually he settled in on the bed, reading in the encyclopaedia about names. There was a lot in there about first names and last names and where names came from but not too much about the process of being named. The boy figured that if it didn't say that someone else had to name him, then he could name himself. It worked for Dru Trip.

He did come across a passage that said that some names had no meaning, that they were just a series of sounds, pleasant to the ear. This was relatively common practice in the United States. Here in America, he thought, they make their own names, their own rules and their own magic.

Something small and hard hit the window. The boy looked out at the overcast sky and it happened again. This time he saw it, dark like a pebble or a big seed. Cautiously, he slid along the wall, trying to look outside while hiding behind the curtain. It wasn't good enough.

"Come on now," called Kelly Lee from outside. "Where else were you gonna be?"

The boy pressed up against the window frame, out of sight. He felt like a fool for not expecting this. He wanted to believe that the Sin Catcher couldn't come unless summoned, or at least couldn't come down off the hilltop, that he was safe down here.

"Boy, you ain't foolin' nobody up there, so open the window. I just want to talk. For now, that is."

He hated to do it but he sure wasn't going to hide in his room until the Sin Catcher went away. The boy unlatched the old window and jerked it up and open. The Sin Catcher stood in the yard, looking human. A Fib stood on either side, the fox-faced Fib and the one sculpted out of soggy puzzle pieces, Puzzleman. Kelly held the orange, frozen heart in one hand and Cinque's face hung from the black chain in the other.

"You got a real ruthless streak in ya, boy," Kelly Lee smirked. "It must come from your mother's side."

"You stay away from her!" he shouted too loud and too quick.

"Maybe." Kelly let the word hang in the air for a second. "If it comes to that, it'll be your fault. Remember that." He swung the boy's old face back and forth on the chain. "Sure, you got out and you got home but what the hell were you going to do next? Seriously? I got your name. I got your heart."

"I'll get a new name, and a new heart."

Kelly cocked his head in disbelief. "A new name? You even understand what a True Name is? What you left here on this hook? What are you going to do? Baptize yourself? It's a tricky thing, dunking yourself in the water. Pulling yourself back up is the hard part.

"As for a new heart . . ." He gave the orange heart a little toss. "A heart's a heart and you only get the one. How long you got without it? I give ya another day tops."

"I'll figure something out."

"You won't. You can't. There's only one way outta this. My way. It's a package deal. You come back up to the meatworks, take the curse and I'll throw in your heart and name for free."

"Not a chance."

"Then what are you gonna do? You gotta come out sometime, and I got Fibs at both doors. They're dishonest and unreliable, but I got enough of them to see the job through. I'm sure you could hold out a while, coming and going with the family. Just ask yourself this . . . When it comes to knocking people down to get what he wants, how far do you think your Pa would be willing to go? 'Cause I can go twice as far."

He'd just been thinking that he could use the family as guardians. Maybe Darren would be able to keep him safe, but Darren sure wouldn't want his little cousin sticking around all the time. "Maybe I'll just stay inside."

"Ho ho!" He didn't expect Kelly Lee to find that quite so funny. "You gonna go the way of Olly Dodds?"

"Who Olly Dodds?"

Kelly Lee shrugged, disappointed. "You surprise me, boy. You don't know the history of this here house?" He shook his head in mock sympathy. "Well let me tell you, this house ain't got a good history of providing sanctuary. You must know that there was some bad times back in 1917?

"Back during World War I, while white men went to war, black folks were brought up from the South to work in the mills. Well, the white folks who stayed behind didn't like that. Hate turned to whispers, turned to rumours of a black man stepping 'outta line'. That was the spark that set off a night of burnings and lynchings. White folks thought they'd save their city from black folks, the city they'd abandon six decades later.

"Good ol' Olly Dodds came a running up here that night, running from one of them redneck mobs fitting to do him some harm. They let him in, the Covington family that is. Good people them, but all it got Mr. Covington was a beating when he tried to stop the mob from coming in an' hanging Olly Dodds from a tree in the yard. That tree, on the other side of the house.

"The spirits of that lynch party, I can call them up for a repeat performance." He put the heart back behind him and took Cinque's face in both hands. "Maybe it won't be a pack of crackers that kills your family. Maybe it'll be you." Lifting the face like a mask he transformed into Cinque, face and body. "You think they'd like that? Askin' 'Why? Cinque, why?' as I carve them up?" The Sin Catcher's lips didn't move when he talked and the nameless boy could see the mask seam around his face.

Horrified, the boy tried to slam the window shut, but the old wooden frame didn't make it easy. As he fought the window closed, the Sin Catcher turned back into Kelly Lee, "You go on an' think about it, boy. I'll get ya one way or another. But it'll be better for you and me both if you come in on your own!" With that, the creature that looked like his father tipped his hat and stepped back though the bushes. The Fibs stayed where they were. The fox-faced Fib scratched himself and sneered.

When he finally got the window shut, the nameless boy jerked the curtains shut and rushed to the other side of the room. There wasn't any place to sit over by the open closet door, so he stood, tapped his foot, chewed on a fingernail and thought as fast as he could.

As a plan came to him, he pulled Willy T's picture out from between the books, stuffed it in the backpack and snuck down the hall to Darren's room. He could hear Black Jesus' second album through the door. The boy waited for the break before the next track, then knocked quietly three times.

"Come on in, little man," Darren said from the other side.

"How you know it was me?" the boy asked, as he pushed the door open.

Darren sat on his bed under his Black Jesus poster reading Rhymez, a hip-hop magazine.

"Because—" Darren hadn't looked up from his magazine. "—you's the only one around here who knock. Some other people around here . . ." He glared down in the direction of Grandma's room. ". . . just walk right in anytime they feel like it." Then, he finally did look at the boy with his backpack.

"What you wearing that for in here?"

"It's 'cause I got to go. Now," the boy said.

"All right then. Go."

"You gotta let me go out yo' window." The tree on Darren's side of the house had a thick branch that reached over by his window. It was how Darren got in and out at night, incognito.

"You definitely ain't taking my window. Like I need yo' fool-ass falling offa my tree and breakin' yo' head. They's likely to cut that tree down if that happens!"

The boy twisted his face in frustration. He needed Darren's permission, since he couldn't force his way past his larger cousin. "What if I had something to tell you? Something you'd wanna know?"

"Let me hear it and I'll see."

"Black Jesus, he used to be in a local group. They called themselves the Cold Money Crew. There's a bridge over the Millsdale Expressway and under that bridge someone sprayed a big ol' picture of them. 'Cept back then he called himself Dru Trip. Most of the picture's all marked up, the only ones you can make out is Dru Trip and MC Groove EEE but they there. Now, was that worth the cover charge for goin' out yo' window?"

"Yeahhhh. See . . ." Darren went back to his magazine. ". . . thing is, you just told me what you was going to tell me. It's like you gave it up for free. Now I knows what I knows, the same as you. So you ain't got nothing to trade no more do you." He smirked to himself.

"I only told you all that so's you'd let me out!"

"We didn't have no deal like that. I just asked and you told me. You gotta learn to keep yo' mouth shut, boy."

The boy was furious. Darren had done it again and when there was so much on the line. He was mad enough to toss them both out the window, Darren first so the boy would land on him. Then he thought of something.

"You know what? You right."

"I know I'm right. That's what I keep telling peoples."

"I should learn to keep my mouth shut. You never know what I'm gonna say and when," the boy warned, trembling as he spoke. "There's a good chance I might just wander downstairs, down by where your grandma's at. I might just say something about that old tree branch and how close it is to yo' window. Accidently, of course."

Darren took a serious look at the boy which broke into a sudden smile.

"Look who's growing up. Ha! Maybe someday you be the one schoolin' me." He swept his arm towards the window showing the boy he was free to pass, but as the boy ran by Darren knocked him upside his head, knocking him down. "Maybe someday but not today."

The boy got back up, pretending that he'd never been hit and opened the window. A wind had kicked up outside and the branch he had to grab was swaying towards the roof and back away. He knew better than to think about it and just stood on the edge of the roof watching the branch and getting a feel for the timing.

One . . . two . . . three . . . JUMP!

Before he knew it he had the branch firmly clenched under an arm, legs dangling in the air, the back of his legs banging into the aluminum gutter with loud, irregular bangs. He quickly pulled his legs up to the branch and shimmied feet first along the underside of the branch to the trunk. The base of the branch was lower than it was by the roof and he just lowered his feet beneath him for a second before letting go, hitting the dirt with a firm plop, teeth clapped shut painfully.

He looked to the front and back of the house for Fibs. The coast was clear, so he pushed through the dying hedge that separated the Williams house from the one next door and climbed through the broken fence that separated that house from the one on the other side, and then he ran.

22

HITTING THE DIRT

When the boy heard the rapidly falling footsteps echoing up and down the street he looked back to see the fox-faced Fib turn the corner between an old firehouse and a pale yellow home. The creature's fists pumped furiously. Its beady eyes locked on the boy with a hate so murderous that it froze the boy in place, costing him precious seconds that the beast used to close the gap between it and its prey.

The boy snapped out of it and started to run before he'd fully turned around. After a few slow, wobbling steps forward he was tearing away from the little monster faster than it could follow.

They ran down the long side of the block, six homes to the side, and when the boy approached the first crossroad, he was turning left, down towards Cairo Avenue, where people still lived, when Puzzleman lurched out from behind a bush at the corner. The boy ran back to the right, Puzzleman's sickening soggy footsteps now behind him too.

He turned down an alley on the next block, not because

he wanted to, but because they were chasing him down into an area filled with blocked streets and sinkholes. There were many dead ends in this part of town and the boy realized that they weren't chasing him down this way by accident. But there was an abandoned playground on the other side of this block. On the other side of that playground there was a road, then an open field, then a train track and finally, a liquor store. He was pretty sure the Fibs wouldn't follow him in there.

Puzzleman and the fox-faced Fib were already falling behind when the faceless boy turned into the playground. He slowed a little. The weeds had grown high and there was a lot of jagged, rusty junk in the grass.

Dark, broken, twisted chains hung from the swing set frame like poisonous vines. To one side, there was a slide with a rusted out track that would crumble out from underneath any child who tried to use it. To the other side there was a jungle gym some big kids had pulled up out of the ground and tossed on its back like the skeleton of a giant beetle. Scattered randomly throughout the park were unidentifiable animal torsos, saddled and mounted on heavy springs.

The neon signs of the liquor store off in the distance was a beautiful sight until the goat-like Fib with the trucker hat jumped up from a crop of weeds on the other side of the yard, blocking his escape.

A clicking sound to his left caught the boy's attention. It was the Fib with the dollar bill mask and the dirty, yellow robe: George Washington. Two pairs of footsteps came up behind him, one wet and one dry. Puzzleman and the fox-faced Fib. The latter smiled and cracked his knuckles, the former had no face to smile with nor knuckles to crack. It just shifted anxiously side to side.

Fox Face was the first to speak, "'Uh oh', he says, 'Seems I done stepped in it here.'"

George Washington's mouth over-enunciated under its

mask. "Ten times worse than he had it last night if it's up to me."

"Let's get 'im!" Goat Trucker shouted, more excited than the others.

Puzzleman stepped closer and started to pace around the boy while the others kept to their four points. Surrounded by this posse of Fibs, the boy looked back and forth for a way out.

"Funny, ain't it?" the fox-faced Fib said to George Washington. "You, me and Cinque all together again after fourteen years." He turned back to the boy, "See kid, we represent sins your Pa committed in the company of your mom, so in a way your mom is our mom too."

"You got nothin' to say about Olamide!" The boy looked about ready to fight. "Just 'cause you're sin that my Pa did to her don't make—"

"No, no, no, kid." The fox-faced Fib interrupted. "We ain't sins he done *to* her. We're sins he done *with* her. Want me to tell you about them?" A smirk slid across its snout.

"You shut up!"

"If you don't come along, then this ain't personal no more. It gets bigger than that. Then it becomes family business—your family against ours."

George Washington hopped forward in an impatient crouch. "And we gots a worse and wider family, that we do." It gnashed its grimy teeth at him. "Can't decide who I wanna bite of first, that's my problem."

Goat Trucker nudged his hat back and spat. "No name, no heart. What we gonna do to him worse 'n what he done himself?"

Fox Face jabbed a finger across the field to the floating Fib. "He's got a point. We got your name, kid. We got your heart. These is the facts. You got no choice."

Puzzleman circled the boy in ever constricting spirals, cutting off his escape route.

He shook his head in frustration. "Then is that all I got? My only road is back up to the meatworks? Take the Sin Catcher's curse? Then what? Maybe get my parts back, if he's feeling friendly?"

Fox Face felt the deal closing in and smiled. "You'll get your parts back, I guarantee. The boss is a forgiving guy. Maybe all that time you spent looking for your Pa ain't gonna go to waste. One Kelly Lee's as good as another, I figure."

The boy had to laugh at that. "The Sin Catcher? Be my pops?"

He kicked the traffic cone up, grabbed it with both hands and swung its base at Puzzleman's head, splattering the Fib from the neck up.

The boy looked back at the Fox-Faced Fib and told him, "No way." Charging at Goat Trucker, he threw the traffic cone, knocking the thin Fib down, leaving a clear path out of the playground and into the field.

The boy raced for the liquor store. The field seemed far wider than when he started running and just as he told himself not to look back, that it might cost him precious seconds, he betrayed himself and looked back over his shoulder. The fox-faced Fib led George Washington. Puzzleman had recovered and trailed far behind. The boy had a comfortable lead over the Fibs. Unfortunately, Goat Trucker had bent down to run on all fours. The boy tried to turn fear into a second wind, but his legs began to wobble beneath him. They seemed resigned to capture.

Across the field a bronze sedan pulled off the road and headed across the field, the front end bouncing along the rough terrain on a path intercepting the boy.

The boy figured that whoever was in that car had to be better for him than who was behind him and as it came to a stop he grabbed the handle to the backseat, but the door was locked. The driver's door opened and Ted Lopez stepped out, looking even more ragged and dangerous than he did on the highway, that old, Hazelwood handled screwdriver held like a prison shiv.

"Hey there, mi hijo. There I was just about to quit on finding you and then, bang! There you are, like we was drawn together. Get it? Drawn together? That's a pun, son."

Goat Trucker jumped between them and faced the Shapeshifter. "Back off, clay-man, this one is our—"

Without looking, Ted's hand twitched out like someone unseen pulled its string, burying the screwdriver deep in the Fib's head and yanked up. The furry body squirmed in the air. As the other Fibs caught up, Ted flicked his wrist and Goat Trucker shrivelled and fell to the ground in a pile of torn skin and broken bones.

While the boy darted around the front of the car, trying to put something solid between him and Lopez, George Washington blustered. "I don't know who you think you are, jackass, but you ain't just messing with the three of us! There's an army . . ." The fox-faced Fib and Puzzleman turned and ran away. Standing alone against the white man who could kill spirits, George Washington ran after them.

Ted hadn't looked at the Fibs, even when he killed Goat Trucker—that crazy stare was fixed on the boy across the car hood.

"Ace of Diamonds, remember?" Ted finally said, giving the screwdriver a dangerous little wave. "But not for me!" He lunged at the boy who skittered along the passenger's side of the car. "There's less of you than there was. What'd you do to yourself?"

"He ditched his name. I—"

"I?" Ted interrupted. "I? You don't get to use that word. Not around me!" He stabbed the car in the grill, the thick, square shaft of the screwdriver puncturing the radiator easily. The hiss of escaping fluids accompanied the rough, uneven sound of the engine. "You ain't no I. You stuck me with your fate, remember? Now I'm gonna stick it back at ya! I gotta throw away all I got, just to get back at ya, but I'd do it in a second. No one gets up on Ted Lopez, pendejo!"

"You ain't Ted Lopez." The nameless boy led the man around the back of the car, if he could make it to the open driver's door . . . "And you ain't Robbie Freegard, you ain't got no name either."

"No, I don't. But I got your fate!"

"You can have it! Fates are for little people!" the boy shouted as he dove behind the steering wheel, dropping the automatic into first while pushing with all his weight in the gas. The car lurched forward as Ted stabbed at him. The boy fell over in the car seat and the screwdriver pierced the aged upholstery where his neck was. Unable to reach the wheel or see through the windshield the boy could only push harder on the gas as the car bounced across the field, back toward the playground. He stared at the Shapeshifter's grip on the screwdriver shifting as the man was dragged alongside for a few seconds before his hand slipped.

Pulling himself up by the steering wheel, the boy jerked the car to the right and ploughed into the playground. The cheap, corroded slide crumbled under the incoming car and brought it to a soft crash. The boy's body jolted forward painfully. In the rear-view mirror, Ted was still staggering up from where he'd fell, halfway across the field.

The boy pulled the screwdriver from the seat, stuffed it in his hoodie pocket and ran.

The boy ran and weaved through St. Jude trying to go the wide way around to the church and lose Ted Lopez. It didn't take long for him to get lost himself, wandering among the back streets until he found an area that had been burnt out by fire years ago. It felt familiar; the boy wondered if Cinque had been here before. He jumped up into a burnt out two-story, looking for a place to hide and rest he came across a bedroom with a pile of concrete chunks in the corner and a light blue t-shirt hanging from a hole in the ceiling.

It felt like an old, forgotten friend.

Picking it up, the wire hanger fell out of it, but the boy didn't notice. He was trying to read the words someone had written across the front in magic marker—CINQUE.

The boy remembered where he was, just as the pile of concrete erupted in movement and colour, turning from rough, gray chunks to the slick, red mottled arms of the Cuttlefish as they lurched forward to grab him. The mouths began their chattering. Silent in ambush, all that pent up conversation burst out in an unintelligible cacophony. The qliphoth didn't have the mass needed for a proper pounce. It hung in the air like a flimsy plastic trash bag stuck on a branch. Instead of enveloping the boy with its arms, it only brushed the back of his left wrist.

That was enough.

A mouth at the tip of one arm bit deeper into his flesh than ever before and drank deep. Pain brought the boy to his senses. He fell to his knees, pulling the Cuttlefish down with him. It pulled the boy's hand in toward its main mouth. The boy's free hand twisted around behind him as the monster's bright red spots pulsed among the black spots of its skin and dulled, taking on a bloody shade. It opened its tentacles and remaining arms wide to take the boy all at once in an engulfing embrace.

"Dressed in your best . . ."

"No hope, not for you—"

"—a little piece here. A little—"

"Tired? Well get used to it."

Frantically fishing around through his hoodie pocket the boy finally got his fingers around the handle and swung the screwdriver around in front of him in an arc. Its flat tip scratched a line across two of the Cuttlefish's arms and along its body, just above its main mouth. The qliphoth reeled in far more pain than such a little scratch should have caused. Its skin flashed hot pink and it screamed with all its mouths, human and mollusk. Trying to get away, it pulled its arms back. All its arms except the one with its teeth sunk in the boy's wrist—that one was stuck.

The boy stabbed at that arm, hoping that the screwdriver would disintegrate the Cuttlefish like it had the Goat Trucker Fib but the qliphoth was stronger, the boy was weaker. As hard as he stabbed, he couldn't pierce the thing's rubbery skin. When the qliphoth realized that the screwdriver wasn't a threat in the boy's hand it brought the rest of its arms around again.

"I mean, that's a long way of saying—"

"It still strikes me as a rebellion."

". . . lady got in trouble because . . ."

"Bring it on, world!"

". . . are when the 'imponderables' come into play."

The boy tried to pry it off, pushing the screwdriver's tip into the mouth, tearing a strip of skin off his arm. He worked the tool up and down as the monster's free arms closed in on him. Tired and scared Cinque felt the heat rising in his chest again, the faster he worked the hotter it got until he dropped the screwdriver and slapped his sternum, instincts trying to beat out the flame that wasn't there. That's when the Cuttlefish's mouth slipped down to his finger, like a suction cup on glass, leaving the bite mark behind on his wrist.

He didn't know how, but the heat worked better than the screwdriver. When he fixated on his missing heart the creature lost its grip. He concentrated and let the heat take him so the Cuttlefish wouldn't. And the mouth slipped the rest of the way off and said, "Huh?"

Arms and eyes wandered and flopped, the Cuttlefish lost track of the boy just a few feet away. He kept the heat in the forefront of his mind as he put the screwdriver in his bag with his good hand. The other was too cold to hurt, its skin was pail and wrinkled. The Cuttlefish lost track of the boy. It searched around the t-shirt, looking for the rest of the boy named Cinque. The boy backed away, leaving it rolling in the air, sluggish and searching.

"Kid, you are crap at hiding." Ted Lopez stood in the doorway, his face scrapped up and bleeding from the drag the boy had taken him on. "I heard you rolling around in here from the next block.

"Now, how about you give me that screwdriver so I can get back to killing you?"

If the boy wanted to run again there were a half-dozen ways out of the building and away from the Shapeshifter but he was too tired, too sore and too angry to be afraid. More dangerous than that, he was inspired.

With a single swing of his arm he picked up the t-shirt and threw it at the man, hitting him in the chest with as much impact as one would have expected. Ted saw it coming and caught it with one hand. The Cuttlefish shot after it. Like the Fibs, Ted didn't see the Cuttlefish.

Ted was saying, "Is that the best you go—" when the Cuttlefish grabbed him with all of its arms, squeezed until he cracked and pulled the shell that was Ted Lopez apart, looking for the emotions within. Robbie Freeguard fell to his knees and dropped the t-shirt as the bits of Ted crumbled in the grasp of the Cuttlefish.

Robbie, confused, felt the ground between his knees, "Where are my glasses?"

The Cuttlefish fell on the Shapeshifter again, and tore Robbie Freeguard off and apart like he was an onion skin revealing another identity.

The boy snatched the shirt, turned it inside out and stuffed it into his backpack, hoping that would cover its scent. He shambled off as the Cuttlefish ripped through layer after layer of the Shapeshifter.

23

TOO COLD TO HURT

By the time he got to Cinque's Place, his right hand was still dead. He had to open the door with his awkward left. Crossing the threshold to his Place felt like a weight lifting off him. Safe at last, the boy leaned against the wall, slid down to the floor and just lay there for a moment.

"I don't know why you're resting. The real work still has to be done," a woman said from the front of the hall.

He knew who it was before he picked himself up over the pews. In the front row a bundle of bone-white dreads hung down the back of the pew, black boots kicked up on the stage.

The White Woman didn't move while he circled around in front of her, eyes following him from behind her sunglasses until he said, "You must be the White Woman."

She stood up, stretched and walked over to the stage, regarding him over her dark glasses. "You lost your name. Interesting."

"Not me, I never had a name. You must mean Cinque. He had some help, Esh—"

She cut him off, covering his mouth with her hand. "I know who you are talking about." She pulled her hand away.

"Are you afraid of him?" the boy asked.

She laughed, loud and sincere, a sound the boy never expected her to make. "No, most definitely not. I'm the only one who doesn't fear him."

"Why's that?"

"Anyone who wants something bad enough to come to him ends up regretting it. He gets his power from his bargains. I have everything I need or want. He has no power over me. But you've gone to him twice now. You're on the edge of the cliff, kid. One more step and it's over."

"What can I do?"

"You owe him twice. When he offers you a third favour, turn it around, offer him a favour instead. That's the only way out of the hole you've dug. The Sin Catcher's been taking you apart, kid. Pastor Akotun's charm held you together for a few days, but that was just a band-aid."

"I know," he said. He scratched his arm but it was still numb. "The Cuttlefish took something too, my hand. I'm worried that it's been hurt for good." He poked his numb left hand absentmindedly. "How'd I get away from that thing? The hole where my heart was started burning and it started to slip. I just went with it but I don't know what happened."

"The qliphoth is after you because of your disjunction. It's almost blind—like a human sees or like a dog smells, its primary sense is for emotion and since you've been broken by the Sin Catcher you've been leaking emotion. That makes you easy prey. Predators usually go after dying prey. You're going to have to fix yourself, and that starts and ends with a new name."

"But I have my old name!" He pulled the t-shirt out of his backpack. "See?"

"That's not a name, that's an impression of a name, like when you press a key against a bar of soap. No, you'll need to earn a new name. This is an opportunity. Not many people get to rename themselves. Names are powerful things."

"Can you tell me what I need to do?"

"You're going to have to work that out for yourself, kid." She leaned back in the pew. "Get to work."

The boy took a seat on the edge of the stage and did what he did best. He thought.

Finding containers for the water took some searching. The boy went from house to house—most abandoned, some showing signs of occupation—until he came across a blue water jug and a red gasoline container in a garage, three gallons each, unused and covered in dust. He found he could carry a jug in his left hand if he used his right to close its fingers around the handle. Somehow it had strength, but no feeling or movement.

The boy carried the jugs up the street, trying to find a spigot with running water, mostly finding them dry or rusted. As the boy came around from the backyard of a ruin of a house with a decrepit pickup truck in the drive he ran into a white-spotted mutt—the dog from the meatworks. He yelled and dropped the gas can.

The dog leapt back, tail between its legs—timid as he had never been before, now almost friendly.

"What are you doing here?" The dog watched the boy unsure if it should run or stay. "Well, if you want to follow I'm not going to stop you." When the boy bent down to pick up the gas can, he discovered a short length of blue nylon rope. He looked at the dog, grabbed the rope and stuffed it in his backpack.

From house to house, the dog followed and watched. When he stopped to check the taps on a house, the dog stopped a little closer each time. When the boy looked directly at the dog, it would turn away, but it couldn't hide the way it licked its chops and stared at the boy's backpack. The bag still held the last steak.

When the boy finally found a working tap, he filled both

jugs with as much as he could drag back to church and then reached inside his back pack. The dog stood up and began to shuffle its feet in anticipation. Discarding the packaging, the boy sat on the ground between the blue and red containers, holding the last steak in his hand. Cautiously, the dog walked forward, a few steps at a time, sniffing the meat tentatively before taking it from his hand. While the animal tore and gulped at its meal, the boy was able to pet its sticky, matted coat. He waited for the dog to finish eating before dragging the nearly full jugs back to the church. The dog followed.

By the time the boy made it back to the church, his arms burned and he could no longer simply carry the jugs. Instead he'd swing the containers forward, letting their weight carry him forward a few steps. When they fell to the ground, he'd step ahead, rest a bit and swing them ahead. He lurched up the hill to the church this way, the dog skipping around him.

The White Woman waited from the stage, watching the boy struggle with his load.

"You know, you could give me a hand with this."

"No." She crossed her ankles and tapped the stage with her heel. "This is your ritual. I'll have my part but this isn't it. If I helped at the wrong time, in the wrong way, it would ruin everything."

The boy dropped the water jugs and his backpack at the door. "Maybe you're just lazy."

"You'll never know for sure, will you?"

The boy dragged the containers, the blue, then the red, up to the baptismal. When he tried to lay down and rest on the stage the White Woman poked him in the ribs with her toe.

"Get up. You can rest when it's over."

"But I'm tired."

"Exhaustion is part of the process. If you're not tired, you're not trying." She looked at the dog, curled up behind the last pew. "What are you planning on doing with that?"

"Take him home and feed him. What else are you supposed to do with a dog?"

"That—" She slowly pointed. "—isn't a dog."

The boy shook his head. "Well, it ain't a cat."

"No, it isn't that either. You don't know, do you? Kid, your *dog* is a guardian spirit. Though to be fair, there's not much difference from where you're standing."

"Why was it guarding the meatworks? For who?"

"No one. That's just what it does. It finds things of value and it guards them. At the slaughterhouse, the border between the living and the dead is softer. That's what makes it magical, valuable. Guardians often take the shape of dogs.

"It would be good to bring him along," she continued. "The dog is mankind's companion, more than any other animal, even the horse."

"I ain't going to kill no dog."

"It isn't alive. Not like you know life. Death isn't what you think it is. If you do this, neither of you will be the beings you once were but neither of you will die. At least as you understand it."

The boy was looking at the dog, reluctantly. "I just wanted a friend."

"He'll be the best friend you ever had."

"He?" The dog rested its muzzle on its forelegs, listening. "So you're a boy, huh?"

"He used to be a boy. He always used to be a boy, but he was never a boy." The White Woman answered for the dog. "There isn't a word for it in this language."

The boy sniffed and rubbed his nose. "I'm starting to have second thoughts about this."

"Go ahead. Back out if you want to."

"Really? That'll be okay?"

"If you're asking if I'd be angry, I don't get angry."

"But will I be okay if I don't do this?"

"Not in the slightest. You'll go crazy and die."

"Then why'd you say it'd be okay for me to back out?" He wanted to shout.

"Because it is. It's all up to you. If you want to do nothing, then do nothing. The universe doesn't care."

"But I care." The boy jabbed a thumb at his chest.

"Then I suggest you get this show on the road because you don't have much time left and you still haven't figured out how this ritual's going to work."

"The hell I haven't!" He dragged the red and blue water bottles with him up to the stage, lifting them up one at a time before hopping up himself.

"So what's the plan?" Iku asked.

The boy kicked the bookcase out of the way and yanked at the pull ring for the baptismal. "I'm gonna make a name for myself, for reals." He reached in to the tub and pulled out all of the valuables, stacking them against the wall and out of harm's way. "I'll talk you through it," he assured her.

The White Woman was intrigued. "You're pretty sure of yourself. Just a second ago you were ready to quit."

"Yeah? That was a second ago. This is now."

"Just like I've been saying."

On the edge of the baptismal, he laid out the Shapeshifter's screwdriver, a bar of Ivory soap he had salvaged from the church's restroom, the stick of Prickly Pear Gum Iku had given him at the Cook County Coroner's Office and the blue nylon rope he'd taken from under the rusted pickup truck. He undressed in front of her, angry enough that he didn't care if anyone saw him naked. Tying the rope around his wrist, he stepped down into the empty pool, its coarse non-slip surface cold against his feet. The feeling kept him in the moment. He put the red stick of gum in his mouth. Expecting a foul, medicinal taste, Cinque was relieved that it tasted like watermelon.

Iku nodded, "Good timing on that."

"What if I'd chewed this when you gave it to me?"

"You'd of died."

He almost spit it out.

"And if you'd taken it in the meatworks it would have been worse than death. Spiritual change, kid, if it doesn't come from within it'll strike from without. That's all I'm going to say about that. What's next?"

The boy wondered about his choice of allies as he told her, "Pour the water."

The White Woman hefted the red container in her right hand and the blue in her left, pouring the water back and forth between them. Her bone-thin arms were deceptively strong.

"You have me playing the part of the angel?" She stopped mixing the water and held both over his head. "This isn't the first time." Slowly, she spilled water from both jugs on him, the streams merging in the air just over his head.

The water was too warm to be cool and too cool to be warm. The boy let it fall over him, seeping into his dry skin. Lifting his open mouth up to the stream, he felt the water run down his throat, washing him inside and out. As the gathering water rose up to his knees, he dipped the bar of soap into it and washed his body free of grime. After his mistreatment by the Fibs, and the labour of collecting the water, this felt like the best bath he'd ever taken. In fact, this was the first pleasant sensation he'd felt all day. The small pleasure left him lightheaded.

The dog had come up to investigate, keeping the baptismal between him and the White Woman. As she drained the last drops from both jugs, the boy finished cleaning himself. He'd even given his dreads a good rinsing.

He considered the soapy water around his legs. The water was filthy, but far cleaner than the dog. The boy coaxed the dog closer, but it backed out of reach and leaned forward just enough to sniff the boy's fingertips. The boy stepped out of the pool and was about to grab for the dog when the White Woman interrupted.

"Stop," she scolded. His foot slipped back in the water. "I'm not going to stand here while you chase a dog around the room, naked. And you!" The dog flinched and dropped his head and tail. "Stop playing around and get in the pool. You knew what you were getting into when you walked through that door."

Admonished, the dog slinked into the pool with the boy. The water was too deep and at first it struggled to hold his muzzle above the water. Eventually it found the lowest step with its forepaws and was able to stand comfortably. It waited patiently while the boy washed years of grime from its fur.

When both beast and boy were finally clean, the boy traced a spiral around the edge of the pool using the dirty water for ink, three times deep in a clockwise direction.

The water was a dark gray-brown with a thin film of black collecting on the top. His fingers stretched down while his neck stretched up as he tried to grip the plug without bringing his face into the water. He could barely touch the top with his index finger. His toes were unable to find a grip on its flat circular shape or the ring. All options exhausted, he resigned himself to taking the dive.

With a deep breath, eyes closed and nose plugged, the boy went under the water. His fingers touched bottom just as his dreads disappeared below the surface. Fingers splayed, he easily found the plug's top and tugged.

The weight of the water was still too much. The boy emerged again, took a breath and grabbed the screwdriver. Going under again, he found the rubber edge and pried it free. The plug came off, floated between his fingers for a brief instant before the bottom of the pool disappeared.

The current gripped the boy and spun him clockwise. His eyes burned in the soapy, filthy water. It filled his mouth with a disgusting combination of organic and artificial flavours. The water quickly lost the frothy texture of bubbles against his skin. Only the tug of the current on his hair and eyelashes told him he was still spinning.

He had swallowed his gum, it still hadn't killed him so he knew he must be doing something right.

24

SOMETHING RIGHT

Feet kicked and hands pulled at the water until he wedged one of them into a thick layer of muck, soft on its surface but harder as he dug deeper. Desperate for air, he jammed his fingers into the sticky substance, climbing up a wall of the stuff. Fingers grabbing with one hand, screwdriver stabbing with the other, he pulled himself up with his good hand. His lungs burned as he ascended. He was full of fear—afraid of drowning and afraid of what might be down in the warm and cloudy water with him. When he felt something slide across his back he pushed off from the mushy wall. Instead of moving back into the water his head broke the surface and came splashing back down. He recognized the feel of air on his face too late and half-inhaled a lungful of salty water instead.

Choking and coughing, he awkwardly reoriented himself, pulling up on shaky hands and knees. The gray, cloudy water poured out of his nose and mouth while he gasped between purges.

Once his lungs settled down, he looked around. He stood in a foot of water over a bed of soft, gray clay. The water came up to his knees and the clay came up to his ankles. Ambient light leaked in from somewhere like an overcast night by the city. Just black sky, cloudy salt water and gray clay in all directions. He got to work.

He shoved the dead hand into the clay like a spade. Reaching as deep as he could the nameless boy pulled up handfuls of clay, piling them in a mound until it rose above the water's surface with plenty to spare. It felt like it took hours but time didn't seem to matter. Caught up in his labour, he excavated a spiral-shaped trench under the water with the mound at its center.

Using the base of the pile as his stage he sculpted a boy lying prone on the table, tall as the nameless boy and just as skinny, but bald. The nameless boy couldn't picture the face the clay boy was supposed to have. Instead he sculpted how he felt the clay boy's face should look, using his hands to mould the nose, mouth and cheekbones and using the screwdriver tip to carve out the nostrils, lines of the eyes and lip lines, until the sculpture felt right.

The handle's other end was flattened, like someone had used a hammer on it, and he wondered if using it like a chisel would create a different kind of magic.

Finally, he used one end of the tip to carefully write the clay boy's name across his forehead. It was exhausting work and when it was finished he sat back in the water for a moment, made circles with his writing hand to work the stiffness out. He waited for the clay boy to stand, sit, shrug—anything. He waited for a long, long time.

The nameless boy decided something more was required. He inhaled deep. Like the Fool, like the Farmer, like the Soldier, he made the act from himself, held it as long as he could, warming the air in his lungs with his heat before he put his lips to the lips of the clay boy and blew. He blew his air into that clay body until a clay hand pushed the nameless boy away.

"That's enough," said the clay boy as he wiped his mouth with the back of his wrist.

The nameless boy stood back and watched his creation rise, in awe of what he'd just done and afraid of what was to come next. The clay boy's feet splashed in the water. He cast a bored look around at the distant horizon, or at least where the gray of the water blended into the black of the sky, and when he noticed his maker watching he glared back.

"What are you looking at?"

The nameless boy straightened up. "I think we both know that."

The clay boy chuckled. "And what am I looking at? What's his name? Can you tell me that?"

"No, I can't." They were only a few feet away but without walls to echo their words were faint and hard to hear.

"That's right, you can't. You gave up your name just to get offa that chain." He smirked and shook his head in pity.

"And that's why I'm here."

"Is it now?" asked the clay boy, sensing a challenge. "Well, here you are and you still ain't got no name. You all a mess and you still don't know jack. Seems to me you came all this way for nuthin'."

The dog from the meatworks barked, interrupting them.

The nameless boy grinned, happy to have a familiar face on his side. "Hey bo—!"

The clay boy interrupted, "I see you brought my dog."

"How you figure he's your dog?" The nameless boy shouted, hoping that the clay boy thought he was shouting to be heard in this echoless place and not out of sudden anger.

"What do you wanna do? Go to opposite sides of the room and both of us call to him? He mine 'cause he'd be better off with me. You'd just let him run wild, like Jaspers and his pets. Letting them run wild in his head, like too many opinions. He'd be owning you, not the other way around."

"This dog's gonna help me fix myself."

"Is that it then? All about you? Then that's another reason you shouldn't have it and I should. I don't need to be fixed, I'm whole."

While the boys argued, the dog stood in the water a fair distance off looking back and forth at the two like it couldn't tell the difference.

The clay boy folded his arms. "In fact, you been losing pieces all week, still haven't figured out what you're going to do about your missing orange heart of . . . courage." He smirked again. "Was that it? You got your fate stolen, lost your name and the Cuttlefish just took another bite outta you. How many parts do you think you can lose before the rest of you burns up and burns out?"

"My losin' days are done. I'm like a starfish, cut me up and I'll just grow it back."

"Like a starfish? Or a worm?"

"I ain't a worm today, I'll tell you that!" The nameless boy folded the fingers of the dead hand into a fist and charged the boy of clay, punching him twice in the gut.

If the clay boy felt anything he didn't show it. "You sure you wanna go down this road, little boy? Beatin' me down won't be easy."

"If it was easy—" he punched the clay boy in his jaw, the handle of the screwdriver lending its mass, "—it wouldn't—" two more punches in the face, "—be worth doing."

The nameless boy brought his knee up into his opponent's midsection, knocking the clay boy down into the water. His hands had given the clay boy his face but his fists couldn't take it away.

"Easy things are worthless things, remember?"

The clay boy slowly rose. The rough gray surface of his face evoked a movie commando, camouflaged with mud coming out of the water for an ambush, a predatory smile lingering. "What's this going to prove?"

"I ain't out to prove anything," the nameless boy sneered.

"That's right. You came here for a new name. But then you gave it to me."

"And now I'm going to take it back. Not because that's the right way to go, but because it's the hard way to go, because I gotta earn it."

While he spoke, the clay boy got back on his feet. "You know, the Shapeshifter does this kinda thing all the time. And he did it easy." He hit the nameless boy in the sternum with his clay fist, slow but heavy. The nameless boy stepped back with it, softening the blow. The dog barked and jumped in agitation.

"That's because he's got nothing inside. He's as empty as that box he was carrying." The nameless boy brought the screwdriver point up between them. "But he did have this!"

He feinted a stab at the boy of clay. The clay boy had let the nameless boy punch and kick him without a care but he stayed out of the screwdriver's way.

"Yeah, you'll go far following his lead." The clay boy kept his eyes on the screwdriver's tip while he taunted. "What are you gonna do when he comes back for his toy?"

"He ain't coming back, the Cuttlefish will take care of him. 'Sides, if he ever did know that this screwdriver was magic he's forgot after rebuilding himself so much."

"And if you can't figure it out?"

"Then this still makes a real good shiv!" The nameless boy lunged, stabbing the clay boy where his heart should be. The nameless boy left the screwdriver stuck in the clay boy up to the handle. The clay boy grimaced in anticipation, clay fingers curled and then . . . and then nothing happened.

The clay boy released his anticipation of pain as laughter. "You . . . you just can't put it all together, can you? You got all the tools but you don't know how to use them." He left the screwdriver stuck in his chest. "And that's been your problem all along—you and your ignorance."

"That's another reason why I'm here," said the nameless boy. "Another thing I'm gonna change."

"What makes you think you can change anything?"

"The White Woman, Iku, that's why she's here, to facilitate."

The clay boy shook his head. "Oh, really? You believe her because . . . ? Because she told you? Is that it? Wasn't she there at the beginning? At the morgue and at the church, right? Where else do you think she might have been? I'll tell you where, because you haven't figured it out and you never will. She was the one that dropped that little ritual into your head, the one that called up the Sin Catcher. She handed you over to him. Does that sound like someone you can trust?

"You trust everyone. You believe everyone. You believed the Sin Catcher and his Fibs when they said you couldn't leave the meatworks. What lies have the African and his Pimp God told you?" The clay boy shook his head and sneered. "I ain't tellin'."

"And I ain't carin'. That'll be for another day. I got today's problems today, but before that I gotta take care of the problem right in front of me."

"Go ahead then, punk, take care of me!"

The nameless boy grabbed the screwdriver handle and gave it a full twist to the left. The clay boy fell apart. Elbows, knees and knuckles—every joint separated. The blocks of clay that had been his body fell in a pile at the nameless boy's feet. He picked up the clay boy's head and told it, "Lefty loosy, righty tighty. In case you didn't know.

"And that's not all I know. I know what the frozen, orange heart is too. It's not courage, it's terror. Because I'd never been able to make it through this last week without any courage. Because when I focused on the heat in my chest, my missing emotion, the Cuttlefish couldn't see me. And like the Cuttlefish, it's easier for the Sin Catcher to pull and grab at negative emotions. I can live without the Orange Heart of Terror, once I find something better to fix me."

He gave the dog a smile. "That's where you come in, boy." The dog was sniffing at the pile of parts that were the boy of clay.

Lips of clay whispered, "You're still a fool."

"I know." The nameless boy wiped away at the clay head's temple. Under the surface he discovered a flat-tip screw and a matching one on the other temple. He inserted the screwdriver and began to twist. "I'll be a fool for a good long time. Juju's easy—look how much I've learned in a week!—but learnin' people, that's hard, but you know me . . . I love to learn."

The screws were carved out of wood. He held them in the webbing of his thumbs and pushed his fingers into the clay again. Behind the temples he found a smooth edge of hardened leather. Careful to leave the name he'd written across the forehead unsmeared, he followed the hard leather edge over the forehead, down past the ears and along the line of the jaw. Free from the clay, the stiff gray mask popped off in his hands.

With his dying breath the boy of clay whispered, "I would . . . have been . . . a better you . . . than you . . . ever will . . ."

The nameless boy shrugged. "Maybe, but you're not me. You can't be me, and you can't define me. Nobody can do that but me, not anymore. You knew that all along."

With that, the nameless boy put the mask up to the front of his head and screwed it into his temples with the screwdriver, righty tighty.

The named boy opened his eyes and licked his lips. They tasted of salt and clay. He found the loose screws in his joints, just under the surface of the skin and with the screwdriver he tightened them up. The aches and pains that had dragged at him since the Sin Catcher took him apart disappeared.

"One last thing." He unwrapped the blue rope from his wrist and tied it into a collar for the dog's neck.

"I don't expect a lot of terror out of you. I think that this'll work out just fine."

Boy and dog smiled at each other in new understanding. He felt the fingers of his left hand unfold. The dog took the hand in its mouth and pulled.

25

NEW UNDERSTANDING

The dog pulled the boy by his hand, through the water and then out of the water, in a firm but gentle grip. The boy reached for the steps and crawled out of the baptismal. He spun around on his belly and leaned over the pool. Clear water poured out of his mouth and into the dirty water below while the dog licked at his face. He vomited water between warm, wet lips until there was no more to give.

Lungs finally empty of water, he took a deep breath, stood and wiped his mouth with the back of his wrist. The boy put a hand to his chest and felt his heart beat for the first time in days. He smiled.

"Tell me you were down there for more than a haircut," the White Woman said. He put a hand to his scalp, confirming his hair was gone. It was bare, like the boy of clay's had been.

"We're not done yet—" she said.

"—the dog still needs a name," the boy interrupted. If this bothered the White Woman, she didn't let it show.

He kneeled and petted his new companion who wagged

his black and white tail appreciatively. "You, boy, I'm going to name you 'Night'."

"Is that with an 'N' or with a 'K'?" the White Woman asked.

"Huh . . . I was thinking with an 'N' but now that you mention it, I think I'll name him 'Knight' with a 'K' instead. How does that sound to you, Knight?"

The dog barked once, as close to an affirmative as the boy expected. "I'll get you a dog tag as soon as I can, okay, Knight?"

"And you?" the White Woman asked. "What's your name?"

The boy looked up at the White Woman. "I think I'll keep that to myself. But you can call me Cinque."

"You're learning." She turned abruptly, picked up her black messenger bag, the one with the white lily embroidered on the flap. She hooked it over a bony shoulder and marched for the door.

"Where are you going?"

She said without turning, "I've done my part here."

"What am I supposed to do now?"

"Whatever you want to."

Cinque nodded thoughtfully. He dried, got dressed and considered how he was going to take care of his problems.

"Knight, how about we go try some things out?"

"Cinque?" As Imani opened her door and said his name the boy she called Cinque knew things were different. She pronounced the name with its one proper syllable—"Sink". Confusion was an expression he'd never seen her wear before. "You cut your dreads?"

"They'll grow back. You busy?"

She squirmed, partially hiding behind the door.

"I guess not."

"Wanna come to the hospital with me?" Cinque nodded out to the street.

"The hospital that you say be haunted?"

"Yeah. I'm-a do an experiment."

"I . . . I guess." She looked around outside before stepping out. She didn't acknowledge Knight standing at Cinque's side, wagging his tail. It wasn't that she didn't see the dog, Cinque realized. She couldn't see him.

As they walked together it felt as if something was missing, the tension that had always been between them.

She stopped. "Your hair's all gone! What up wit' you?"

Knight barked at her, but Cinque purposely walked a few more steps before half-turning back.

"Why does it matter?"

Imani tightened up her eyes and her attitude and pretended that she didn't care anymore, but Cinque guessed that maybe she did. He kept walking up to Memorial Hospital and Imani followed.

Cinque didn't wait by the parking lot. He didn't hide behind an unsuspecting group of visitors. This time, he walked right up to the security office and found Gus reading the sports page.

"Hello, Gus."

The security guard looked up from his newspaper and blinked twice.

"I need to ask you a favour. I need to get back to that store room. I think I got a good shot at clearing it out, sending Michael Bentley's ghost on to whatever's waiting for him next. And if I don't . . . well . . . you know I ain't here to steal so I can't say you'll be out much of anything."

Gus twisted his mouth, considering for a moment before he nodded slowly. "You go on then. I'll be back there in fifteen minutes. Be gone by then."

Cinque smiled and walked back to where Imani was waiting out of sight. "I got fifteen minutes."

"Is that gonna be enough time?"

"If I can't fix this in fifteen minutes then I can't fix it at all." He led Imani through the halls back up to that last door, the last barrier between ghost and boy. Knight ran forward to sniff at the crack under the door. Imani stopped at the last intersection, reluctant to step out of the light and into the shadowed hallway. Cinque smiled back at her. "That's okay. You wait here."

"What you gonna do in there?"

"Some Juju." As he pushed through the door darkness and the smell of flowers enveloped Cinque. Knight ran ahead into the room. Cinque drew the screwdriver and waited for the sobbing to start.

"Is he here?" the ghost of the boy whimpered.

Cinque turned to face the door. "Not yet he ain't."

"He's here to kill me."

Knight padded around in the dark, ignoring the ghost of the boy.

"I know," Cinque answered.

The ghost sounded surprised. "You do? How you know that?"

"'Cause that's what he always does, every night since the first."

"The first what? What are you talking about, man?"

"Why you asking?" Cinque asked. "You ain't gonna listen to anything I say anyway."

"He killed—"

"Your family, I know, it's ancient history. I'm here to help you, Michael, I really am. But I'm also here to help myself and you and all your crying is distracting."

"He killed—"

"The Cloudy Man, I know all about him." Cinque locked eyes with the ghost. "If I tell you what you don't wanna hear, if I tell you he was your father, will that do it? Will that bring him here?"

The door that lay over the door, the door of gray light, pushed open, revealing the man with a cloud for a head and a hammer in his hand.

"I guess so. Well, here we go." Cinque pushed down his fear, imagining hands that reached into him, scooped it all up and pressed it into a little harmless ball and kept it down and out of his way.

Knight barked at the man with the hammer.

"Knight. Stay." He ordered. "This one's for me."

Behind him, Michael started screaming and crying. Cinque put it out of his head. Sympathy wasn't what the ghost needed right now. The Cloudy Man stepped slowly forward and the phantom door swung closed behind him. When the Cloudy Man was close enough, Cinque stabbed forward with the screwdriver, penetrating the spectre's chest, just below the sternum. It sounded and felt like there was nothing there, but the Cloudy Man was pinned, arms and legs flailed, mindlessly trying to move forward, towards his prey, the ghost of the boy. What interested Cinque was what he didn't do. He didn't attack Cinque or try to free himself. He just twisted around the screwdriver's point in his single-minded drive to get to Michael's ghost.

Cinque flicked the Cloudy Man off the screwdriver like a rotten piece of fruit. He hit the wall, staggered back to his feet and resumed stalking Michael's trembling ghost as if Cinque wasn't there.

"He's like a robot, ain't he?" Cinque asked Michael, but Michael was too terrified to answer.

"I feel stupid for being scared of him. Not no more though!" Cinque lunged at the Cloudy Man's back, stabbing with the screwdriver and twisting it to the left. Again, the screwdriver went in easy. It met some resistance when he turned it, like it was stuck in peanut butter. Half a turn and the Cloudy Man disintegrated before his eyes.

Then Michael Bentley surprised Cinque—he stood up. Mouth hung open in disbelief, he slowly approached Cinque. Knight huffed in warning.

"What . . . what just happened?"

"I took apart the Cloudy Man. It wasn't that hard, you didn't build him very well. But I guess he did the job."

"You say I . . . built . . . him? Why did I do that?"

"To keep from facing the truth, I guess. It doesn't matter now that it's gone. Now it's your turn."

Michael's fearful eyes stared at the screwdriver in Cinque's hand.

"Heh. No, don't worry. You'll go all peaceful-like. By Egungun I command you."

"What is—"

"By Egungun I command you."

"Who is—?"

"By Egungun I command you. Rest, Michael Bentley, rest in peace."

The ghost that had spent thirty years in this room torturing itself rather than face the truth faded in silver light.

Knight rubbed up against Cinque's leg and the boy reached down to scratch his dog behind its ears. "Maybe I do know what I'm doing, huh, boy?"

Outside and down the hall Cinque noticed Imani clutching herself and trying to look anywhere but in the direction of the haunted room. He couldn't resist walking up to her in her blind spot and whispering, "Boo." He smiled when she jumped. "What?"

She punched him in the arm. "What happened?"

Cinque led her back out the way they came. "What I said. I fixed the ghost problem. It was two ghost problems actually."

"You send the ghosts to heaven then?"

"I don't know, maybe. If there is a Heaven I haven't seen it yet. Someone told me there's a Hell. Someone else told me there's a Heaven. But both of them was liars."

They passed by Gus's office, Cinque held out his fist in acknowledgement toward the man. Gus responded in kind, but slowly, unsure.

"Well this was just target practice. I gotta bigger fish to fry, and then a bigger fish after that. But that's life, isn't it? One damn fish after another."

Imani ignored him and said, "Do that mean you did what you came to do?"

Cinque thought on that for a brief moment and nodded with a confident smile, "Yeah. I'd say the experiment was a success. What do you think?"

"What do I think? I don't know what to think."

"You ain't gonna put me in my place like you used to do?"

She looked down and kicked at the ground in front of her. Cinque couldn't be sure but it seemed to him that she might even have been a little ashamed of being called out like that. He smiled. "Then I'd say the experiment was definitely a success."

"Stop it, Cinque." She mumbled.

"Stop it? Stop what?"

"Stop doin' what you're doin'!" He thought she was making a joke but her eyes snapped up full of fear and fire. "I can't tell if you're messin' with me or you're just crazy. And I don't want you to be crazy so if you ain't then stop it!"

"I wish I could. But I gotta be crazy, it's a crazy world I live in."

She turned and ran home. Cinque wanted to run after her, but he still had more work to do.

Cinque decided on the abandoned auto shop on Randsburg Avenue: a boxy, cinderblock shell with two garage doors, blue pedestrian doors and orange, broken, boarded-up windows. Boxes and trash littered the floor. Weeds pressed up on all sides. The weather-worn sign on the ground proclaimed the place to have once been Boreas Gas and Fixit.

A cold wind pulled down from the north. He pulled up one of the garage doors and went inside to prepare.

The fox-faced Fib led his diminished posse up Randsburg Avenue. Puzzleman and George Washington walked with him. The group headed straight for Boreas Gas and Fixit, surrounding the building. George Washington licked his lips as he crept around the left. Puzzleman staggered slowly around the right, while the fox-faced Fib watched the garage door that Cinque had left open.

George Washington and Puzzleman circled back around to the front after finding all the other doors locked. Without a word, the fox-faced Fib nodded to the one way in, the three foot gap of the open garage door and waited for the others to go first.

They picked through the mess inside, hoping to catch the boy by surprise. It was a small shop, and if the kid was in here, he was under something. George Washington stalked up on a heavy wooden crate in the middle of the room. Built to ship a transmission, it was long and wide, about the size of a coffin for a fourteen year old boy. The other Fibs watched, prepared to pounce, but when George Washington threw open the lid, the only thing inside was packing foam. The masked Fib dove in anyway. He dug and tore at the insides with his claws, shredded yellow foam pieces flew up and out like a fake snow machine. Long after the rest of the Fibs came to the same conclusion, George Washington jumped out of the box, yellow bits of foam were stuck all his over yellow robe. It shouted, "Nothing!"

"All right," the fox-faced Fib shouted. "We know you're in here and you know we're in here and we all know you're busted. I'm sick of this hide-n-seek, so come on out while I still have it in me to be a gentleman about this!"

"There's no way out 'cept our way," George Washington hissed.

Puzzleman helpfully pointed toward the door they'd just come through, still open behind the fox-faced Fib.

Their leader growled at Puzzleman, slammed the garage door down and barked back at the soggy Fib. "Not no more there's not!"

The other Fibs stared his way.

"What? Get back to business. Let's turn this place over!" They stayed frozen, transfixed on something behind him.

The fox-faced Fib turned to face the closed garage door. Someone had drawn a life sized stop sign across the door in thick, black ink.

"Damn," he whispered.

He turned and ran to the boxes piled against the back wall and knocked them down, uncovering another door with another drawing of a stop sign.

Puzzleman found another stack along his wall, and another door, and another illustrated stop sign.

"What do we do?" asked George Washington. "What happens if we open a door?"

Fox Face glared at him, "You wanna know? Go ahead and find out." But none of the Fibs moved a foot or finger.

Cinque had been watching the Fibs from the roof, through the skylight. He had seen enough. They were right where he wanted them. He dropped an old car battery through the skylight's aged glass, showering the room in bits of broken glass. The Fibs ran for cover, under desks and among the piles of trash, hiding from further assault from above but the only thing that came down from the roof was the boy's laughter.

The fox-faced Fib looked up from under cover. The boy who was supposed to be hiding *in* the garage had been hiding *on* the garage. The Fib leader was so angry he couldn't form human curses, he could only bark in rage up at the boy. Something barked back at him from up on the roof, a bigger bark, a bigger canid. He shut his muzzle out of reflex and punched himself in the face out of shame for it. He took a breath and forced the words out. "You think you're so clever."

"Naw," Cinque smiled wide. "I ain't all that clever. Y'alls just stupid."

George Washington jumped on top of the edge of the long crate and tried to jump again up to the broken window's frame. "We'll show you stupid when we get a hold of you, you little butt-snort! We ain't gonna be trapped forever, you know!"

Cinque feigned confusion, "Trapped? No no no, little figment. You're not trapped, you're bait."

He spit into a rag and tossed it down onto the garage floor. The fox-faced Fib snatched up the rag, a worn light blue t-shirt with "Cinque Joseph Williams" written across it in magic marker.

Cinque and Knight sat on the garage roof and waited, ignoring the shouts of the Fibs until The Cuttlefish came. Flaring red, it raced through the trees on the other side of the road, faster than ever, its colour more vibrant, it must have found some dark, powerful emotion at the heart of the Shapeshifter. It rushed the garage and swept along the front of the building, tasting with its many tongues.

". . . switchblade on me."

"I've spent my life holding in—"

"Time's up! Sucker."

"—can't love this!"

"You didn't draw that."

The more it licked around the windows and doors the more it wanted in. Gripping at one of the boarded windows with some of its arms, the soft flesh oozing in between board and frame, it pushed against the wall with the rest of its limbs. Nails creaked, wood groaned. The creature easily popped the window open.

Cinque heard the screaming of the Fibs down below. He

hadn't expected this—real terror. Morbid curiosity pulled him to the edge of the broken skylight just in time to see the Cuttlefish grab Puzzleman, hold the Fib up off the ground and twist. The brown fluid that kept it soggy sprayed from the little monster in all directions.

The fox-faced Fib tried to run past the Cuttlefish while it was busy killing his comrade, but the qliphoth slapped him in the face with a free tentacle, pushing him into the ground. The fox-like skull cracked against the concrete floor and it lay still in shock until the tentacle grabbed him by the face and pressed. The Fib clawed at the Cuttlefish's limb as it smothered him.

George Washington went on the attack, climbing up something out of Cinque's view and jumping onto the long upper side of the Cuttlefish's body, little clawed hands gripped the ridge between body and head. The Cuttlefish's eyes were as big as the Fib's mask and he slid down face-to-eye with it and bit into the w-shaped pupil.

Now it was the Cuttlefish's turn to scream, a cacophony of voices, from every mouth on every limb. The tentacle that had been slowly smothering the fox-faced Fib jerked the Fib up and smashed it down, crushing its skull. What was left of Puzzleman was thrown aside as arms and tentacles whipped up, grasping at the tenacious Fib attacking it.

George Washington lost his mask—the Fib had no head above its mouth, his skull just tapering to a point where its nose should have been. The Cuttlefish rolled. The Fib's grip on the body ridge and on the eye weren't enough of a hold; it fell to the floor, limbs spread eagle as it hit the ground and the Cuttlefish tore into it from above.

Cinque pulled back from the edge of the window, trying to keep quiet, scared that the sound of his racing heart and lungs would give him away.

The voices of the Cuttlefish took a long time to fade to whimpers and then to silence. Cinque stood on the street in front of the garage. Inside it was dark in spite of the broken skylight. He ordered Knight to heel and took a few experimental steps away. The dog followed. Maybe the spirit-in-the-shape-of-a-dog had been taught these commands by a previous owner, or they'd been imposed on the creature when he'd recast it as his pet, but he was grateful for it.

Climbing through the window frame, his mismatched sneakers stepped on something soft and wet, a lump of soggy cardboard pieces. The remains of Puzzleman were scattered all over the room. As Cinque's eyes adjusted to the dark, the only sign of the fox-faced Fib was a red stain on the floor that trailed behind the transmission crate. The bloated form of the Cuttlefish lay on the other side, flat and sagging on the ground like a plastic bag half-filled with rain water, its skin now a spotted pattern of dull purple and black.

Cinque felt like he should be cautious, that the Cuttlefish might lurch out and grab him again, but the monster wasn't intimidating anymore—it looked pathetic. It didn't move when Knight ran up and sniffed at it. The mouths along its limb arms and tentacles gasped weakly at the air or, if they were close enough, licked at the pools of brown liquid it had wrung out of Puzzleman.

The trail of blood that started where the fox-faced Fib died led to the Cuttlefish's main mouth which futilely tried to swallow the remains of George Washington. The Fib's skinny gray legs stuck lifelessly out from a maw that couldn't get past his waist.

The creature looked the way Cinque felt on Thanksgiving afternoon. He stepped up, next to Knight. Both of them were easily within grabbing range but the arms lay limp. Poisoned, engorged—or both—the qliphoth wasn't in an eating mood. It was helpless before him.

Cinque lifted the transmission crate by its rope handle, moved it to the side, and retrieved the picture of Willy T and his girl from where he'd hidden it.

Then, he drew the screwdriver from his hoodie pocket, the way a butcher draws his knife, and went to work on the Cuttlefish. He pinned the monster, straddling it with his legs and grabbed one of the limp arms. Some of its mouths moaned and whined, complaining sounds without words as he lifted it back and stabbed into the base of the arm with the screwdriver. Tough, rubbery flesh gave way to the metal tip. The creature cried and writhed weakly while the boy patiently explored deep inside its body, through the soft mushy stuff until he found something small and hard. With some tapping and scrapping he found the slit. The screwdriver slipped right into it and the boy twisted.

Turning the screwdriver was like turning a rusty screw in a metal door. Cinque had to lean back and put his legs into it before the screw would even budge. He switched hands—one holding, one turning—to keep going. When he finally came to the end of the threads he inspected the connection. Instead of the wooden screws of the clay boy's mask, or the air screw of the Cloudy Man, screws of bone held the Cuttlefish together. Yellow and pocked with age, Cinque knew it was ancient, possibly older than the world.

In time he reduced the Cuttlefish to a pile of flabby, lifeless limbs. One of the eyes had been torn open by George Washington, but the other he popped out of its socket using the screwdriver as a lever. He stuffed the sphere with its unseeing, w-shaped pupil into his hoodie pocket.

Cinque smelled flowers just as Knight started barking.

"Weeee—oooo! You mess all these niggas up yo' self?" Willy

T was leaning against the open window frame, arms crossed, smile on his face, a nervous glace at Knight.

"Willy." Cinque was sad to see his friend. He knew how this was going to play out. "Knight! Quiet!"

He ordered the dog and it pulled back to stand by his side. Knight stopped barking, but it kept a suspicious eye on the ghost.

"Guess you done checking in on your girl then?"

"I ain't never done checkin' in on my girl, boy, you know that. But I figured I could spare some time to check in on you, too." He looked at the pile of limbs that used to be the Cuttlefish. "But it looks like you don't be needin' no checkin' in! Is that—was that what I think it was?"

"Yep." Cinque looked down at the pile and smiled. "One less problem I got."

"And that be the dog that ran you offa the hill?"

"That's two less problems I got." Cinque gave a confident smirk. "I been busy while you been lounging around at home, but I can't say it's been easy. If I could I'd go back so I never had to do any of this."

"See, none o' this would a happened if you'd just forgot all about your pops like I said you should." Cinque nodded agreement, though he didn't remember Willy ever saying anything like that.

"So whatcha gonna do now then?"

"I'm going wrap things up with the Sin Catcher."

"Think you can?"

"I just killed a spirit that was older than the earth itself." He pointed at the parts of the Cuttlefish. "Yeah, I think I can. Besides, at this point do I have a choice?"

"Guess you don't. Whatcha got to work with?"

Cinque emptied the backpack, setting the magic marker and bottle of whiskey on the ground. Willy was disappointed.

"Why you gotta be the only nigga without a gun?"

Cinque rolled his eyes.

"You just gonna walk in like this then?"

"I'm not going in alone," Cinque said. Knight let out a short woof. "And what are you going do? Watch? You're not going help me? We were supposed to be crew."

Willy reached down, his hand passing through the ground. "What am I gonna do? Spook 'em? Spook a bunch a monsters? Maybe I can walk along with 'em an' wave my arms, if that'll help."

"Then what do you think I should do?"

"You got a bottle, empty it. Get blasted. An' maybe you'll wake up back on Auntie Em's farm an all this bad dream'll be gone."

"That's all you got? Getting drunk? Is that going to solve my problems?"

"It's always worked fo' me! Ha!"

"There's got to be something better than that."

Cinque stuffed the bottle back in his backpack. Willy pointed at the remains of George Washington and Puzzleman. "How'd you mess up all o' them?"

"I didn't do anything to them. I locked them down with this." The boy held up the sharpie. "I just wrote something on the inside of the doors that kept them from going through."

Willy was shocked. "Wa—? What kind of jack was that? Magic?"

"It wasn't any kind of magic unless you mean magic marker. They didn't know any better and that did the trick." He looked at the pen in his hand. "Maybe that's what magic is all about." He glanced back at the ghost. "Does magic scare you?"

Willy straightened up, and the nervous look that crept up while Cinque spoke of magic fell from his face. "Naw, naw, man. I was just, I was just wonderin'. Jus' tryin' to figure out what's goin' on around here, that's all."

Cinque put the sharpie, the bottle and his other possessions back in his backpack and zipped it up. "Let's go."

They didn't say much as they walked. At least Cinque didn't say much. Willy tried to get a conversation started time and again but when he did the boy never said more than an occasional grunt. They stopped at the road up to the meatworks. Cinque stood and stared up the hill until Willy tried talking to him again.

"So whatcha got in mind, boy?"

"I'm going to walk up that hill, into the meatworks and put an end to all this."

"Keep it simple, huh? What about all them monsters they got up there?"

"Knight and I will take care of them."

The dog barked again at Willy T, either in agreement with Cinque or maybe the ghost had gotten too close for the dog's liking. Willy scowled.

"You think you're that bad, huh?" Willy laughed. "Didn't they kick yo' ass when you first come here?"

"That was then. This is now."

"Yeah, heh, all o' one day, I guess I missed the part where you hooked up with them ninjas, learned their secret ways." Willy kicked the dirt road by his feet. "You want some advice, boy?"

Cinque still stared up the hill. "Whatever."

"If you ain't gonna drink that whole bottle of booze to let it take you away from all of this jack, at least drink half of it. If'n you need to pound some motha fucka's it'll help. I kicked many an ass with that extra drunk-strength that I never woulda if I'd a been sober."

Cinque pulled out the bottle and let the backpack fall to the ground. He stared at the label—Four Houses American Straight Whiskey—and considered the bottle with suspicion. "What's in it for you if I drink this, Willy?"

At first the ghost said nothing. The question hung in the

air. Nobody moved until Cinque shot Willy a look, a look that said he wasn't trusted. That started the ghost to talking, "Wha—whatchu mean?"

"You've been trying to get me to drink this since you found me. Why? What's in it for you, Willy?" At his feet, Knight growled and barked at the ghost. "And why'd you come find me anyway? Our deal been done. You're off the hook."

Willy relaxed a little at that. "Come on now, Cinque. You know you still got that picture of me in your pocket. I'm kinda attached to it and . . . I like you, kid—"

"The picture?" His free hand pulled the picture out of his pocket. "This picture right here?"

"Yeah, you know the one—"

"The picture of you and your girl?"

"Yeah—"

"Funny thing about that picture, whenever I had it with me, the Fibs were on me at every turn. If I was running across town they were there. If I went back home they were there. If I was in a run-down old gas station that I'd never been to before, never been in my whole life, they knew I was there. Why you think that is, Willy?"

Willy just looked back at him, and Cinque could tell he was trying to think of something to say. He drew the screwdriver out of his pocket and pinned the ghost to a telephone pole.

"By Egungun I command you be truthful."

"Wha—?"

"By Egungun I command you be truthful."

Eyes wide in fear, Willy tried to pull away but the screwdriver had him stuck.

"By Egungun I command you be truthful." Knight bristled and looked ready to tear into Willy. Cinque let the ghost go and he fell to the ground.

"Please," he begged, shivering.

"Why? Why did you come back?"

The ghost held his hands up, protecting and pleading. "Because I can't!"

"Can't what?"

"I can't touch her!" Willy whimpered something, his arms covering his face from the truth.

"And you made a deal with the Sin Catcher against me? What's he got that you want?"

"He said he was goin' to use you to get back at your pops, take over your pops' life and then he'd bring my girl back to me."

"How?"

"He'll kill her, capture her ghost and give her to me. We'd be together forever."

Cinque felt weak in the knees. Willy was going to have his girl killed? The girl he claimed to love? The man Cinque thought was his friend? "And that's love to you? You set me up. . . . How long have you been in on this?"

"From . . ." Willy's voice was forced, like he was trying to keep the words in. "From the start."

As he twisted the cap off the bottle of Four Houses' whiskey with his free hand, Cinque shook his head.

"Willy, you been lying to me all along. You been lying to yourself even longer. She don't want you, never has. Now your lying days are done."

"Whatcha gonna do to me?" Willy asked through his fingers.

Cinque easily pinned him to the ground with the screwdriver and poured the bottle down the ghost's throat. "Willy Thompson. I'm going to make you something you've never been. Useful." The ghost struggled but his ethereal body had no strength. When the bottle was empty Cinque kept it in Willy's mouth until he was sure the ghost would keep the whiskey down.

"The liquor was supposed to soften me up, right? Maybe you were supposed to soften me up? Possess me? I read about that in my pa's book. That gave me an idea."

When Willy's eyes lost their focus and his flailing limbs lost their direction, Cinque let go. Willy twisted around on the ground, stupefied. His eyes spun dumbly around.

Cinque retrieved the photo from where he'd dropped it in the scuffle and his calculator from his pocket. He folded up the picture of Willy and his girl and stuffed it inside with the batteries, holding them together with his thumb. He pushed the combination into the ghost's chest and made the act from himself.

Like water down the drain, Willy T's spiritual form spiralled into the battery compartment with the picture. Some of Willy's substance wasn't pulled into the grou-grou. It dropped to the ground in thin black fibres: white man's hair. Willy had done a deal with the Sin Catcher, maybe more than that.

If Sin Catcher's magic had been holding Willy together maybe that's why he had it together more than the other ghosts, Cinque thought. Maybe Willy's spirit was supposed to go on, and the Sin Catcher had tied it down. Maybe the Sin Catcher had killed him in the first place. It didn't matter anymore. Willy T wasn't working for Kelly Lee any more. *From now on he'll be working for me.*

"Remember, Willy T, numbers don't lie. Now neither will you. I know I'm easy to lie to, so now you're gonna help me tell the lies from the truth." He flipped the calculator over and powered it on. The display flashed 59 then 14 then 5 then nothing. Cinque put the calculator back in his pocket.

"Any fool can do it." He'd made his first grou-grou. Like the Fool's. Except Cinque planned to be very careful how he used his.

26

TELL THE LIES

As dawn broke Cinque and Knight walked up the long dirt path to the Armour Meatworks. He locked the chain link gate behind him with the padlock he'd picked up from His Place.

Boy and dog wandered into the meatworks. Cinque felt a shiver of fear and he half-hoped that all of the Fibs would be out looking for him, that the building would be empty. Then he remembered: *When you're someplace you're not supposed to be—act like you own it.*

Cinque stopped and waited—longer than he thought he would have to—until finally a mob of Fibs spilled out of the back door. He recognized some of them from before: Mustard Man, Band-Aid Mummy and the one who'd slapped him. Some of the Fibs lingered around the doorway and some surrounded Cinque and Knight. The dog stood by his side, looking back and forth, buffing at a Fib that got too close. They chattered amongst themselves again. It wasn't as intimidating a sound this time. This time the crowd was more that of a confused spectator than a cruel tormentor.

Cinque waited.

"Good to see you again, son," came the Sin Catcher's familiar voice from behind him.

Cinque twitched at the sound of Kelly Lee's voice. He turned to face the creature. "I'm not your son."

"Force of habit. I can't help but play the part when I wear his face." The spirit again appeared as his father, human. The Sin Catcher stood on top of a stack of I-beams. He still had the copy of The Black Arts tucked in his waistband. A second mob of Fibs gathered at his feet.

"Take that face off," Cinque ordered. "You're not impressing me."

"I'm just getting used to it. Seeing as I'll be wearing the real thing soon an' all. But if you want it gone . . ." The Sin Catcher resumed his true form: black wire, rough cloth, an old picture and an old cork. "Then it's gone. It's the least I can do." His voice was as charming as could be. Cinque could almost see himself forgetting what this creature had put him through, if he wanted to. "Truth to tell, you caught me with my pants down here. I figured that we'd have to drag you back." He snapped at two of the Fibs, "You an' you! Get my tools. We gotta get everything set up like it was last time—"

"Don't bother," Cinque told the Fib, keeping his eyes locked on the Sin Catcher.

Puzzled, Kelly leaned back, tilted his hat. The picture that was his face looked confused. He then hooked his wiry, black thumbs into his belt and asked, "Just what do you mean by that, boy?"

"I mean that I didn't come here to bargain with you." It was a statement of fact.

Kelly brushed his confusion aside with a wave of his hands. "All right then. What did you come back here for?" He jabbed a finger at the meatworks. "Maybe you want me to sweeten the deal? I know most of what he knows. I can fill you in on all the details, the true story of how you came to be. It might not be pretty, but it's yours, and you're entitled to it. Now I suppose if you were to step back up to the bargaining table, maybe we could work something out."

"No." Another fact.

The Sin Catcher shook his head and matched his tone of voice. "Well, then I don't know whatcha came here for, but I can tell you what you're gettin'. You're gettin' tossed back in that hole, 'cept this time, I'll hog tie you too."

"I'll tell you what I came here for. I came here to pull a thorn from my paw. I'm done with you and your puppet show, and I'm putting an end to it."

Diplomacy over, the Sin Catcher got to business. "Well well, we'll just see about that." He gestured for Fibs to move in.

"Yes," Cinque said to the Sin Catcher, "you will."

He casually turned to face the biggest, closest Fib. It lumbered forward, its long arms uncurled, blocking Cinque's exit route. But he wasn't interested in escaping. Knight started to growl at the thing stepping forward, but Cinque ordered him to stay as he pulled the screwdriver from his hoodie pocket and stabbed the Fib in the chest, piercing the rib cage like an egg shell. The Fib froze; Cinque turned the tool to the left and the Fib fell, shrivelling like an empty costume.

The other Fibs stopped, astounded.

Kelly Lee, face twisted with displeasure, was defiant still. "Well, look who's got himself a new little toy. I'm sure that's handy for taking apart these little losers but I hate to break it to ya, I'm in a whole 'nother class. Your real pa's ten times the sorcerer that I am and I've had years of sucking up sin to run on. I'm the big dog around these parts, kid."

Cinque pulled the Cuttlefish's eye out of his hoodie pouch and tossed it at the Sin Catcher's feet, the w-shaped eye's dead gaze cast up from between Kelly Lee's feet. Cinque didn't have to tell Kelly Lee where it came from. The Sin Catcher's astonished look said it all.

"You're right. You are the big dog, now that I took the

Cuttlefish out of the way. Speaking of dogs . . . Knight?"
The dog snapped to attention and stood, growling, suddenly
looking three times bigger and five times meaner. "Sic 'em."

The dog became the demon of fur and teeth that had chased
Cinque through this very field. He pounced on the closest Fib,
a fat thing in a jumpsuit of old leather patches. He pushed
it to the ground and tore out its throat with a lightning fast
snap and jerk. Expecting flesh, Knight was befuddled when
he found himself with a mouthful of paper. The dead Fib was
hollow.

The remaining Fibs panicked and ran any way that was
away from the dog.

Knight regained his composure and ran down his next
victim, a spiky black Fib with a dozen empty beer bottles
hanging from its belt. He knocked it over, turned back on it in
a quick circle and tore into it, the thin shell crumpling in the
dog's jaws.

Cinque stood calmly and stared at the Sin Catcher as
it watched like a spectator at a street fight while Knight
destroyed its army.

"When the Cuttlefish tore into them they were flesh,
because that's how the Cuttlefish saw them—bad feelings,
food—but I know that they're empty. Not just made from
lies, they're nothing but lies." The Sin Catcher looked at him
dumbly. "They only have strength when I give them strength,
I see that now." Cinque stepped towards the Sin Catcher. "The
same goes for you. I coulda walked right outta the meatworks
when you tossed me in there. Chain or no chain, name or no
name. Isn't that right?"

A Fib with a boney body and a big, tear-shaped head tripped
on a rusted pipe as it ran from Knight. The dog grabbed the
fallen Fib by the back of its neck, and shook to pieces.

The Sin Catcher seemed to get over the shock at the carnage
being inflicted on his Fibs. "Oh, there's somethin' to me, you
little punk." He reached behind his back and pulled out the

orange, frozen heart. "It happens to be somethin' to you too!" He laughed as he squeezed, fingers cracking the organ's surface, pressing in. His wrist shook from the effort. The boy was unaffected—he considered his fingernails for a moment and took casual steps closer, close enough to backhand the heart out of the Sin Catcher's hand. The upper part snapped free and shattered on the ground. The lower half stuck, uselessly, between Kelly's fingers.

"Oh. Was that yours?" Cinque feigned innocence. "Because it sure wasn't mine."

Kelly Lee stared at the worthless lump in his hand. The photo of the original Kelly Lee pictured Cinque's father with hands pressed to the sides of his face, mouth agape.

"Maybe it was some other kid's," Cinque suggested, helpfully.

The Sin Catcher dropped the broken heart and bolted into the meatworks, slamming the door behind him. Cinque walked up to the door and waited for Knight to finish off the last of the Fibs. When the screams died, the dog trotted up to the boy, a proud look on its muzzle.

"Good boy."

Dog and boy walked around the building until Cinque found Knight's secret way into the building: an old ventilation cover that had rusted out, concealed by the overgrowth that hung down from the roof.

"There's one more, boy." Cinque pulled back the dangling vines and pointed in. "We got to finish the job." The dog was on its toes in anticipation, looking in the hole and back at Cinque.

"Go get him!"

Knight disappeared into the meatworks. From inside Cinque heard nothing, then cursing, and then screaming. The screaming got closer until Knight backed out of the ventilation shaft, dragging the Sin Catcher by his ankle. Kelly Lee protected his face with his arms.

Cinque pinned the spirit to the ground with his white

sneaker, the creature's woven substance spongy under his weight. The Sin Catcher moaned.

"I don't know if I should be angry at you for making me think you were bad, or at myself for letting you," said Cinque. From behind his protective arm the creature with his father's name said something, the sound muffled by the twist of thick hair that made up its limb. Cinque leaned forward, putting more weight on the creature's chest. "What was that?"

"I'll give you whatever you want! Anything! Just name it!"

"Really? Can you find buried treasure?"

"Huh?" The Sin Catcher snuck a confused peek up at the boy between his defending arms. "Buried treasure? Sure! If that's what you want . . ."

Cinque reached into his pocket, touched the grou-grou he'd crafted from a calculator. A scratchy, twisting sensation ran up his finger, as if he had stuck it in a whirlpool of sand.

"I didn't think so." Cinque pulled the empty whisky bottle from his backpack. The Sin Catcher cried and pleaded, but Cinque wasn't listening. He lit one of Mr. Jaspers' matches, dropped it in the bottle and pressed the bottle's lip into the Sin Catcher's face. The cork's spongy surface formed a seal around the bottle's opening. Like a plastic bag, the Sin Catcher's clothes sucked up around his woven shape, sticking to the contours of his body. Kelly Lee screamed as his legs and arms curled and his torso sunk. His head began to collapse in on itself. He pushed against the bottleneck, but his legs sucked up into his torso just before it all pulled through his head and into the bottle. Cinque sealed it shut with three quick turns of the cap. Inside the bottle, the Sin Catcher was reduced to his original size. The thick black wires of his body were now braids of straight black hair, his head a wine cork, his shirt was a roughly hand-sewn outfit with the pockets drawn on in ink. The little figure banged at its glass prison with its woven fists, shouting at Cinque, the face on the picture full of anger and fear.

"Funny, your head's too big for that bottle neck," Cinque said as he gave the bottle a shake, knocking Kelly Lee to his little knees.

The Sin Catcher righted himself, his rage subsiding to a quiet hate. He shouted through the glass. "You may think you kicked my ass pretty good, and I gotta admit you surprised the hell outta me. If you were my son I'd even be proud of you, but I'm one crafty S.O.B. just like our dear old dad, and you're just a kid on a lucky streak. You let me outta here and I'll just walk away. No harm, no foul. If I gotta bust outta here myself then some serious payback is gonna happen. You understand?"

While the bottled imp ranted, Cinque slipped his thumb on the calculator grou-grou in his pocket again. The scratchy, twisting sensation told him that the Sin Catcher was bluffing.

"Little Kelly, serious payback has already happened. Get used to it." Cinque couldn't resist giving the bottle a little shake, knocking the Sin Catcher off his feet. "All in all, I ain't even all that mad at you. Sure you tried to con me but I let you do it. If I was gonna be mad at anyone it'd be at me, and what's the point in that?"

He picked up his father's copy of *The Black Arts*, stuffed the book and the Sin Catcher's bottle back in his backpack and headed down the road into St. Jude, Knight at his heels.

The boy and his dog walked down the unnamed road, away from the Armour Meatworks to where it crossed another nameless road that led downtown. Someone was waiting for him. A giant in a black and red suit held the head of his silver ant head cane in both hands before him, a proud smile on his face.

"Well done, young master, well done!"

He gave Cinque and Knight a quick look over. Despite their concealment, his eyes obviously stopped to look at the calculator in Cinque's pocket and the bottle in his backpack. "Any loa that chooses to stand in your way is in danger of becoming an accessory. I should watch myself." Eshu Wara chuckled at his own joke.

Cinque didn't. "What happens now?"

"Now?" The word radiated innocence. "Now you will learn. You will learn from Pastor Akotun, about Juju and about your place in this world as my worshipper. You've accepted my help twice now, your faith is strong."

"Did I accept anything? Cinque Joseph Williams, the boy I used to be, he accepted those favours." Cinque tested.

Eshu's innocence slid away replaced by warning. "Don't forget that the 'boy you used to be' still owes me for those favours. Don't think that your new name absolves you of your debts." Eshu pointed his cane at Cinque. "You may think that you've undergone some grand metamorphosis but from where I stand this is nothing more than a change of clothes." He punctuated this by driving the tip of his cane down into the ground between them, cracking the pavement.

Cinque ignored the god's display of power. "I'll pay you back, don't worry about that, but I won't be asking for any more favours. I got enough hanging over my head as it is." He took the calculator out of his back pocket and deliberately held it in his palm. "If I do ask for another favour, what'll happen to me then?"

Eshu Wara scowled at the grou-grou in the boy's hand. "Put that away. Now."

He put the tool back in his pocket, hiding his smile of triumph under an apologetic one. *The charm was a threat to the god.*

The loa was still angry. "Try to use that on me and I will take it and the hand that holds it."

"I think you might be bluffing."

"And if you think wrong?"

"If I'm wrong then you wouldn't be asking me if I was wrong. Right?"

Cinque didn't see the cane that struck him across the face.

Suddenly, he was sitting down, trying to hold on to the ground as it spun beneath him as his jaw ached fiercely. Knight growled and then yelped as Eshu Wara grabbed the dog by the throat. Not because it was a threat, Cinque could tell. He held the fifty pound dog at arm's length like it was nothing, to show that he could.

"There was once another little shaman who spoke to me as you do now. I used his arm bones to stake him to a tree and made him watch while I took my cruel pleasures with the men, women and children of his tribe. You have some use to me, but only if you know your place and your place is very, very low. I've softened since those days, but test me again and you'll discover how hard I can be. Are we clear? Or should I demonstrate on your pet?"

Holding a hand to this thumping head, Cinque stood but kept his head bowed. "No, sir. You've made your point."

Eshu Wara dropped Knight, who landed on his rump with a yelp. Ears pressed to his head, tail between his legs, he slinked around to Cinque's side.

The Loa's anger cooled. "You seem to think you have it all worked out. Go then, but remember, you have a long, difficult path before you. I'll see you further down that road, when you need me."

Cinque had recomposed himself, cockiness behind. "Thank you, sir." He walked back down the unnamed road to downtown St. Jude, his head held not quite so high as a minute ago.

From the crossroads Eshu Wara called out, "I warned you, my lessons are harsh. But harsh lessons are quickly learned."

"Oh I'll learn quick, little godling." Cinque muttered. "Quicker than you'll know what to do with."

27

LEARNED

Cinque had eaten a plate of leftover spaghetti, two peanut butter and jelly sandwiches and drank four glasses of milk by the time Darren came home. Without a word, Darren went right to the refrigerator and helped himself to the pre-sliced package of American cheese-food, peeling them off and stuffing them in his mouth while he sat with Cinque. With a mouthful of cheese he finally noticed Cinque's hair.

"You shaved your head? When'd you do that?"

Cinque dodged the question. "It'll grow back."

Darren shrugged and pulled a pair of envelopes out of his pocket. "Check this out. This here's some applications for those gas cards. I figure we both get one, then I take yours and you take mine and buy gas for people and get them to get us cash."

While his cousin talked, Cinque leaned back in his chair. Touching the calculator in his pocket with his thumb, he felt the scratchy, twisting feeling up his thumb while Darren spoke.

"We keep usin' them 'til they cut 'em off. And when they

come lookin' for me I'll say, 'That ain't me on that video tape.' And when they come lookin' for you you'll say—"

"You're wasting your time." Cinque interrupted.

Darren stopped talking, his hands froze in the middle of the closing gesture he used when selling an idea to a sucker, the one where he brought his hands down in the space between him and the mark, half begging and half presentation.

A second later he dropped his hands back to his sides and smiled nervously. "What?"

"Time," Cinque repeated as if Darren hadn't heard him. "You're wasting your time. I'm not buying it. You're going to get a card in my name, throw out the card in your name, rip off the gas company and make it look like it was me. I know you and I know me, so I know what's what."

Darren stood fists ready. "Boy, you better watch your mouth or I'm a—"

"What? Beat my ass? You think that'll convince me you ain't lying?"

Cinque could tell that Darren didn't understand why his lies and his threats failed. The only other tool he had to manipulate his younger cousin was a beating and the first step of a beating was intimidation. In the past, when Cinque flinched then Darren knew he'd already won the fight. He swung across Cinque's face, missing his jaw by less than an inch. Cinque didn't flinch. He stayed in his chair, unimpressed, "Is that all you got?"

They both heard Cinque's Ma's car pull up in the driveway. Darren pretended like that saved Cinque. He grabbed what was left of the cheese food stack, threw it back in the fridge so hard that it thumped against the back wall, slammed the fridge door and pointed at Cinque. "You lucky," he shouted before storming upstairs.

Ma and Grandma came in from the car, both carrying bags of groceries. When his Ma saw him sitting at the table she let into him.

"Where have you been all day, boy? You better have been at school. And what happened to your hair?"

"I got rid of it is all."

"Good," she nodded at last. "I never liked those dreads anyway. Now get out to the car and get the last two bags. We got frozen foods in there and they're gonna melt." She tossed him the keys and Cinque went out to the car, returning with two bags while the women were putting groceries away.

"Hey, Ma," Cinque interrupted, "I been thinking about what you said to me out by your school."

Olamide stopped what she was doing and carefully turned to Cinque, "That's good."

"I got a question: If knowledge is good—" She nodded, "—and ignorance is bad—" Again she nodded. "—then why didn't you ever tell me my pops was white?"

His Ma stopped cold. Her mother gaped at her: one hand held a can of beans, one held a can of corn—both slowly stopped moving. With a quick glance over at him to judge his seriousness she looked back at her daughter and asked, "Olamide? What does he mean by that?"

Careful not to show it, Cinque was surprised that his Grandma didn't know. He wasn't the only one not in on this family secret.

Olamide turned away from her mother and couldn't look at her son so she stared at the floor. "How—how did you . . . ." She did a little nervous fidgeting and finally looked up again. "I . . . was going to tell you when you were old enough."

Cinque's thumb was on the calculator in his pocket. He felt a slight twisting sensation. He asked, "How much older? Ain't fourteen old enough?" He tried not to enjoy having the upper hand over his Ma. "Not that it matters. I wasn't gonna join the Black Panthers' junior league or nothing. You was right about him: white or black, he ain't a good man. But I'm better off knowing than not knowing and the best way to learn was to find out for myself."

"Is this why you've been acting up?" She asked the floor.

"Yes and no. I can't say things is goin' back to normal, I don't think normal's gonna be in the cards for me, but I can say I'm done doin' what I was doin'. I know enough about where I came from to know where I'm going and that just 'cause he is like he is ain't gonna make me be like him if I don't wanna be. I need you to be straight with me from now on and I'll be straight with you. But I needed to learn what I learned to be ready for when he comes back."

"Comes back?" His Ma sounded less surprised than worried. "How's he coming back, baby?"

"Bad pennies always do, don't they? You don't really think he's dead do you?"

Olamide said nothing, but Cinque could tell that she believed it now that he'd said it aloud.

He went to get the last of the groceries from the car. When he left he felt Grandma turn on Olamide, still holding a can of beans and a can of corn. When he came back in the women stopped talking as he crossed the threshold. He left the bags on the table and went up to his room without being told.

He lay in bed, staring at the ceiling. In an odd way the fact that his Ma had lied to her Ma about Cinque's father and had held true to that lie for fourteen years made Cinque feel better. Better about all the lies he'd been told, all the lies he was about to uncover with his grou-grou. Better because the lies of the world, the lies people told, they told to everyone, not just to him.

28

THE LIES OF THE WORLD

The air smelled like rain on the plains of St. Jude, plains that dreamed of Africa. Cinque sat cross-legged, concentrating on the broken pebble in his hand until Pastor Akotun appeared. His iron staff lay by his side, the drum in his lap and the mirrored sun glasses on his face. Today his robe was a dark blue and green pattern. The Pastor stopped playing the drum and put it aside.

From the young shaman's hip, Knight jumped up, barked twice and charged at the herd of squirrel-gazelle scattering them away from the water hole. A pair of possum-elephants ignored the yapping little spirit and kept drinking.

The boy said, "I thought you weren't going to teach me about Juju."

"And I did not. The lessons I taught you were about life. If you misinterpreted my lessons it is no fault of my own." The African somehow smiled without using his mouth. "What did you learn?"

"I gue—" Cinque corrected himself. "I learned all the wrong

things. Like the Fool, I learned how to make a grou-grou from meaning and thought. Like the Farmer, I learned how to reach a ghost by way of the All Ghost. And like the Soldier, I learned that I can remake myself if I want it bad enough." Cinque spread out his hands, embracing the stories. "I learned to make the act from myself."

A large flock of small, dark birds arrived, touched down by the possum-elephants, picked up again and touched down by Knight. The dog gave a loud bark, and they scattered into the sky, landing again on the far side of the watering hole.

The African idly handled his iron staff, not doing anything with it, but seeming like he did. "I did not teach you these things, but did you find them useful?"

"Less than they should have been." Cinque drew a single dot in the dirt in front of him. "The Fool should have showed me that a little power is a dangerous thing and should be used carefully." He drew a second dot next to the first. "The Farmer, that a stranger is a stranger, even if they're family, and that if someone seems untrustworthy they probably are." He drew a circle around the two dots. "And from the Soldier, I should have learned that when touched by spirits I should surround myself with people. Isolation leads to madness." He drew a line through the circle and between the two dots. While playing with the dirt Cinque was subtly looking at the ground around him. There were no signs of any ants, black or red.

One of the possum-elephants began rubbing up against a tree and Cinque could hear the trunk straining and cracking against the pressure.

"If I had learned the right lessons I would a stayed away from spirits because they can be worse than people, especially ghosts. I would have known that Willy T was no good when I first figured that his girl wasn't really his girl. I would have stayed with friends and family and stayed away from guys like the Shapeshifter and Mr. Jaspers."

Cinque looked into the African's sunglasses and locked eyes where the man's eyes should have been. "I got a feeling that these were your lessons too. The ones you say they weren't, but I know you ain't gonna tell me if that's so.

"I learned my lessons the hard way, but easy things are worthless things, and I'm stronger now because of it. I even used Juju to fix myself." He looked at Knight. The dog was digging for something in the dirt nearby. "For good this time, not a jury rig."

The African nodded. "I never intended to fix you for good. It was a temporary solution to carry you over until you found your own." With a twisting sensation the calculator told Cinque that the African had just lied. Another one of the many lies told to him by teachers and preachers, peers and parents. He'd been practicing with the ghost in the calculator, keeping a thumb or a finger on the device while in conversation was enough to tell him if someone was being truthful. His cousin lied so often that Cinque was surprised when he told the truth whereas his Ma lied rarely and only to keep Cinque in line.

Once he realized that everyone was lying to everyone else, Cinque stopped taking it personally. The grou-grou in his pocket told Cinque what was true—the African never intended to fix Cinque for good—and what was a lie—his temporary solution was not supposed to carry him over until he fixed himself. To Cinque's newly suspicious imagination, it was the first in a series of temporary fixes the African had in mind, to keep the boy dependent on him. *The first one's free.* He'd heard that one before.

"And your search for your father. Will you continue?"

Cinque shrugged. "He's a dangerous man and I don't think I'll be ready to meet him face to face for a good long time." Cinque brushed the dirt flat and slowly traced a spiral. "You know . . . first I wanted to find him outta curiosity. Then I wanted to find him for money. Then I wanted to find him for healing and for power. It turns out I didn't need to find him at all. I already had everything I needed, except the will to use it."

"You have come a long way in a short time, little boy. But there is much left for you to discover."

In the distance, Knight chased after some rats in the shape of zebra.

Though Pastor Akotun had selfish intentions, Cinque realized there was still knowledge to gain here. He just had to be careful.

"Well, I do love to learn," Cinque said with a smile.

discussion
questions

1 At the beginning of the novel, Tone Milazzo describes Cinque as wearing one black shoe and one white shoe. To what extent does this image foreshadow his heritage and his position as a boy with one foot in Black America and one foot in White America? How do other characters (Darren, Imani, the George Washington Fib, Mr. Jaspers) reconfigure the image of shoes throughout the narrative? What do their misunderstandings reveal about their characters and values? What lessons do these misunderstandings teach Cinque?

2 Olamide describes St. Jude as a "tough little town" and much of its descriptions centres around images of simultaneous decay and tenacity. How is the Williams family history entwined with the history of St. Jude? How has growing up in St. Jude shaped Cinque's life experiences? In what significant ways does Cinque grapple with the social and economic legacies of the city?

3 In *Picking Up the Ghost*, magic takes on a different form and operates by different rules for Cinque, for Kelly Lee and for Pastor Akotun. Why does Cinque's magic take the form it does compared to his two teachers? To what extent does cultural conditioning alter the way Cinque sees the world?

4 After he receives the letter announcing his Pa's death Cinque finds himself thinking, "If his life was a river, and his family, all his family including his Pa, was its source then he knew he'd better find that source soon because it was drying up." How does family play an important role in *Picking Up the Ghost*? How are Olamide and Darren both obstacles to overcome and sources of comfort and protection? What relationship does Cinque have to his family—Kelly Lee included—and how might his practice of magic threaten his familial ties?

5 Throughout the text language is a continual marker of social class and background. Discuss moments when Cinque or the characters he meets adapt different speech registers; how do they manipulate or change the expectations of those around them? How does magic alter Cinque's need to be precise about the way he speaks?

6 Cinque encounters two magicians in his journey: Mr. Jaspers, the keeper of the Store of All Wants, and the Shapeshifter. How do both of these figures relate to the theme of identity? What allows Cinque to navigate the dangers of doing magic that these characters represent?

7 "Ghosties always want something. That's what makes them ghosties," Mr Jaspers remarks as he and Cinque bargain for the bottle of Four Houses American Straight Whiskey. What is the nature of desire in this chapter, and what does it mean for Mr Jaspers to make a play for Cinque's desire?

8 When Cinque meets Kelly Lee, he is surprised to learn

that his father is white. How does this discovery change the way that Cinque thinks about himself? Discuss the racial and cultural politics of identity in *Picking Up the Ghost*. What does it mean to practice magic in "a gray America"? To what extent does the fact that the author is not African American change the politics of cultural representation?

9 After telling the last of his tales, Pastor Akotun warns Cinque, "You have missed the point, but found your own." To what extent are many of Cinque's crises structured around him "finding his own point"? How do Darren, Olamide, and the Sin Catcher each manipulate Cinque by letting him believe what he wants?

10 "Names are powerful things," Iku tells the nameless boy before he takes on a new identity, yet she never discloses her own "true name." What is the nature of the power that naming offers? Does Cinque truly change and, if so, why is he still under an obligation to Eshu Wara?

ACKNOWLEDGEMENTS

If I'd had known back in 2006 that this novel wasn't going to be finished until 2011 I probably wouldn't have tried. The fact that you hold this book in your hand is a testament to my ignorance. Thanks to all the people who took the time to read the previous, painfully clumsy drafts.

Melissa Milazzo, Carly Catarcio, Rachel Bellinsky, Jake Arky, Sam Carr, Justin Hudnall, Justin Bedwell, Tara Raines, David Schmitt, Daniel Palacio and Eric Nunes.

Also thanks go to Brett Savory, Sandra Kasturi and Helen Marshall at ChiZine Publications for taking a chance on an unproven, unpublished, barely literate author such as myself.

Another debt is owed to my primary sources: Harold Courlander's *Tales of Yoruba: Gods and Heroes*, Bab Ifa Karade's *Handbook of Yoruba Religious Concepts*, Robert Farris Thompson's *Flash of the Spirit* and Sharon Caulder's *Mark of Voodoo*.

ABOUT THE AUTHOR

As a child Tone Milazzo wanted to be a writer and a Green Lantern. But then he grew up and lived his life as a Marine, a cab driver, a software engineer and a teacher before coming back around to writing. His power ring is still pending. When it does arrive you'll hear about it first at tonemilazzo.com.

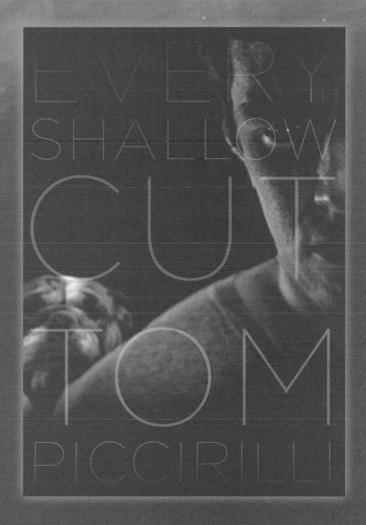

**AVAILABLE MARCH 15, 2011
FROM CHIZINE PUBLICATIONS**

978-1-926851-10-5

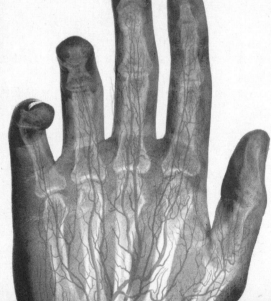

NAPIER'S BONES DERRYL MURPHY

AVAILABLE MARCH 15, 2011
FROM CHIZINE PUBLICATIONS

978-1-926851-09-9

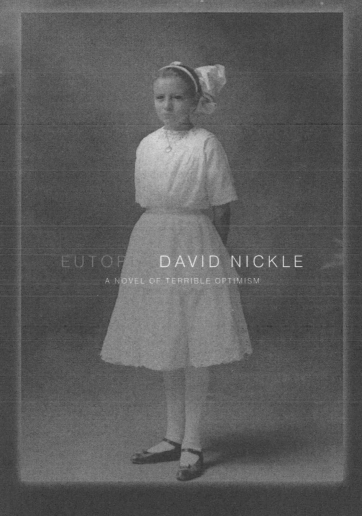

EUTOPIA DAVID NICKLE
A NOVEL OF TERRIBLE OPTIMISM

AVAILABLE APRIL 15, 2011
FROM CHIZINE PUBLICATIONS

978-1-926851-11-2

THE DOOR TO
LOST PAGES

CLAUDE LALUMIÈRE

**AVAILABLE APRIL 15, 2011
FROM CHIZINE PUBLICATIONS**

978-1-926851-12-9

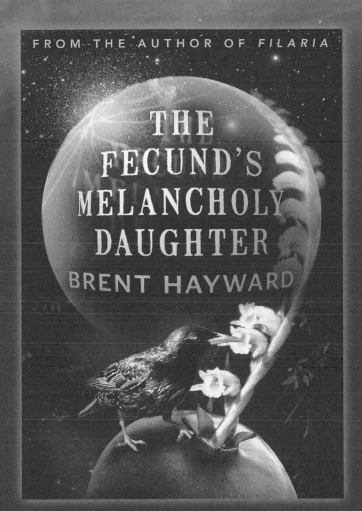

AVAILABLE MAY 15, 2011
FROM CHIZINE PUBLICATIONS

978-1-926851-13-6

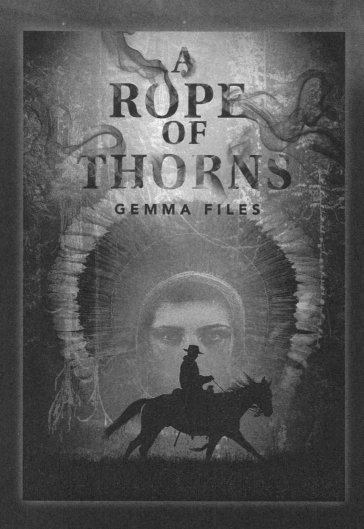

AVAILABLE MAY 15, 2011
FROM CHIZINE PUBLICATIONS
978-1-926851-14-3

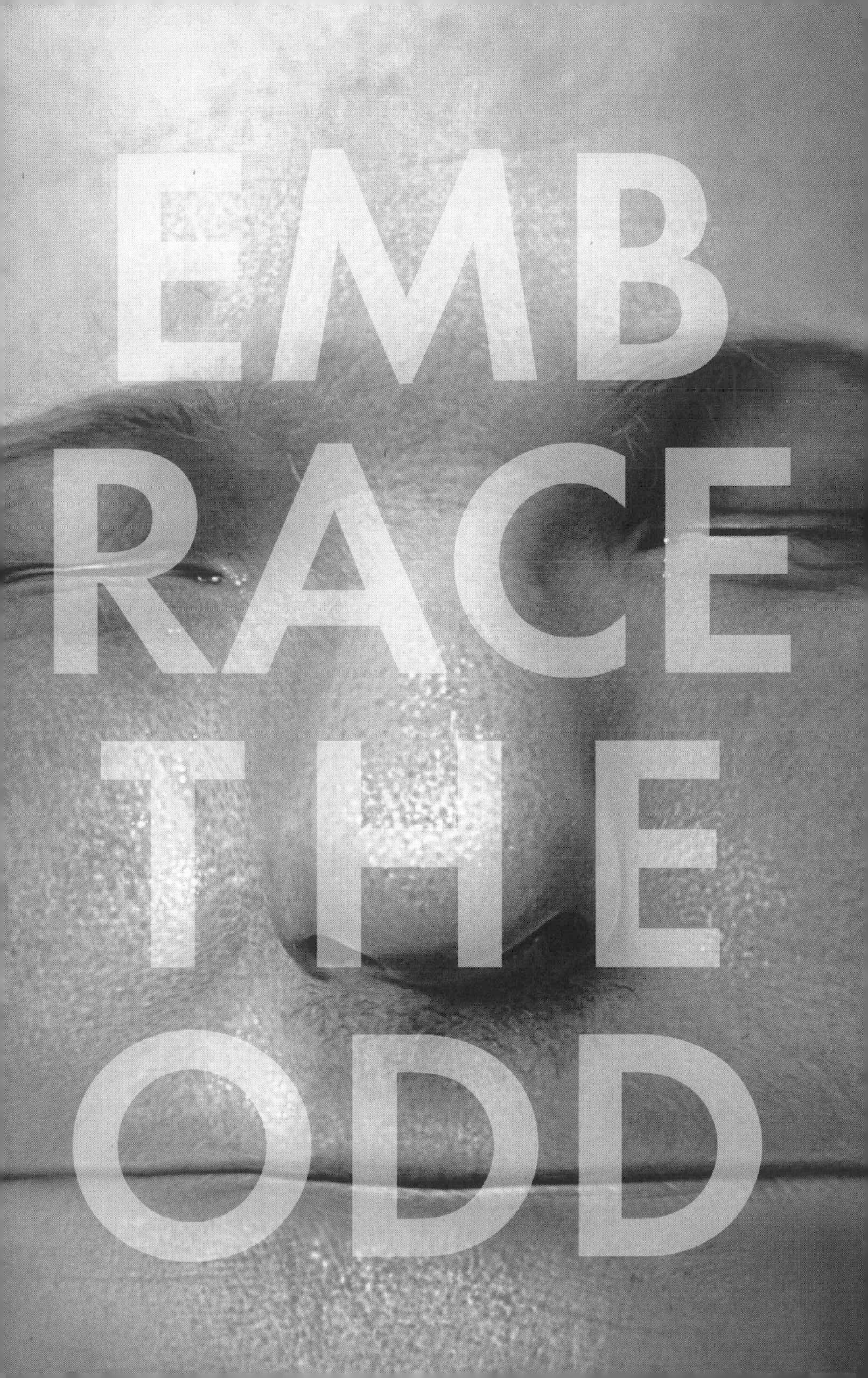
EMB
RACE
THE
ODD

978-0-9812978-9-7

TIM LEBBON

THE THIEF OF BROKEN TOYS

978-0-9812978-8-0

PHILIP NUTMAN

CITIES OF NIGHT

978-0-9812978-7-3

SIMON LOGAN

KATJA FROM THE PUNK BAND

978-0-9812978-6-6

GEMMA FILES

A BOOK OF TONGUES

978-0-9812978-5-9

DOUGLAS SMITH

CHIMERASCOPE

978-0-9812978-4-2

NICHOLAS KAUFMANN

CHASING THE DRAGON

"IF YOUR TASTE IN FICTION RUNS TO THE DISTURBING, DARK, AND AT LEAST PARTIALLY WEIRD, CHANCES ARE YOU'VE HEARD OF CHIZINE PUBLICATIONS—CZP—A YOUNG IMPRINT THAT IS NONETHELESS PRODUCING STARTLINGLY BEAUTIFUL BOOKS OF STARKLY, DARKLY LITERARY QUALITY."

—DAVID MIDDLETON, JANUARY MAGAZINE

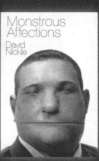